THE
NEW WORLD OLIGARCHY

DESTROYING THE UNITED STATES
THROUGH GLOBALIZATION

A Novel by

JOHN R. KRISMER, MHA-LFACHE

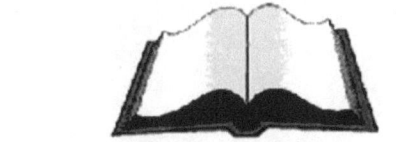

CCB Publishing
British Columbia, Canada

The New World Oligarchy: Destroying the United States Through
Globalization A Novel

Copyright ©2009 by John R. Krismer
ISBN-13   978-1-926585-36-9
First Edition

Library and Archives Canada Cataloguing in Publication

Krismer, John R., 1927-
The new world oligarchy: destroying the United States through globalization : a
novel / written by John R. Krismer.
ISBN 978-1-926585-36-9
1. United States. McCarran-Ferguson Act--Fiction.
2. Medical care--United States--Fiction.
3. United States--Politics and government--1933-1953--Fiction. I. Title.
PS3611.R46N49 2009   813'.6   C2009-903996-6

Publisher: CCB Publishing
             British Columbia, Canada
             www.ccbpublishing.com

Contents

Actual Events and Fiction

At the beginning of the last century, a powerful group of *International Bankers* decided that if they could ban together as a tightly knit Oligarchy, they could command the enormous wealth, power and status the United States had acquired through its working class. But to achieve this, they had to clandestinely establish a *New World Order (NWO)* as their front, so these proponents of a socialistic society could furtively maneuver and eventually control this nation's open market by deregulating and decentralizing our once world renowned infrastructure. They'd already found it to be a simple matter to control the world's industrialists' and this country's politicians through their trickle down bank loans and under the table gifts and benefits. But what's so frightening about all this is, *We the People, the Myopic Herd as they refer to us,* seemed entirely unaware of this powerful Oligarchy's existence — even though we frequently proclaimed we'd never live under the rule of an Empire; a Monarchy; or a Kingdom. In fact, it seemed as if only a few Americans still remembered that more than two hundred years ago we all escaped to this country from a similar Kleptocratic Aristocracy that also suppressed the working class to increase their affluence and power. Nor do we even seem concerned that we inadvertently allowed this country's Federal Reserve to become privately owned by this same group of powerful multinational bankers, who are currently not even subject to oversight by either our Congress or our President. Worse yet, when this Federal Reserve Act was unlawfully approved by Congress, as a result of the 1907 Bank Panic — and later regretfully signed by President Wilson — few realized that this closely knit clique was seeking to enslave not only the United States but eventually the entire world market. And if we take a moment to identify who this International Oligarchy really is, we will readily recognize the powerful Rothschild of London and Berlin; the Lazard Brothers of Paris; Israel Seiff of Italy; the Kuhn and Loeb Company of Germany; the Warburg's of Hamburg and Amsterdam; and the Rockefellers, Lehman Brothers, and Goldman Sachs of New York - all currently maintaining controlling ownership of this nation's Federal Reserve under the cloak of the 1907

Bank Panic. And perhaps few of us even recall that this takeover was skillfully coordinated under the leadership of Senator Nelson Aldrich, the father in-law of John D. Rockefeller Jr., who persuaded Congress to appoint a National Monetary Commission, composed of J.P. Morgan, Paul Warburg, Otto Kahn, Jacob Schiff and the then infamous monopolist John D. Rockefeller himself — all playing a major role in creating this country's privately owned Federal Reserve System, which was in direct conflict with our Constitution. And isn't it ridiculous that at the same time this was all happening, the Supreme Court declared John D. Rockefeller's Standard Oil an illegal monopoly over this country's natural oil resource. And now, as a result of all these concessions, this Oligarchy currently makes its own policies and buys or sells our government securities whenever they wish to make a profit. This same Aldrich Commission also illegally promoted our first income tax in the year 1913, to secure their interest on the multinational bank notes they extended to our government — notes which today earn this Oligarchy almost two billion dollars a day in interest from our tax payers. And since they now control almost all of the international industrialists, as well as our politicians, they are now able to create depressions or open new markets whenever they desire. In fact, by hiding behind their fallacious NWO slogan of *"World Trade through World Peace,"* this NWO has blamelessly maneuvered the U.S. into some nineteen unwarranted conflicts including: World War I, Vietnam, Cambodia, Laos, Philippines, Somalia, Haiti, Croatia, Bosnia, Chechnya, Albania, Kosovo, Serbia, Sudan, East Timor, and Afghanistan and Iraq, which have served them well in their money making interventions and war provocations that have gained financial control over so many other nations and their natural resources. And now, with all their multinational banks loaning out today's valueless fiat money, which they can create from nothing; and our income tax providing a means to repay the inflated debt and their huge interest earnings, these Invisible Money Baron's have actually forced us to accept their deceitful *Trickle-down Philosophy*. And although very little ever *trickles down* from this Inter-national Oligarchy, it doesn't stop there — since we've even allowed them to lower the tax on their earnings in this country, by allowing their tax exempt foundations to serve as repositories for their divested interest, making almost all of their assets non-taxable along with their estate and gift tax. And now, with this enemy of capitalism tapping directly into our treasury through their unwarranted interest payments and their ridiculous corporate welfare and tax bailout scams, these proponents of a free market have become totally dependent on big government. But it doesn't stop there, in that during the last century these false prophets of capitalism have instituted policies that are antithetical to free markets, thereby placing themselves in an ideal position to increase earnings during positive times while gaining equity during recessions, all under the ridiculous concept of this *New World Order (NWO)* — clearly leveling this once great nation to that of others. But what's even more frightening is one of our own once respected financial giants, David Rockefeller, supported this *NWO* and their openly stated aspiration of *leveling the United States to that of other nations* under the misleading ploy of globalization. David has also been financially linked with the internationally powerful Bilderberg Group, who has close ties with the Saudi Oil Czars and their corrupt cult of terrorists that strategically bombed the World Trade Center — providing still another unjust deception to go to war with Iraq. And in addition to all this, this Rockefeller dynasty *Overlords the Council on Foreign Relations* (CFR) and the powerful *Trilateral Commission* (TC), which David himself created to take the place of today's dysfunctional Congress that once looked after this country's working class. But more importantly, their more recent deregulation and decentralization of our infrastructure is now applying the final blow to our sovereign nation. So this is where my novel begins.

This novel, *The New World Oligarchy*, is based on actual events that show how this powerful Aristocracy has taken total control over our once respected and cost effective nonprofit healthcare system. It also describes how their destructive Master Plan is now mushrooming throughout this once sovereign nation's entire infrastructure – causing our economy to grow weak and the world more fearful, unfriendly, and certainly less united.

The N W O's
$$$ COSTLY MASTER PLAN $$$

WHICH PROMOTED: Deregulation - Endless Wars and Torture Tactics - Devaluation of the Dollar - Global Manufacturing - The Ridiculous Bail Out of International Banks - The Housing Crisis - Fiat Money - The Great Cover Up - The Buying off Congress - The 2008 Recession - and is currently promoting the 2012 Depression

DISREGARDED: International Law - The Environment - The Nonproliferation Treaty - and Business Ethics

OWNS OR CONTROLS: The Federal Reserve - Most of the World's Natural Resources - and all Bank Loans

AND BANKRUPTS: The Sick and Disabled - The Economy and Jobs - The Public Treasury - and This Nation's Infrastructure

---

Looking back, the imbalance in this country's vitally important healthcare service first reared its ugly head when this controlling Oligarchy coerced our politicians into passing the 1946 McCarran Ferguson Act, which deregulated and decentralized FDR's world-renowned single nonprofit prepayment healthcare service to our sick and disabled — all occurring right after FDR's death in 1945. In fact, healthcare in the United States was then still ranked 1st instead of 37th by the World Health Organization (WHO).

In this novel, Doctor Bill Warner and Mary Swanson, an RN — represent two real life healthcare professionals who tried to confront this *Oligarchy*. And if one will only take a closer look at this nation's infrastructure, including our entitlement programs, our energy services, our environment, our airline industry, our schools, our highways and bridges — as well as our cost of living and our outsourcing of commodities and jobs — they're all now failing in order to support this upper crust's contrived inflations, depressions, and wars of aggression —

all skillfully designed to make *big bucks* while controlling the world's natural resources under the fallacious parody of freedom. Worse yet, this International Aristocracy now controls our powerful military complex, our intelligence and homeland security system, the news media and all its influential propaganda networks, as well as their own privately controlled international banking system — all under this nation's puppet like government, which was once admired as a leader throughout the entire world. Yes, this novel describes in shocking detail what first took place at the grass roots in healthcare, and what has now been repeated over and over in almost every other facet of human service. And as a result, we're failing as a democracy, just as the Athenian Culture was sapped of it's strength and unity by the wealthy Persians in 45 BC — and our future now depends on *We the People* waking up and getting this *Enemy Within* out of our craw, if we ever hope to regain our sovereignty. And remember, this time we have no place to run!

Chapter 1

A Fresh Start

As Doctor Bill Warner sipped his morning coffee he recalled Susan's love for the mountains, and even though the fresh snow offered him a different outlook for that day, he still couldn't look at Pike's Peak without deeply missing her pleasant smile that had greeted him for so many years. And since her murder, he often found himself grieving over those trips into the mountains to see the golden Aspen. As he sat absorbed with these painful thoughts of the past, he recalled when the Catholic Sister's he'd worked for demanded he and his wife Susan take a fully paid vacation to Hawaii as their gift to him for a job well done. As he thought about that vacation, he remembered how the phone jolted him from a sound sleep, and how completely disoriented he was as he reached out several times before grabbing the phone and finally saying, "Hello?"

"Hi Dad."

"John? Is that you — is everything all right?" He'd asked, wondering why his son would be calling in the middle of the night, but sensing that something was terribly wrong.

Then John sobbed, "Dad, Kate's dead."

"Dead! Oh God no! — John, what's happened?"

"She drowned in her apartment swimming pool. They tried to revive her at the Hennepin Hospital in Minneapolis — but they couldn't," he gasped. "I guess they were able to restart her heart, but only for a short time, and she was pronounced dead at nine-thirty last night. Dad, Donna told me there were abrasions on her head, and that the police were concerned about that."

1

Bill recalled how his mind was racing wildly, thinking back to the phone threat he'd received. *I … I can't believe this … what should I do?* He'd thought to himself.

"John, where are you?"

"I'm in Texas, but I'm leaving for Minneapolis in about an hour and I don't know too much about what happened just yet."

After they'd finished talking, Bill remembered how he and Susan sobbed in each other's arms, neither one speaking before he finally gathered enough energy to call the airport. Since it was an emergency, they were assigned the next flight that would return them to the mainland, but it seemed like an eternity before they were able to finally sit down with their three children and talk as a family at Kate's apartment. Donna explained how the police had secured Kate's apartment until just a few hours before they arrived, and John and Peggy also shared whatever information they could, but none of them believed that Kate would have willingly gone into a swimming pool with her allergy to Chlorine. They also were concerned that Kate couldn't tolerate cigarette smoke, and yet there were several cigarette-butts in that dish on the end table. As Bill sat starring at the floor, he finally told Susan and the children about that threat he'd received, and the corrupt doctor organization the FBI had been investigating. Terrified by all this, they talked about it for a good hour before Bill finally decided to call Joel Wilson at the FBI. Joel was shocked and asked Bill to meet with a Mr. Donald Anderson, their investigator in Minneapolis.

Taking another sip of coffee, he recalled how this tragedy was a torturous ordeal for the entire family and how he'd gone to Anderson's office almost daily, only to pace the floor and stare at the huge Catholic Basilica on Hennepin Avenue from his second floor office window. Anderson was an elderly gray haired man that was obviously suffering from some type of burnout before Bill ever met him.

"I prefer to work from my office," Anderson had told him. "But I'll assign a very capable private investigator to do the leg work on your daughter's death." Later, that investigator told Bill how a young lady had pulled Kate out of the pool and ran to the apartment store to get help before finally giving CPR. "I guess she almost saved Kate's life," he explained.

Bill also remembered how concerned he was that Kate was found in the shallow end of the pool, in that she was a very capable swimmer.

"My Agent looked through all the police records and the only reason he could find as to why they were investigating things further was because they were concerned about those abrasions on her head, and now that they've checked everything out properly, they've closed the case," Anderson told Bill.

Then as Bill sat thinking about all this, he remembered how Donna was throwing some things out from the apartment when she found this weird man with long hair crouched inside the dumpster. He'd obviously been going through Kate's things, and quickly climbed out without saying a word, as he leaned casually against a tree smoking a cigarette. Later, Donna pointed him out to Bill just as he was climbing into a red Corvette, with California license. Bill recalled how he was short and thin with dark brown hair pulled back into a ponytail, probably weighing less than a hundred and fifty pounds. After he left, Donna recovered his crushed cigarette, which matched identically with the one found in Kate's ash tray. Later Bill gave the man's description, the cigarettes, and the car's license number to Anderson, who said they'd find this guy and check him out — but they never did. *So why did the police close the case? —* Bill had asked himself over and over. *And thing's still aren't right,* he whispered to himself, as he thoughtfully took another sip of coffee. Then as he thought about how the family went their separate ways after their tragedy, tears once again filled his eyes — a reoccurrence that had been happening far too frequently, clearly rekindling the deep loss that was always there now.

Then as usual, his thoughts jumped to another traumatic time, when Susan and he were sitting down to dinner, and the phone rang.

"Hello, is this Doctor Warner — are you the father of Peggy Downey?"

"Yes I'm Doctor Warner," Bill replied, again sensing something wasn't right.

"Doctor Warner, my name's Doctor Kilbride. Your daughter Peggy has been in a car accident, and we have her at the Brakenridge Hospital in Austin, Texas. She's in ICU, and we've stabilized both her and her unborn child."

Once again Bill couldn't believe what he was hearing.

"Although things were touch and go for a while, she's now in no immediate danger, but you need to know she did have a serious concussion. At this time we don't feel she'll require surgery, and her prognosis should be for a normal recovery." As he continued he explained, "She has no recall of the past or the accident, but we expect things will clear up in a few weeks. In fact, she would most likely not even recognize you if you were here right now."

"Oh my God," Bill said. "Doctor, we'll make arrangements to get down there right away," as he turned to explain to Susan.

With that, Susan just dropped her fork and covered her face with both hands, unable to respond.

"Doctor Warner, since your daughter's not in any eminent danger you shouldn't have to race down here right away!"

"Oh no, we'll definitely get there as quick as possible," Bill responded, "In fact we'll leave as soon as we're packed."

As Bill hung up the phone he recalled how he turned to Susan and yelled, "If that God damned Lanin had anything to do with this, I'm driving to North Dakota and kill that bastard."

"My God Bill, how much more of this can we take?" Susan had shouted.

* * * * *

In that these accidents were more than a coincidence, Bill had talked with the FBI, demanding tighter security measures for his family. Then later that evening, after leaving the hospital, he remembered turning onto Westgate Drive near Peggy's home, when he heard an explosion that shattered the glass on Susan's side of the car. He recalled the odor of gunpowder as he struggled to wipe the dust particles of glass from his eyes, and slamming his foot on the brake he instinctively hunched forward to protect himself.

"What in the hell was that?" He'd screamed — his eyes still not able to see clearly. Then after blinking several times he could finally make out what looked like a small bullet hole in Susan's window. At first he thought a car had hit them but there was no impact, and as he stared at the hole it slowly became larger with each piece of glass that fell. Finally his eyes cleared enough so he could see the blood covering the side of

Susan's head and as her body slumped forward he screamed her name. Fumbling to get his seat belt off — his hands were shaking so badly that it took several attempts before he was finally free. Then after checking Susan, he whispered, *that bastard killed her,* finally screaming at the top of his voice, "I'll get you — you son-of-a-bitch."

Just then the FBI security car that had been following them screeched to a halt and it took both men to hold Bill back. Finally one of the agents ran up the steep wooded embankment where Bill had been pointing.

"You've got to get him," he'd shouted. "He shot Susan in the face — and I think he killed her," he screamed, hopelessly fighting to get away from the agent who was restraining him.

After the agent stared at the spattered blood and pieces of flesh on Bill's shirt, he finally let go and ran to the car. Checking for a pulse, he turned toward Bill. "Bill, she's dead," he whispered, as Bill pushed him aside and grabbed Susan in his arms. Touching her, he remembered that hopeless feeling, and then he realized that everything important had now been taken away. "How could I have been so stupid to feel that my family wouldn't get hurt," he remembered shouting at the top of his lungs. "I risked my family's lives to save a hospital, when life and death means nothing to these money grabbing bastards. They'd sell their soul for a buck," he'd sobbed, pulling Susan tightly into his arms.

Bill also remembered how it took several days before he was again aware of his surroundings after Susan's murder, and how his life had become a maze of confusing thoughts — mostly revenge. Over and over he'd thought of how he'd like to get his fingers around Lanin's throat and choke the life right out of that bastard. In fact, that same intense uncontrollable hatred had automatically taken over almost every time he thought about Susan or Kate. And now — even after more than a year — he still couldn't sleep.

Damn this cruel world, he muttered to himself.

But Susan wasn't a damning person, and his bitterness would usually fade after he thought about the positive influence she'd been. Bill had accepted a few consulting jobs since he'd rescued the Sister Hospital from a hostile takeover, but his real hope was to still try and expose this greed that was now plaguing his entire healthcare profession — a human service that was almost completely shattered by this endless grabbling for more money. And although he'd probably fail in his promise to Sister Gerome, to expose these outrageous crimes, his recent writings had at least given him the opportunity to vent some of his anger over what had happened to both him and his family.

All their damned money making schemes are destroying this whole country, he cursed.

As he backed away from the window, the phone suddenly jolted him back to reality. Setting his coffee on the table, he apprehensively said, "hello," since it was still early in the morning.

"Hi Bill, how are you?" A familiar voice shouted.

Bill paused, wondering who'd be calling him at such an hour in the morning.

"Dave Nelson?"

"Yes, it's me," Dave replied rather uneasily — "how are you?"

"Oh shit," Bill snarled. "The last time I talked to you it cost me way too much — you're no friend of mine!"

"Oh yes I am," Dave quickly retorted, lowering his voice to a whisper. "Bill, there's no way I can ever make up for what happened to your family — and you know that."

"Bull shit!" Bill growled, showing his revulsion at what his family had been subjected to — then after a short silence he finally whispered, "Oh to hell with it all — maybe I am still trying to find a scapegoat for all the guilt I carry."

Bill hadn't heard from Dave since he'd persuaded him to move to North Dakota to help get that Sister hospital back on track — but that damned experience hadn't been without an enormous cost to his career, let alone the damage to him and his family.

"I understand, "Dave whispered. Then after chitchatting for several more minutes, he finally had the courage to once again ask, "Well — are you okay?"

"It's not been a bed of roses, but I still get up each day and try to understand this whole damn mess."

"I'm so sorry," Dave said. "I understand the FBI is still looking for that bunch of crooks. But I hear they just suddenly disappeared from the planet — and the FBI isn't making much headway."

"I guess so — but I'll tell you this — I'm all done worrying about them."

"I can understand that, but it sure makes you wonder what's going on. I thought the FBI had them in their sights," Dave scoffed. "By now, all those con-artists have probably high-tailed it back to their own countries. You know Bill; someday we're all going to maybe realize this damned globalization isn't everything it's supposed to be."

"Perhaps you're right," Bill growled, casually pulling back a chair and sitting down.

"All right Dave — let's have it — you haven't called me just to chitchat. What's on your mind this time?"

"Hey buddy, I'm concerned about you. I guess it's just this damn business we're in," he mumbled, rethinking his approach to what was now clearly a very touchy subject. "All right, so I do need your help! You know there aren't too many Bill Warner's running around, and I've got a serious problem you could help me with."

"I knew it," Bill choked, reaching for his coffee. "Damn it Dave — what do you want this time?"

"Bill, I flew to Colorado Springs last night, and first thing this morning I had breakfast with the Administrator of your local pediatric hospital, a Mr. Bakencamp. Then after our meeting I called the Director of the State Health Department and he scarred the hell out of me."

"I'm not familiar with that Administrator," Bill explained, taking a quick sip of his cold coffee. "I didn't even know his name, until you just told me."

"From what I can gather, Bakencamps done some real stupid things, and as a result he's gotten his ass in a jam."

Bill fidgeted uncomfortably, anticipating what might be next. "Well, at least you chose my home town," he scoffed.

"Listen, I'm staying at the Broadmoor. Why don't you meet me for lunch in the Tavern? I'll get a reservation for twelve thirty, and we can visit."

As Bill hung up the phone his mind flashed back to Doctor Lanin, screaming for his life.

Damn it, I should have told Dave I'm not interested. I just can't go back to that type of salvage work again — but I need to tell him that face to face. Hell — I don't need anymore skeletons in my closet — I can't sleep now.

* * * * *

7

The Tavern resembled an English pub, and it took Bill a moment for his eyes to adjust to the dimly lit room. After he pushed through the crowd, he dodged several waiters dressed in starched white shirts with black bow ties, scurrying from table to table. And as he greeted Dave it was obvious his suit needed a good pressing, which of course was the result of living out of a suitcase.

"I suppose you've heard James Baker, our former President retired," Dave said.

"Dave, you know I'd never work for that bastard again — after what he did to me."

"Bill, it's a whole different organization without him." Wrinkling his forehead, he stared squarely into Bill's eyes. "In fact, I'm beginning to enjoy my job again," he smiled, swiveling his chair a bit so he could face Bill directly. "I had no idea he was dealing from the bottom of the deck. I guess he wanted to retire so bad he'd do anything."

Dave had already ordered a cold draft beer, and as he tilted his head back he took a deep swallow from the freshly iced mug. Bill just stared at him until he set the mug back on the table.

"I should have followed my intuition," Bill snarled, shaking his head from side to side. "I knew he was using me as his straw man. Dave, if you ever pull that type of shit on me again, you can go straight to hell."

"I'd never do that, and you know damned well I wouldn't," Dave quickly retorted. "I honestly had no idea what we were getting into, and to be very honest, no one else could've accomplished what you were able to do for those Sisters. At least you stopped those corrupt bastards in their tracks, and the Harrington and Associates, and the whole country for that matter are indebted to you. The sad part is Baker exposed our strategy to those bastards for some sort of kick-back, and sold you and your family down the river, which I promise you — I will never do."

"I guess I have to blame myself for that — I knew he was using me right from the start and it was all very stupid on my part to ever agree to help him out in the first place. Look, I'm just not ready to consult for you again. I'm too busy trying to tell the world about our crises in healthcare — that's if the public will ever listen to what I have to say — but I guess nobody wants to hear bad news. That dammed Oligarchy that's running our country, thinks the myopic herd will just hide its head in the sand and hope it'll go away."

Tensing his jaw, Dave bristled, "Bill, this insidious money grabbing is growing by leaps and bounds all over the country. What's worse is it seems like everyone wants to market the hell out of the poor sick and disabled, and it's not just these God damned insurance companies and the pharmaceutical houses, it's these international bankers that want to control everything, including the entire world market. Hell, we don't have a clew as to where this *New World Oligarchy* is taking us, and no one seems to give a damn as long as it doesn't hurt any of these wealthy bastards that are benefitting from it all. Every place I consult I'm seeing more and more executive fraud, and with all these damned CEO's and politicians stealing from our public treasury, we've got a monster starring us right in the face." Dave paused to look around the Tavern — then leaning closer he whispered. "And the damned public acts as if nothings going on! No one seems to give a damn about the *Great Cover Up* that's playing out right in front of us. It's almost as if we don't care that some entrepreneurial fat cat is picking our pockets. What a con job!"

"No wonder we're all becoming so apathetic," Bill snarled, feeling his emotions rise as he sat back to take a quick swallow of the cool draft beer the waiter had just set in front of him. "Shit — we could talk about this crap all day, and it wouldn't change a thing. What is it you wanted to see me about?"

Dave waved his hand at the waiter saying, "Hey, we'd like to order."

As soon as the waiter took their order, Dave slid his chair closer, so he wouldn't be overheard.

"All right, let me tell you what's on my mind. In the not to distant future, the *Denver Post* is releasing an explosive story that's going to blow the lid right off Mr. Bakencamp's hide out — and its all got to do with this damned deregulation this crooked Oligarchy's been promoting. Then in a few months, a national news network is going to feature a story called, *The Epidemic that Never Was.* It's all about a neurosurgeon and his young resident who've been performing a very radical surgical procedure on hundreds of infants, without the parents ever really understanding the risks involved."

"What kind of risks?" Bill asked, looking confused.

"Apparently they've removed and reshaped hundreds of infants' entire skull caps, to correct a questionable cosmetic problem called *Craniosynostosis*, or CS. And at last count, they've done more than a thousand of these major surgeries without following any surgical standards. Doctor Hanes, the neurosurgeon who started all this, apparently developed this fifty thousand dollar procedure all on his own — and he's been getting very wealthy from it — that is until the Center for Disease Control blew the whistle on him and began to investigate the situation. Rumor had it that this very extensive procedure was even being done on infants who had no documented symptoms — and apparently he's left a trail of babies that have grown up with terrible physical complications, and a batch of lawsuits that are now skyrocketing. In fact, if the hospital loses too many of these lawsuits, they just may have to close."

"Sounds like they should," Bill snarled, rubbing one hand over his unshaved chin. "Just what the hell does Bakencamp have to say for himself? Was he hiding in a closet when this was all going on?"

"That's exactly where he's been. And now he wants me to save his ass!"

Dave took another quick swallow of beer as the waiter set their sandwiches in front of them.

"Can I get you anything else?" he asked.

Again Dave waved him off, briefly staring at his sandwich before he unconsciously picked it up to take a bite.

"Why are these characters removing the infant's entire skull cap?" Bill asked.

Dave paused, slowly putting down his sandwich. "Well as you well know, CS involves the premature fusing of the skull plates, which can eventually cause some really bad deformities. And Doctor Hanes was terrifying these parents by telling them their child would have increased pressure on the brain and would probably become mentally retarded, or even insane — when there was no real evidence that could ever substantiate that." Pausing just long enough to finally take a bite of his sandwich, Dave continued. "But what responsible parent would ignore the physician," he mumbled through a full mouth. "They do just what all worried parents would do — they listen to this profound God-like creature. And Bill, as you know too well, some of these guys think they can walk on water. And since the parents are afraid of irritating this guy who might be performing major surgery on their child they just accepted everything he says. They don't even get a second opinion from another qualified neurosurgeon — doesn't that sound familiar?"

"Yah — it sure does," Bill frowned, swallowing a bite of his Rueben.

"After the Center for Disease Control and the Health Department became involved, they did a study of some two hundred of his CS surgeries, and determined that Hanes and his resident were falsely diagnosing CS symptoms in over sixty percent of their cases and totally ignoring surgical standards.

"You can't be serious!" Bill shouted.

"Oh yes I am. And on top of that, it appears that Hanes has a huge referral network of former residents who refer him all kinds of candidates."

With that Bill stopped chewing. "So you're saying there is no justification? Is there some sort of kickback?" he asked. "It always comes down to the almighty buck, doesn't it? So was money the reason?"

"I'm afraid you're right," Dave moaned. "And now Bakencamp has hired me to protect his treasure."

"I don't get it — what possible help do you want from me?"

"Hell, what I've described is just the tip of the iceberg. Some of these infants are now showing the results of his butchery. They have scars and lumps in their skulls, which they're teased about in school, and they get headaches and a whole bunch of other physical problems. Worse yet, just three years ago a *six-month*-old infant with a known cardiac problem had a cardiac arrest on the surgical table. She's now retarded and almost totally blind. Another infant died from the procedure, and a dozen or more parents are lining up in the wings to initiate lawsuits against the hospital and this self aggrandizing surgeon and his resident, Larry McGrath. And what's even worse is this *Young Turk*, McGrath, recently signed an agreement to buy out Hanes, and now he intends to continue this money making fiasco. Bill — it's just one big nightmare!"

"Well, at least the public is starting to show signs of standing up to these hoodlums," Bill smirked, with a small tinge of satisfaction. "Yet, you say McGrath is still doing this surgery?"

"Yes! — And that's the frightening thing about this whole damned deregulation mess we have on our hands today. But that's not all," Dave paused again, raising one hand. "One of the residents in training, a

Doctor Rahn, stood up and fearlessly challenged both McGrath and Hanes, knowing full well he could have been thrown out of his residency. But by the grace of God, the national neurosurgeon's organization got wind of it and saved him by threatening to investigate the lack of diagnostic criteria that the CDC had already identified. In fact, neurosurgeons from all over the country are now disagreeing with this procedure because there's just too much blood loss. Bill, they often transfuse the infant's total blood volume two or three times in this procedure — and as you know, the tissue that separates the skullcap from the brain can hemorrhage extensively when you remove the entire skull cap. In fact, the neurosurgery society has decided this type of procedure is far too extensive and dangerous for what's been previously known as a simple cosmetic procedure. And from what I've been told, Hanes is lucky those babies haven't been dying left and right. I heard that at the last national meeting of neurosurgeons, the whole professional society was up in arms on this issue, and they really took McGrath and Hanes to task."

"Stop right there!" Bill said raising both hands. "You mean the neurosurgeons, *as a group*, are willing to openly oppose what these guys were doing?"

Dave nodded.

"Boy, that's a positive change from their usual code of silence," Bill chuckled, quickly washing down another full cheek of Rueben. Then suddenly he shouted, "Damn it!" Causing several other patrons to look his way — "Just what the hell is this administrator doing? He's supposed to be acting in behalf of the patient, and all that crap is going on right under his nose?"

Dave quickly put his forefinger up to his lips, hoping to quiet Bill down as he reached over and patted his arm. Then cautiously looking around the room to see that nobody was still listening, he explained what he wanted Bill to do.

"Bill, I can't put my name on any consultant report without knowing the facts, so here's the bottom line. This administrator is so preoccupied with saving his ass that I need someone to investigate the situation and find out just what's been going on here. I need you to go and talk to people and get the facts." With that Dave pushed his empty plate away, again leaning closer to Bill. "I need someone I can trust," he whispered.

"Someone who can go out and visit with the parents, the residents, the members of the medical staff, and check out the condition of these children they operated on — and you're the best in the business. You don't have to take sides, or fight another corrupt organization this time, just get me the facts, and find out what the hells been going on."

For a long moment Bill sat with his eyes staring at the ceiling before he finally looked back at Dave with a sly grin on his face. His disgust at what Dave had told him was obvious, as he thoughtfully nodded before he spoke.

"Perhaps I could help you," he said, gazing once again at the ceiling. "In fact, if I don't have to take sides, it may even prove to be enjoyable — and I could use some extra money right now."

They both talked for at least an hour, discussing in detail what needed to be accomplished before Bill came back with, "I'm really surprised that things have worked out between us — because I had no intent of ever helping you again when I came in here."

Dave laughed. "Bill, I don't mean to change the subject, but Bakencamp's Nursing Director walked out on him last week, probably because he's asked her to help him cover his tracks. She must've anticipated the level of scrutiny they're going to be under, so now he needs a top notch Nursing Director — one who has no ties with the past. He needs somebody like a Mary Swanson," Dave whispered, looking ill at ease as he uncomfortably shifted his position. "Have you kept in touch with her?"

With that Bill sat back and laughed so loud that almost everyone in the restaurant looked his way.

"You sure know how to use a guy!" He howled, biting at his lower lip and shaking his head from side to side. "Yes, Mary and I have kept in touch. In fact, she's one of the few people I still trust." With that, he looked directly into Dave's eyes with a crafty grin. "Why do you ask if I've kept in touch?"

"Well, I want you to persuade her to take a sabbatical from her retirement and help get some standards back at this hospital. As you know, this *New World Oligarchy* is trying to deregulate everything so they can steal with impunity."

Bill could only think of how wonderful it would be to have Mary working with him again, but he also knew that she was now financially set for life, and he already suspected she'd have almost no interest in getting back into this ridiculous rat race for more big bucks.

"You know damn well my chances of getting Mary to help us would be far greater if you were to call her," Dave explained with a wily grin.

"Well, you better not get your hopes up. I doubt very much if she'd ever get back into this rat race. She's worth several million dollars and seems very comfortable with her present life in Florida."

"Wasn't her husband a well known surgeon?"

"Yes he was," Bill, said thoughtfully. "In fact, he was a very close friend of mine — but sadly he died of a stroke shortly after they retired to Fort Myers."

"Oh my God — I'm so sorry to hear that. How old is Mary?"

Bill frowned, looking away for a moment — "Perhaps late forties, maybe forty-six or seven."

"Why don't you at least call her, and see if she shows any interest at all. Even if she'd only take on a short term assignment, she could be a big help right now."

Pausing a moment, Bill finally said with a sympathetic smile, "all right — I should call her anyway. I really need to see how she's been handling Doc's death." Folding his napkin and placing it neatly on the table he continued. "Yes, I agree, she could really straighten things out fast — but I just don't feel she'll take on this can of worms."

* * * * *

As soon as Bill arrived home he called Mary. The phone rang several times before she answered.

"Mary? This is your old friend Bill Warner."

"Bill," she cried, pleasantly surprised. "It's good to hear your voice. I think of you often."

"Mary, I've been meaning to call you for some time. But as you know I'm not very good at that. How have you been?"

"Oh, pretty good. My friends have been a big help since Doc's death. They certainly haven't given me much time to think about myself. How about you? I worry about you."

"Mary, I've been busy writing, but I'm not sure anyone wants to read what I have to say. I guess I'll have to get my name on the front page of the *New York Times* before they'll realize I have something worthwhile to say."

"Hey, that powerful *Oligarchy* doesn't want the public to ever understand what's really going on in this country — do they? But we're all going to have to face up to the facts someday, or go broke — and I don't know anyone that can tell the truth better than you," she added. "So what's up?" she asked, knowing Bill would never have called just to chitchat.

"Mary, do you remember Dave Nelson, with The Harrington Associates?"

"You mean your good friend who was as wide as he was tall? Wasn't he the one that played football?"

"Boy — that photographic memory of yours is still working, isn't it? — Yes, that's the guy. We just had a three-hour discussion on a very serious problem at one of the local hospital here in Colorado — and I promised him I'd call you and ask if you'd be interested in helping us out. I guess you'd call it a crisis."

"Now that sounds interesting!"

Although Bill hadn't anticipated it, he could sense an excitement in Mary's voice.

"In fact, that's the most interesting thing I've heard in a long time. It would certainly be an improvement over golf, bridge and shopping. When can I start?"

Bill was so shocked at her immediate response he didn't know how to react. And after he described what Dave wanted, he finally answered her question. "And I believe you could start as soon as they agree to hire you."

"I'd need to keep my home in Florida, but I'd love to help you guys out. In fact, I think I've needed something like this."

After discussing a few more of Dave's concerns, Mary agreed to meet with the Administrator.

"You know, the most satisfying years of my life were the years I worked with you," she whispered before hanging up.

Chapter 2

Another Time – Another Place

Bill was so surprised by Mary's response, that he just sat there remembering the perfect Nursing Director he'd accidently hired with those remarkable blue eyes — but more importantly he thought back to how much she'd helped him to save that damned hospital in North Dakota. Then as he thought about her actually moving to Colorado, he recalled the time when he'd just returned from a trip to Chicago and Susan said, "The Swanson's want us to meet them at Lake Sakakawea on Sunday. Apparently they've got a boat, and they'd like to take us out on the lake. I think they also want to discuss some things concerning the hospital. In any event, they gave me directions with the hope we could make it. I probably should've said I needed to check with you first, but I said we'd meet them. Is that okay?" she'd asked.

"Yes, that's fine, I hear their boat is really something to see. Guess what? — I've talked to James Baker about recruiting my replacement, in that I've now just about completed everything I came here to do, and it looks like I can turn this job over to someone else in a few months," he'd replied.

Bill recalled how Susan smiled, not knowing if she could depend on what she was hearing, since they were both anxious to return to Minneapolis — but Susan wasn't about to get her hopes up too high just yet, knowing it would be difficult for Bill to keep his usual job enthusiasm if they both were anxious to leave, so she just said, *Oh - really.* Then he remembered how on Sunday they drove west toward Garrison, looking for the first dirt road going south toward the bay, when he spotted Doc's boat.

My God, his boat is huge. It looks like a small steamboat, Susan whispered as they stepped onto that rickety old hand made dock that groaned with each step. Doc's powerful diesels had no problem pulling the huge steel hull from that shallow bottom as the reverse props churned up the mud until the bow of the boat was pointing out towards the mouth of the bay, and the open water.

As Doc powered up the diesels, Bill recalled how this respected general surgeon had grown up on a ranch just north of Lake Sakakawea, which his father eventually left to him. Each year Doc had leased out thousands of acres of land, farming only a small section himself, while maintaining less than a thousand head of cattle and a few riding horses. And in spite of his busy surgical practice, the ranch still remained profitable and his surgical practice soon became one of the best in the state, supporting the Sister's mission at the hospital for over thirty years. Because Doc had been involved in hiring Bill, he was one of the very few that knew Bill intended to leave after he'd salvaged the hospital — but more importantly he'd kept that a secret and Bill knew he could be trusted with this. As he stared at him, he noticed how Doc's green eyes always had a twinkle to them. Suddenly Doc yelled over the diesels, just as they crossed under the New Town Bridge, "The water's so deep here they've yet to find the bottom," pointing at the depth finder, which was wavering up and down below the hundred foot mark on the gauge. Then pointing up at a cliff on the north end of the New Town Bridge he yelled, "That's called lover's leap, and you can almost see the entire reservoir from up there." Then as he turned the boat south he explained, "I'm heading for our favorite beach where we can hike a bit and swim in some very refreshing cold water, if you're up to it."

As the boat glided toward the south shore, Doc idled down both diesels. "I'm planning a fresh walleye dinner tonight," he grinned. "While you and Mary talk over some business, Susan and I will take the fishing boat and catch some fresh Walleye for dinner."

Then driving the square nosed bow onto the sand beach he suddenly powered up both diesels, climbing a full five feet onto the shore before shutting things down and heading back to change into his swimsuit, just as Mary casually walked into the room in a very brief bikini, saying, "Well it looks like we've finally landed."

Bill remembered how stunned he was, seeing her in a bikini. It was hard to believe he'd been meeting daily with her in a starched white nursing uniform that had concealed such an attractive body, as he awkwardly attempted to continue with some meaningless conversation. It was fortunate they were the only two in the room since it took Bill a while before he felt comfortable with her nakedness. Her tan also suggested she must've lived in bikinis during her time away from the hospital, and it was obvious that her Las Vegas show girl experience had conditioned her to be completely at ease without much on. Later, as both Doc and Mary casually strolled along the shoreline, it was even more difficult not to notice her hour glass shape while trying to pay attention to the peaceful surroundings that Doc was describing in great detail.

When they finally returned to the boat, Doc said, "Susan lets go catch those Walleye for dinner. Mary and Bill have some business to discuss, so we'll let them talk while we fish."

Bill remembered how both Mary and he stood watching their small boat slowly disappear around the point before she turned to Bill and laughed, saying — "Bill, it's good to see you relaxing in a bathing suit. I don't think I've ever seen you in anything but a suit and tie."

"I must admit," Bill chuckled, "seeing you in a bikini is a shock compared to that damn white nursing uniform I see you in every day."

Laughingly Mary looked away, flipping her hair off to the side — then as she turned back to talk, her face suddenly became very serious, and her jaw visibly tightened. Pursing her lips tightly she stared at him. "I've got several things I need to discuss with you, and I know it's not good to mix business with pleasure, but what we need to talk about would best be discussed away from the hospital."

"Alright! — What's on your mind?" Bill asked as they both sat down.

"Well, first let me tell you that on Monday we're putting the ranch up for sale, and we thought you should hear about that before it happened. We're building a home on a golf course in Fort Myers, Florida, and Doc's retiring in about eight months. We've also purchased a manufactured home to live in after we sell our ranch — for when we return to North Dakota in the summers. As you know, Doc will be seventy-five years old, and it's time he starts winding down his practice. Bill — I've certainly enjoyed my job with you, and I'm really going to miss working with you — very much," she added as an after thought — again pursing her lips with one hand over her mouth to cover her obvious emotions.

"Bill, I want you to know that the last few years have been the most fulfilling years in my entire life," she whispered as tears filled her crystal blue eyes. "Damn-it, I knew I was going to cry," she mumbled to herself— turning away to hide her feelings.

As Bill reached out to console her, she grabbed his hand and squeezed it tightly. "I'm so sorry. I guess I wear my emotions too close to the surface."

"I know — but that's what I respect about you," Bill had replied.

She didn't have to say any more as she awkwardly tried to wipe away her free flowing tears with the back of her hand. Then after several moments of complete silence, they both stood up and without saying a word put their arms around each other. Her soft body sent chills down Bill's spine, as his hands carefully moved across her bare back. It took everything he could muster to keep his hands from moving any further, as he felt goose bumps rise on her back in response to his touch. Finally they released just enough to look at each other. There was no need for words as their lips touched briefly in a soft but affectionate kiss. It was apparent that neither one of them wanted to end their relationship as Mary backed away, still holding his hand tightly as she stared off into the distance.

"Bill, There's much more that I need to say," she finally continued, slowly letting go of his hand and again staring intently at him before they sat down.

"My respect and support for you has recently been deeply challenged, and as you probably know to well, it's also difficult for Doc to do anything that would alienate his colleagues, or that damned code of silence you doctors all hold so dear. And to be very honest, he doesn't want to be involved in what I've recently trapped myself into. That's why he thought it best you and I discuss things before we eat, and then he wants to visit with you after we've had a chance to talk."

Not knowing where this was heading, Bill recalled how uncomfortable he felt.

"You know Red Hinkley — don't you?" she continued.

Nodding, Bill remembered saying, "Yes, I've played golf with him, and he's eaten with our town house group at that Spanish Inn Restaurant."

"Are you aware of his background, and my relationship to him?"

"I guess I'd have to say no. I had no idea you even knew him."

"Bill, in a small town everybody knows everyone. And I feel it's important you know about my past relationship with him, particularly if you're going to understand what I want to share with you," she'd whispered, again looking intently into his eyes. "I've been thinking about how I might tell you this and all I can say is I'm going to tell the truth in the simplest and most honest way I can," she stammered uncomfortably. "I first met Red when I was a showgirl in Las Vegas. He worked as a dealer at Caesar's Palace, but he had all kinds of other things going on with many of the other showgirls. At that time, he'd fly back to North Dakota to manage the entertainment and gambling for the annual golf tournaments at the country club, which he now does full time."

"Yes, I've heard some pretty rough stories about prostitution and gambling in those upstairs rooms of that clubhouse. And I understand he pays the police to overlook his underground syndicate."

"Yes — that's not only true, but it's probably much worse than you'd ever dream."

Bill recalled how she paused, tilting her head as she drew in a deep breath to relax a bit. "I feel close enough to you, that I'm going to say some things that I probably shouldn't, but you need to know where I'm coming from. My marriage to Doc wasn't initially based on love, it was a marriage of convenience based on money. Doc had seen me in a show in Las Vegas, and because he knew Red, he'd asked him to introduce me to him. He'd recently lost his wife to cancer, and he and his children were devastated by her death, and he needed both a companion and a caregiver for his children — and of course a female relationship with what he perhaps considered some type of trophy wife."

As she spoke, Bill remembered how she kept shaking her head from side to side.

"I was young and foolish, and to be very honest I was looking for someone with money. My goals were simple — I wanted someone to provide the things I never had, and I wanted to travel — and I saw that in him."

Bill remembered how very uncomfortable he felt with what Mary was saying, since he had no idea as to why she was even telling him all this.

"Red was always helping some showgirl to make ends meet, as long as he could benefit from it. So, some ten years ago, he flew four of us to his annual golf tournament. The other girls did tricks, and Red split the money with them and paid all their expenses. Of course he brought me along as a surprise for Doc, and we were married shortly thereafter. Later I found that Doc paid Red a fee for arranging this get together." As Mary talked, she stretched out her shapely legs, staring at her feet. "Bill, my first five years in North Dakota were not only a culture shock — they were a nightmare. Here I was, a show girl trying to raise three strange children who really didn't accept me in the least, and we lived on a ranch that was so remote I almost went crazy. Finally Doc persuaded me to go back to school and train as a nurse, so I'd be able to help manage his office, and that's what I did — and that was the only thing that kept me from going insane."

Bill recalled how shocked he was at what she was telling him, "My God Mary, your life looks so stable from the outside. I hadn't a clue," he'd replied.

"Much of my happiness has been my challenge in nursing. And now I see so much more purpose in life having worked with you. To be very honest, money's not the answer to happiness. I'd give anything to have placed love above money, even though I eventually grew to love and respect Doc over the years."

Again taking a deep breath, she appeared visibly relieved to have this out of the way, but she still looked disturbed.

"Okay, let me get to the point as to why I'm telling you all this and why I wanted to talk to you." Bill remembered how her eyes were even more determined, as she once again stared at him.

"Last week, Red asked to meet alone with me at the ranch. He said he needed to ask me a very important favor, and like a fool my inexperience trapped me. He wanted to know if you were working for the government, and I told him you were flying to Washington every so often, but I didn't know what you were doing there. Doc tells me Red and Lanin are very close friends, and Red sets Lanin up for gambling, girls, and booze regularly on his wife-less trips to Las Vegas — and let me tell you, Red Hinkley isn't the type of person you'd ever want to cross swords with. He's been known to serve as the middleman, like hiring a torpedo to take people out of the picture. Doc's been able to distance himself from Red, but Red keeps acting as if he did me a big favor. Recently, Lanin told him that you represent a real problem to what they call their Dinosaur Club. In fact, he and Lanin would've gotten rid of you a long time ago, if they didn't suspect you were involved with the FBI or someone in Washington. Bill, he's asked me to find out just why you came here. He wants me to learn more about you, even if I have to seduce you — and he's willing to pay me if I can find out what makes you tick. Pausing she said, Bill, I just can't sell you down the river to that leach — not for any amount of money, which I'm sure the Lanin clinic and his big international bankers would pay."

With that she uncrossed her feet, and sat up straight. Then leaning closer she whispered, "Bill, I think you're safe as long as they think you're an informant for the government, but I get the distinct feeling your days are numbered if they learn you're really here just to help these poor little Nuns."

"Mary — Doc knows why I'm here, in fact he helped hire me. He also knows that Lanin's clinic, or these Dinosaurs as you call them, intend to eventually acquire the hospital and I've been hired to stop that type of hostile take-over. But I still have to reorganize the emergency service before I leave, and that's going to become a real peeing contest — as you well know. Anyway, I've just started to recruit my own replacement, and it now looks like we're both planning to leave paradise at about the same time now that the hospital is back on a sound financial track. That's unless they plan to kill me before I can get out of harm's way."

"Bill, that's exactly what my meeting with you is all about, she whispered. I think they do plan to kill you!"

Startled by what she'd just said, Bill stared out at the water speechless, as Mary grabbed his arm, shaking it to get his attention. "Bill, you know that Doc, like anyone else, must protect himself. If he even attempts to expose that Lanin clique — that damned Dinosaur Club would blackball him forever, but I'm sure you already know that. However, he's willing to secretly talk to you in confidence — after we've had a chance to visit. So I guess we both need to talk to you off the record, and he asked me to find out if you'd be willing to keep his confidence, before he tells you anything about what's really going on here."

"Mary, you know Doc has my assurance of that," Bill said to her, "and you can tell him that neither I nor Susan will abuse that confidence. I also understand what you're trying to tell me, and I'm very appreciative. Hell, I'm really very thankful to you for what you're telling me — but you need to know that there is much more behind this than meets the eye. To be very honest, I can't share with you whether it's a government investigation or not, but the Harrington and Associates have asked me to find out more about all these powerful doctor organizations that are intentionally cooperating with that Washington clique in de-regulating healthcare in America. We know a little bit about all these elite aristocracies trying to deregulate and decentralize our healthcare system through their monopolies, but they apparently include much more than health insurance and these corrupt pharmaceutical houses. Worse yet, they already have far too many politicians and corruptible physicians in their pocket, and believe me their pockets are very deep. But whoever they really are, they're totally ignoring the medical ethics and the basic principles of our profession, let alone this country's democracy we've held so sacred for so many years. Hell, this powerful aristocracy is completely caught up in an endless feeding frenzy, and they could care less about the working class that built this country. And there appears to be a new breed of doctors that are acting like a bunch of God damned Witch Doctors. Fascists use these same terror tactics to keep people confused while they get what they want, and that's exactly what Lanin's cronies are doing. They don't want medicine to remain a professional science with standards. They just want to be a part of that wealthy upper crust that completely controls our dysfunctional politicians in Washington."

"You sound just like Doc, Mary said finally grinning to relieve the tension. Bill, I'd like to tell Red that you told me in complete confidence that you're investigating things for the government. I'd like to tell him the government sent you here to stop any takeover of this nonprofit hospital. It just may give you the time you need to get your butt out of here, before being killed."

With that, tears once again filled her eyes — "Bill, I just don't want you to get hurt," she'd whispered softly.

23

"Alright — you can do that — but I have a favor to ask."

Bill remembered how she looked at him and nodded, not knowing what that might be.

"Please don't let Susan know that Lanin and Hinkley have me on their hit list."

"That'll be our secret," she smiled, nodding to confirm their agreement.

* * * * *

After Susan and Doc returned from fishing, both Mary and Bill ran to check if they'd caught dinner, and once again Bill recalled Susan's beautiful smile as she lifted a stringer of fresh Walleye out of the holding tank — but it also hurt him deeply to think back to those happy days.

"Guess who caught the first and the biggest Walleye?" she'd yelled, laying the fish down and diving into the cold lake.

"You shouldn't have to perform surgery on Sunday, — I'll filet them," Bill remembered saying to Doc as he picked up the stringer and carried them to their fish-cleaning table where he made fast work of ten thick boneless filets, while the others changed for dinner. When Doc returned, Bill watched him soak the fresh filets in a mixture of milk and eggs before shaking them in a plastic bag filled with flour, salt and breadcrumbs — explaining all the time how an Indian guide had taught him how to make the best shore lunch in America. Then after melting a pound of lard in a huge skillet, they all watched each filet sizzle as he carefully lowered one filet at a time into the pan, which Bill recalled was spattering in every direction.

Mary had prepared everything but the main entree while Bill and Susan helped set the table as they snacked on some hors d'oeuvres, happily drinking and talking about Susan catching the largest Walleye. Then Bill remembered how Doc walked out on the deck and smugly rang a large silver dinner bell, yelling — "Let's eat."

It took only a few minutes for them to ravenously devour the delicious Walleye filets, and then as the sun began to inch closer to the horizon, Doc once again started the powerful diesels, pulling the boat off the beach. As the chill of the lake took over, he powered up the boat yelling, "We'll have some warm coffee and dessert once we're safely docked." Slipping on their jackets, Mary, Susan and Bill found a comfortable place at the stern of the boat where they were protected from the wind, watching the rolling wake reflect a spectacular sunset. Then as the sun finally disappeared below the horizon, Doc carefully guided the boat along the stick-like markers back to that shaky dock. Bill could still remember that deathly silence when the diesels stopped — just before the sounds of the night once again felt it safe to take over as the frogs and crickets resumed their evening symphony. Even though they were protected from the wind, Mary hurriedly shut the cool evening air out by closing all the windows, before she served coffee and dessert.

After some casual conversation, Bill remembered how Doc held up one hand to get their attention.

"I apologize for changing the subject," he'd explained, "but Mary's probably told Bill that we'll be leaving North Dakota in January, and the hospital will need to hire a new Nursing Director and a new General Surgeon. Mary and I have talked an awful lot about our retirement years, and I've concluded that if we're to ever enjoy retirement, we need to do it now. I've been fighting these Dinosaurs for so long, I'm completely exhausted, and I need to get away from it all. I also have some real fears about what's going on with these healthcare monopolies, and both you and Susan need to hear some of my concerns." And as he looked at Bill he whispered, "I hope that what I'm going to tell you will somehow protect you and your family."

That caught Susan's attention as Doc paused, taking a quick Scandinavian swig of scalding hot coffee.

"Bill, you're one of the best damn administrators I've ever seen, and I can't stand to see you get trapped by that stupid-ass Lanin. But let me start by saying it's very important for me that no one knows what I'm about to share with you."

"Both Susan and I can assure you of that," Bill answered as he looked to Susan for approval.

Then after Susan nodded rather cautiously, Doc continued.

"All right, let me tell you I've been under some severe pressure to sell my practice to Lanin's clinic, and I've never caved in to his demands before, because I consider his clique to be the biggest conglomerate of corrupt ass-holes on the face of the earth. There's no one at that damned clinic you could ever trust, and as you already know, many new physicians are either run out of town by their boycotting, or they eventually bow to becoming submissive to those bastards. Because I came from a wealthy local family, my practice was well established before they came into power, and they haven't been able to hurt me — although that's not to say they haven't tried. I could tell you stories that would curl your hair, but our time can best be served by telling you only what you need to know."

With that he paused just long enough to finish one last spoonful of cherry dessert.

"Dick Lanin is an inept GP who could hardly qualify for his license to practice after he finished his general internship. About nine years ago he sucked up to his controller buddy Collier and the Sisters, whom he hates, so he could get appointed as Board Chairman at the hospital. We've all known that Collier was an original plant from that huge Nashville monopoly, but none of us had the guts or foresight to do anything about it back then — nor did we ever think it was even going to be a problem. As a result, Lanin and Collier have been stealing the hospital blind, and you've been successful in finally cutting off their water. If they had it their way, they'd bankrupt the hospital so they could take it over. You also need to know that Sister Jean, the former Administrator, and Sister Catherine the former Nursing Director, before you came here, were murdered by that son-of-a-bitch. Bill, that's the absolute truth, but nobody is ever going to accuse him of that, if they want to live very long. You also need to know that those two Sisters were fed up with Collier's crooked accounting tactics, and were about to blow the whistle on him. In fact, Sister Gerome, the Provincialate, told me they were driving to Denver to explain what was happening when their car ended up in the lake. They'd also told Gerome they were leaving the convent, and that was final — all because of the hell Lanin and Collier had created for them."

"Later," Gerome said to me, "she'd placed Jean and Catherine in two of her most responsible positions, and had told them they couldn't just walk out on them — she told them they needed to drive to Colorado, so they could at least talk before they made any decisions that involve the hospital. If we lose that hospital, we lose our mission in healthcare she'd said to them just before they were murdered.

"Then after Lanin concocted that damned accident on their trip to Denver, Gerome flew here to visit with me. She told me she was searching for a solution to what was rapidly becoming an impossible situation. As you know, they're a small order of just over three hundred nuns, and they'd already lost two of their smaller hospitals in the same type of hostile take-over. Bill, it was going to be impossible for them to survive if they lost this hospital. I remember standing there and watching her nervously pacing back and forth as she agonized over the predicament she was in."

With this, Doc paused, taking one last swig of coffee.

"Then she told me she should've seen this coming. You know how our hospital's costs have been spiraling out of control since those profit-centered HMOs have taken over our once nonprofit healthcare system, she'd said. And it was probably Jean's only way of getting out of an impossible situation. Just as soon as she earned her Masters Degree, I moved her right into one of the toughest jobs we had — and that was wrong, she explained to me."

"Yes, but you had no choice — you had no one else who was even qualified," I replied.

"I know, but she was just too young and inexperienced, and it was a huge mistake. Worse yet, we've kept her in that position way to long. In fact, she told me she couldn't tolerate another day in that hospital because of these two thieves, which she referred to as Sodom and Gomorrah. Doctor, do you realize both Jean and Catherine were asking me for dispensation from their religious vows — can you believe that? She'd said to me — I can remember when a Sister's vow was for life, and if we keep losing our younger nuns, it's going to be hopeless for us to continue to help the sick and disabled."

"Bill, for as long as I've known Sister Gerome, she'd always been a very efficient and capable decision maker, but this time she was clearly at a loss as to what to do. In fact she asked me if I'd pray with her, and as I watched her lower her tall aching body to her knees her voice echoed through the room in a way I'll never forget. It was just as if she had a direct line to God. I'll never forget the way she said Dear Lord, when will I acquire some problem solving skills? Please give me your divine guidance. I just don't understand what you want me to do. Then she lowered her head and prayed out loud — saying a prayer I'll never forget."

"Lord, make me an instrument of Thy peace; where there is hatred, let me sow love; where there is injury, pardon; where there is doubt, faith; where there is despair, hope; where there is darkness, light; and where there is sadness, joy. O Divine Master, grant me that I may not so much seek to be consoled as to console; to be understood as to understand; to be loved, as to love; for it is in giving that we receive, it is in pardoning that we are pardoned, and it is in dying that we are born to eternal life."

"I can't explain it but I felt like the Lord was right there in the room with us. It was scary. I don't know if you know this about Sister Gerome, but she's half Lakota Indian, and she loved working on their Indian Reservation at Wounded Knee. She felt far more at peace swinging a hammer, or helping to build a home for a needy tribe member than playing corporate politics. But since much of her life had been spent helping the sick and disabled, she'd often said to me that she'd be damned before she'd let another group of entrepreneurial fat cats take over their largest hospital. Bill, when she finished praying her entire body seemed to relax as if she was finally at peace with herself — just as if an answer came to her without any doubt as to what had to be done. I could see the pain in her eyes as she maneuvered her large frame into a standing position, inhaling deeply to relieve that constant hip pain that had always plagued her."

Then she looked at me and said, "Doc, we're not licked yet. We're not going to give up our mission, or let some corrupt group of fat cats profit from these poor sick and disabled human beings."

"Bill, I can remember how her brown eyes were flashing in defiance as she hurriedly walked to Sister Jean's office with me right behind her."

"Dave Nelson, that consultant we hired, has just completed a Role and Program Study for us," she muttered, searching for his phone number. "He's familiar with our problems. I'm going to ask him to get us a professional administrator who can salvage this hospital."

For a moment, I'd felt like I'd just witnessed a miracle. Fortunately, Dave Nelson, the Vice-President of the Harrington and Associates was at his desk, as she blurted out, "Mr. Nelson, this is Sister Gerome. I'm sorry to bother you, but something has come up that urgently requires your help."

Since she had him on a speaker phone I could hear him say, "Sister, that's no problem. What's on your mind?"

"Mr. Nelson, I've got a big problem and I need your help. Sister Jean and Sister Catherine were killed in a car accident Friday night. They were both driving to Colorado to meet with me on Monday, and they were planning to resign if you can believe that. In fact, they told me they were planning to leave the order immediately."

"Sister, I'm so sorry to hear that — that's terrible! Please accept our sympathy."

"Thank you, but this has been a terrible set back to us as you can well imagine, and I can no longer let our hospital problems continue this way. I need to take the necessary steps to protect our ownership, and I want you to get me a top notch lay administrator who can put things back together. I know the church won't like that, but that's the way it is."

"Sister, this day was inevitable," Dave said to her, "and I'm glad you're finally ready to face up to your problems. What you're going to have to do is get somebody who can go in there and play hard ball — and you know what? You're going to have an even bigger problem when these new Medicare Caps control your hospital's reimbursement, which goes into effect in just eighteen months. Actually, you have less than two years to reduce your expenses, or your hospital is going out of business."

"I'm just beginning to realize that," she grumbled. "Worse yet, Mr. Simms, our Provincialate Controller, feels there have been some huge amounts of money disappearing from that hospital. He thinks it's been going on since that Controller, Mr. Collier, and the new Board Chairman, Doctor Richard Lanin have taken over the Board of Directors. In fact, we've become one of the highest charging hospitals in the nation. Just the other day he showed me how the hospital's expenses have been increasing at an average of twenty percent annually since those two came on board. And this year, they expect an increase of more than thirty percent. We've been asking Sister Jean about this for months, but she can't, or won't give us any answers. But that's what this was all about. Mr. Nelson, we're beginning to feel like outsiders in our own hospital. And you're absolutely right, we're going to lose another hospital if something isn't done to turn things around — and I mean right now!"

"Well, that's not going to be an easy assignment," Dave replied. "In fact, I can only think of a couple men in the entire country who might be persuaded to handle that type of combat — and I can tell you right up front — it'll be very difficult to persuade them to take on that bunch of hoodlums and their powerful international bankers that have bankrolled them."

"Mr. Nelson, I want you to contact them immediately. You do whatever it takes to get a qualified administrator to help us reclaim our hospital. We just can't continue this way any longer. And Mr. Nelson, it's time we hire someone we can trust — someone who can look out for our interests."

"Sister, I'll get right on it," Dave replied, "and I don't want you to get discouraged, I'm sure we'll find someone who can measure up to the task. I'll discuss it with our staff this afternoon and I'll call you first thing, once I find a candidate for the job."

"And Bill, as you know — we were fortunate enough to hire you," Doc said. "But now you need to understand that Lanin is going to make you pay dearly for what you've accomplished. As Board Chairman, Lanin has used his position, and the hospital's financial wherewithal to move up rapidly in the informal ranks of his Dinosaur Club, which represents a sizable group of corrupt physicians throughout North Dakota, Montana, South Dakota, Nebraska, and I believe Colorado."

Bill recalled looking at Susan, who was glaring at him. "I've heard about that wealthy Oligarchy that wants to make some big bucks off healthcare, but I had no idea that many doctors were mixed up in this thing," Bill scowled, starring at Doc.

"You can bet your sweet ass it's big, and you better pay close attention to what I'm going to tell you. I now understand this Dinosaur Club has just appointed Lanin to some top position, and the officers of that illustrious aristocracy meet secretly every quarter in Las Vegas. And I suspect that the hospital has been unknowingly paying for all of Lanin's previous frivolity — at least until you arrived on the scene. You may not know this, but it's now mandatory for every member of your hospital medical staff to routinely pay a substantial amount of money in cash, to their organization if they want referrals from Lanin's clinic. This money is then used to accomplish their political agenda."

Bill recalled the sour look on Doc's face as he continued.

"From what I've been told, they keep no minutes, and their financial power and influence is growing every year. So far, I've refused to pay one damn dime to them because I just can't swallow their strong-arm tactics. But recently, Odoroff, who's short on ears and long on mouth told me I'd have to contribute three thousand dollars in cash, and that's what persuaded me to get the hell out. Hell, those contributions go right into some God damned politician's pocket, so that healthcare can be shoved out into the open market, where only those who can afford care will receive it. That's nothing more than a two level system where the poor will get pissed on — and that's called trickle down healthcare."

"My God Doc, what type of professional image is healthcare getting? What are they going to do for an encore, screw all our sick and disabled in America?" Bill snarled. "Americans have already paid billions of tax dollars to develop a quality nonprofit healthcare infrastructure, and it sounds like these bastards intend to rape and pillage the poor sick and disabled patient into oblivion."

"It's much worse than that, and it's not just healthcare we're talking about. Our utility companies, our airline industry, our schools, and many of our large corporations have all been deregulated so this wealthy upper class can create their New World Order and monopolize the global market under the deceitful heading of globalization. And the only thing their HMO's and their corporate practice of medicine look at when they see a patient is how many dollars can we squeeze out of this one. So as a result, our once nonprofit, legally licensed private practice of medicine by professional doctors is going to hell in a hand basket, which doesn't sound like an open market to me. And on top of all that, the patient doesn't have a damned thing to say about what's being done to them anymore. But what else is new? Hell, these guys don't know what democracy means — I can't tell if it's a democracy or hypocrisy. Worse yet, my once respected Republican conservative party and this Dynasty have all been bought off by these bastards, if you can believe that."

Bill remembered how Susan had been squirming in her chair, and finally out of complete frustration she blurted out, "Doc, what's happened to that Hippocratic Oath you all thought was so sacred?"

Doc looked at her and shrugged. "Hey," he chuckled. "The Dinosaurs will tell you to shove that where the sun don't shine. They've spent years going to school, and they want to get paid for their hypocrisy — not some damned Hippocratic Oath they've all taken back in their school days. Susan, Lanin's so damned mad at Bill right now it's

31

unbelievable. We constantly hear at coffee, how he's going to get both Sister Gerome and Bill if it's the last thing he ever does."

Bill recalled how Mary physically flinched at that, knowing Doc had said much more than he should have.

"Well that's nice to know," Susan interrupted. "You come in and work your butt off to improve things, and they're going to get you for cleaning up their mess. Sounds like they want to control more than the practice of medicine to me," she snarled. Then gritting her teeth she added, "Maybe, 'We the People,' really don't have any rights anymore."

"I agree," Doc replied, "and on top of all that, they've been doing things that have been scaring the hell out of me and many other ethical physicians. Now their damned monopolies are acquiring nonprofit hospital ancillary services as their own private business in almost every part of the country, and that use to be considered a conflict of interest — a no-no — beside being far too costly to the patient. In fact, if a physician prescribed something they'd receive money for, it was once considered unethical. But what the hell — it's a sweetheart deal if the upper crust can triple their income without any regulation or intervention, all because they've paid off some crooked politician. That's how they're baiting these younger doctors into joining their Dinosaur Club. And don't tell me they don't have power. But you know what? They don't realize that someday the consumer's going to bite back at them — and stop paying them when the sick and disabled all go broke. They just don't seem to realize that most empires fail because of people revolutions. That's why more experienced countries have gone to a single nonprofit prepayment system, so they can control this type of abuse. And that's not some damned profit insurance system, like we have today."

Bill nodded, "Your absolutely right Doc, and I agree with you."

With that he recalled how Doc paused, sucking in a deep breath before blowing it out in a long frustrated whistle.

"Bill, you're very much aware that Lanin's Dinosaurs have already taken over two of the Sister's poorly run hospitals, aren't you?"

"Yes."

"Well, I bet you don't know it was Lanin who orchestrated those take over's in Nebraska. And once these Managed Care Monopolies take over, the public will never prevail again. When I asked Lanin if he wasn't creating an illegal monopoly, he said — we've got the consumer by the balls, and just what the hell can they do about it? Are they going to put us all in jail, where we can't treat them when they get sick?"

"That may be just what we need to do," Bill growled, puckering his mouth tightly. "At least it would help cut down on the current excess of some two hundred thousand physicians in this country."

"The other thing I was going to tell you, which should be extremely important to you is they're forcing hospital boards, under the threat of boycott, to replace highly qualified administrators with their yes men, like Collier. Today, every new administrator must be capable of sucking-up to the Dinosaurs to keep their job and their big salaries, or they get rid of them. That's their way of controlling things. I don't have to tell you that you've walked into a buzz saw, and that's what's going to happen all across America over the next few years. Ever since we won the cold war, America has been to strong for these bankers to control, and that's how they are going to weaken this once great nation — so they can take over."

Susan and Bill looked at each other as if Doc had just touched a hot wire.

"Susan, it looks like I should be the one to retire, not Doc," Bill grumbled.

Frowning, Doc picked up his empty coffee cup and then quickly set it back down. "Bill, these wealthy noblemen have set up the largest administrative blackballing system in the world, and you're probably pretty close to the top of their list, right now. They don't want ethical Presidents that lead; they want yes men. Perhaps you can now see why I'm ready for retirement. No practicing physician would dare tell anyone what I'm telling you, because they'd be castrated — but I'm in a position where I can still get out, before I contaminate a lifetime of ethics with this Lanin bullshit — and so are you."

Bill thought Doc was finished, but then he continued.

"Now I'm going to really break their God damned code of silence," he snarled, leaning forward in his chair and lowering his voice. "Richard Lanin's a very close friend to the man that first introduced me to my wife."

Bill remembered how Mary's face flushed with that remark.

"You probably know Red Hinkley, don't you?"

"Oh yes, I've played golf with him a few times."

With that Mary looked at her feet, embarrassed — trying to ignore what Doc was about to say.

"Well, Dick Lanin and Red are the best of friends. Red's been involved in some sort of Las Vegas underworld for many years, and I can't stand the bastard, even though he helped me meet Mary. And recently I've been told by a very reliable and close colleague of Lanins, that Red paid a Las Vegas mechanic to do away with those two Sisters."

Mary was visibly relieved as she glanced at Bill.

"That was their attempt to place their yes man, Collier, in the top position at our hospital. And although that take-over backfired on them when you fired Collier, they'll be patient for the time being, and they'll acquire another yes man once they find a way to get rid of you. No one knows that you plan, or even desire to leave once you have things in place, so they think you're here to stay, and they're really afraid of you." With that Doc rubbed his chin, staring stoically at Bill.

"That paranoid bastard thinks you may have some type of government connection, and that you intend to expose their mischief — Bill, he's afraid of you, and I'd advise you to keep him thinking that way. But I'd also recommend you at least look over your shoulder now and then, and I'd damn well not get caught in any corners if I were you."

"Yes, I guess I'd better watch my hind quarter the way it sounds," Bill replied, clenching his fists as he glanced at Susan to check her reaction.

With that, Bill recalled how Mary stood up and began to gather the dishes, smiling at both Bill and Susan as she moved quickly around the table. Yes, Doc had confirmed Bill's worst suspicion of what was happening in healthcare, and he now knew it would be next to impossible to get any hard evidence on Lanin's informal organization. He also was certain that this corrupt aristocracy was growing like a cancer across the country.

After Bill and Susan gathered their belongings, Bill remembered shaking Doc's hand and saying, "thank you, I now have a much better understanding of the magnitude of this thing."

As they all began to make their way along the shaky dock, Bill once again turned and thanked both Mary and Doc for alerting them to what was really going on, agreeing to meet again if and when they found it necessary.

"They've shown considerable courage in trying to help me," Bill thought as he drove away on the narrow dirt road.

Chapter 3

Mary Wants to Help

One week after Bill had contacted Mary, she flew to Colorado Springs. Dave had made arrangements for her to stay at the Broadmoor, and Bill agreed to meet her at the airport. As she walked out of the gate she smiled and threw her arms around Bill, giving him a big hug. Their frequent glances conveyed their pleasure at once again being together, and after getting her a room they sat at the patio bar overlooking the lake, where they had a drink and caught up on what had happened to both of them since they'd last seen each other. Although they'd always maintained a professional relationship, which had only grown since their years in North Dakota, their strong support for one another was also very apparent. As they enjoyed the beautiful mountain scenery surrounding them, it was reassuring for both of them to be back together.

Bill had anticipated the administrator would be impressed with Mary, and therefore had made all the necessary arrangements for her to rent a furnished townhouse close to his, in the foothills of the Cheyenne Mountain. Then after she was formally hired they both realized her schedule was going to be extremely busy, so they agreed to routinely have brunch at the Hatch Cover on Sunday mornings. The Hatch Cover was a small but popular restaurant nestled picturesquely amongst the tall pine trees just down the street from where they lived. Each Sunday they sat where they could watch their favorite Scrub Jay peck at one of the many huge seed laden pinecones that lay on the ground just outside the restaurant's window. Eventually they began to feel like this bird was a part of their Sunday ritual, as the glowing logs in the fireplace provided the warmth they both enjoyed in their recently rekindled relationship.

"Doctor McGrath seems to do just as he pleases, and Mr. Bakencamp isn't about to challenge him," Mary said, sipping at her cup of hot green tea. "Bill, from where I sit, it appears this young man has the entire medical staff under his thumb, as well as my nursing staff, and I think it's all because of the big bucks he and Hanes have brought into that hospital. They must be averaging a CS case a day at fifty thousand dollars a case — and you have to admit that's quite impressive."

"You've got to be kidding," Bill scowled. "At that price, they must all be making millions! No wonder no one wants to challenge them," he growled, raising both eyebrows. "Have you had a chance to visit with any of the parents?"

"I certainly have, and it seems like these two characters had frightened many of the parents into this surgery. I also found that not one of the parents was ever informed of the severe hemorrhaging or the long-range implications involved. It appears these guys have not only violated the patient's right of informed consent, they may well have deceived the parents into believing their child would actually become retarded if they didn't perform this miraculous procedure immediately. On the surface, it appears these two have no regard for any of our hospital standards or regulations at all. Bill, I've never seen anything like this," she frowned, quickly swirling her spoon to scoop up a small tea leaf that had just floated to the surface. Then after finally looking up, her striking blue eyes appeared even more troubled.

"I also know that Hanes hired McGrath right after he'd finished his residency, and then somehow persuaded this young inexperienced student to buy his practice," she scowled — glancing over her shoulder to see that no one was listening. "Dollar wise, that had to be quite a windfall for this Young Turk just starting out in practice. And worse yet, I think he now believes he's Jehovah, saving all these poor little infants. In fact, I could find no evidence he'd ever performed a single Total Calvarial Reconstruction before he was appointed to our hospital staff. And from all the information I've been able to gather, he'd only completed a general pediatric residency. Yet, during his first year in Colorado, he performed more than a hundred CS surgeries, without ever being properly supervised or even boarded in neurosurgery."

"So during this supposed epidemic, you're telling me he wasn't even boarded — is that right?"

"Yes — I'm almost sure of that — and yet to talk to him, you'd think he's the nation's leading expert."

Bill's eyes narrowed recognizing the impact this could have on any hospital.

"What does Bakencamp say about all this? Is he even aware that the patient has the right to select a qualified surgeon, and at least consent to or decline any research procedure? Does he realize the patient's family should also have any research procedure risks fully explained to them before they even attempt to obtain their consent?"

"I asked him that, but he must've had his hearing aid turned off. He told me they are the leading hospital in the nation for this procedure, and it's not research. He says every hospital in the country will soon be performing this same procedure, and I shouldn't worry about it. When I asked him if this procedure was classified as routine, or if McGrath's formal training in this procedure was documented, he just glared at me — In fact he didn't even respond."

With that Bill threw his napkin on the table, pushing his plate away.

"That gutless son-of-a-bitch is supposed to be responsible for affecting the mission of the hospital, and yet that untrained horse's neck is using infants as guinea pigs, without telling the parents the facts — talk about deregulation!"

"I know, but Bakencamp is not a Bill Warner — I guess you've spoiled me. I don't think I'm going to last very long in his camp," she smirked, curling the corner of her mouth disdainfully.

"Bakencamp is the one who shouldn't last very long," Bill grumbled. "I just talked with the Health Department about all these abnormal skulls their seeing, and they say they've been concerned about this epidemic for some time now."

"That's probably true," Mary nodded. "Haven't unusual shaped skulls been with us since ancient times? Tell me — just what's a normal shaped skull?"

Pausing a moment, Bill finally shook his head in disgust — "I can't!"

"Does the Public Health Department even know if the Colorado ratio of CS cases to population is the same as in other states?" Mary asked, already anticipating the answer.

"No, they don't," Bill, explained as his finger tracked over his notes. "I looked that up and the average throughout the country runs at around three and a half cases for every ten thousand births. After McGrath arrived, the Colorado rate jumped to almost eight and a half, and then after he was there a while it peaked at fourteen and a half," Bill explained, looking both concerned and confused as he thought about that — "So I guess it all changed about the same time McGrath arrived on the scene."

"Oh my God," Mary shook her head in disgust. "I suppose Hanes had another mouth to feed, so they went out and created more patients."

Bill placed both hands behind his head, stretching back in his chair as if defeated. "God, I hope not," he growled, glancing at Mary for only a moment. "Listen to what they say here. *Colorado identified what they referred to as clusters of cases, occurring at various times in different locations throughout the state. For example, a cluster of several cases was reported in an area just north of Denver, and then that same year a cluster of ten more cases was found in a small area just to the west.* I guess that's when the state first launched their study. At the same time they also asked the Center for Disease Control to become involved, and the CDC agreed to conduct a comparative study to further investigate the problem. And for a while they even thought it might be the altitude. Anyway, the CDC initially considered it to be a full-scale epidemic, and since Colorado had no disease registry for CS it was almost impossible to even track the patients or the physicians, so that fourteen and a half percent ratio is totally an unreliable figure. In fact, they told me they were really starting from scratch."

"I've got to be honest with you, I feel the same way — as if I'm starting from scratch," Mary frowned. "In fact, I'd never even heard of the problem until I came here, so I guess I'm really starting from scratch."

"Welcome to the club," Bill replied, "you're certainly not alone on that. The frightening thing is those CS figures continued to increase until the CDC finally opened it up to public scrutiny," he explained, flipping past a few more pages. "Here's where it really gets interesting. In their CS study, several neurosurgeons from both Atlanta and your hospital were asked to submit X-rays of their most recent cases, and an unbiased radiologist was asked to review the patients' X-rays to determine if they met standard diagnostic criteria for the disease. The origin of each X-ray wasn't revealed to the radiologist, and he reviewed over ninety-three percent of some six hundred cases, finding that two-thirds of McGrath and Hanes cases did not have CS, according to all known diagnostic criteria."

"So you're telling me McGrath and Hanes misdiagnosed as much as sixty-six percent of their cases?"

Bill nodded. "And what's even worse is several other independent comparative studies confirmed the same thing. So as a result, the CDC concluded the epidemic was a result of their overly aggressive diagnosing."

Mary inhaled, letting out a long-drawn-out whistle at the injustice of it all. "That's criminal negligence — that's malpractice. He needs to be stopped now, and fast."

"You're right, and you're going to do just that by reinstating some hospital standards."

"Bill, I'm really having trouble believing any capable surgeon would take a normal infant and perform major surgery without a confirmed diagnosis, or at least a second opinion by a qualified consultant," she groaned. "This pains me deeply!"

"Mary, they don't even know the cause of this disease, and that's what makes this whole thing such a neat con-job if these doctors are completely free to do what ever they want for more bucks."

"I agree, and it really scares me when my staff tells me McGrath is God's gift to children — how can we be so blind?"

As tears filled her eyes, she quickly forced them back, turning her head to regain her composure. Her sensitivity had always been obvious to Bill, and it was easy to understand why people liked her so much. You always knew where she was coming from because she was at all times an open book, and that's what Bill respected most about her — besides also being a very attractive and likeable person.

"Mary, I feel just as you do. I don't know how any ethical human being could feel any different. Here, let me read their final decision to you." *Eventually, the CDC confirmed the high rate of CS as being attributable to inaccurate diagnoses, rather than an epidemic.*

Mary looked squarely at Bill. "My God," she cried. "Just how am I going to approach this mess? This is a medical staff disaster, for which it appears their doing nothing about." Glaring defiantly out the window, she looked confused.

"Sure it's a medical staff disaster," Bill quickly responded. "But you can still demand basic standards be met. And you should also require the medical staff to provide accurate supportive information such as comparative skull measurements, or at least documented evidence of the progression of the disease over time, before you schedule any more of these major CS surgeries."

Looking at his watch, Bill suddenly realized they'd talked away most of the morning as he signaled the waitress for their check.

After the waitress left, he continued. "Mary, you need to confirm that all CS cases have been validated by X-ray, and that all supportive subjective and objective information is recorded in the patient's chart. In fact, each surgeon should be asked to provide a written plan of accomplishment, clearly stating the specific type of surgery they intend to perform to resolve the problem, before you schedule anymore CS cases."

Pausing, Bill thoughtfully bit at the inside of his cheek. "Mary, the fusion of one single sagittal suture should never justify a total removal and reshaping of the entire skull, let alone the forehead of any infant. And more importantly, the hospital needs to define what research is, and then document and approve all these major surgeries before they're ever done. I feel any Total Calvarial Reconstruction is just too damned risky and extensive, and each procedure needs to be clearly defined and monitored — I'm not sure if your hospital's policy also requires an unbiased second opinion by another qualified neurosurgeon with that type of major surgery, but it sure as hell should. And that's what you'll need to enforce. You need to put those regulations back in place."

"Okay," Mary said with conviction, quickly wiping a last tear from her cheek.

Taking Mary's hand, Bill squeezed it tightly, trying to ease her agitation. "That's enough discussion on the good doctors and this fallacious epidemic."

Neither spoke as they both thought about the impact this was going to have on the hospital. Finally Bill said, "You might as well accept the fact that McGrath is going to retire wealthy, right on the heels of Hanes if this continues, all because the consumer remains so damned submissive and uneducated about their own well being and the importance of having trustworthy physicians and standards in medicine. Corrupted physicians know better, but some of them just can't deny their voracious appetites, which they'll never satisfy. Taking advantage of the sick and disabled is nothing more than that same old *Witch Doctor Syndrome* we suffered from years ago."

Mary gave Bill's hand a final squeeze before she blew her nose.

"You're right. I wonder what ever happened to those doctors that entered medicine with the high ideal of helping the sick. I know my husband was one," she said, sliding her chair back so she could stand up.

"There just aren't too many of those left any more," Bill, replied. "And yes, your husband surely was one. But we still have to educate the patient so they can at least become aware of those few bad apples, and that's why I'm writing."

As Bill picked up the receipt for brunch he continued, "Well, unless we plan to eat dinner here we better quit for the day. It sure seems like old times, working weekends to improve the system."

As they left, Bill said, "I guess we both have a little better understanding of CS."

"Yes, I think I finally understand it. In fact, I think I now understand it too damn well," Mary scoffed.

"With that photographic memory of yours, I bet you do. Why don't you tell me what you've stored on CS in that head of yours, while we walk home?"

"Okay, let me think a moment," she laughed, as Bill pushed open the massive Mexican door. Once Mary read something, she had almost one hundred percent recall, and as they started to walk home, she said, "Alright — let me see — at birth, there are four sutures or fissures of the skull that separate the five membranous bones on the top of the head. And because the infant's skullcap is very flexible at the time of delivery, it provides nothing more than an elastic type cranial vault that surrounds and protects the brain. And those four major sutures serve an important function in resisting the separation of the five bony skull plates, while allowing for brain growth." After hesitating a moment she continued. "It's also important to remember that the brain's largest growth period occurs during the first three years of an infant's life — and the premature closure of any one of those sutures potentially results in this very rare birth defect, called CS disease."

Bill laughed, for it sounded like she was reading from the text itself.

"Abnormal suture closure results in the skull bones fusing together before the brain growth is completed." She continued. "When that happens, the brain will grow through whatever sutures are still open; causing what is referred to as morphological abnormalities and deformities. Increased pressure on the brain perhaps can result in brain damage, or developmental delays, but currently there's very little knowledge about that. Surgical intervention most often requires the surgeon to cut artificial cranial sutures where they're absent, but even that simple procedure isn't always necessary."

Stopping, she stood silent for a moment.

"The most common deformity of the skull usually involves a single suture repair, such as the sagittal suture located right on the top of the skull," she explained as she again starting to walk slowly. "To reopen this single suture is normally considered a minor cosmetic procedure, and that's been the usual approach to this problem. And that's what I believe should've been done in the Keppler case. Bill, Mrs. Keppler is the first family to sue the hospital."

"I suspected as much," Bill frowned. "By the way, I've scheduled a meeting with Mrs. Keppler next week. Apparently they're bringing a claim against both the hospital and Doctor McGrath, and she seemed willing to meet with me, since I'm not representing the hospital. I'm also going to meet sometime next week with that resident who challenged Doctor McGrath."

"I've met Mrs. Keppler, and I think you'll be quite impressed with her — I'd say she has a claim that's going to be difficult to deny." With that, Mary stopped to kick a pebble off the sidewalk. "There's another case that involved an infant by the name of Shana Fry, where they did what they call a multiple strip craniectomy. That was back when Shana was a fifteen-month-old infant, which is rather late to perform such a procedure. Apparently he removed way too many strips of bone and left a very large opening in the skull. After more than a dozen surgeries, the bone never grew back and they had to use several of her ribs to close her deformed skull."

Bill grimaced — spinning completely around as he visibly flinched at her comment. "Wow, that's horrible," he snarled.

43

"From what I understand, the infant was at an age where the bone wouldn't regenerate as fast as in a newborn and here again they only found that out by trial and error."

"If that isn't research, nothing is," Bill whaled. "Dave told me the hospital may well have to close its doors with all these lawsuits — and you know what? I'm beginning to think they should."

"Oh great, I move here and they close the hospital," Mary howled — letting out a hysterically loud squeal. "All right," she giggled, "let me tell you something else about Veronica's case. The blood loss exceeded more than twice her body's blood volume, which is unbelievably dangerous — particularly with a six-month-old infant who had a previously diagnosed cardiac problem. And worse yet — her X-ray clearly indicates that only the sagittal suture was fused, perhaps only slightly elongating her skull, which would have normally suggested further observation. Bill, he told the parents that the deformity was probably causing pressure to her brain, and she could experience very severe deformity and brain damage. He even told them their daughter might die, which just doesn't happen with a single fused sagittal suture."

"For God's sake," Bill shrieked, "That's unbelievable. But you have to admit that's one hell of an incentive when presented to a terrified mother."

"That's for sure. But the most frightening thing about the Keppler case is he then elected to do a Sub-orbital Restructuring in addition to a Total Calvarial Restructuring. Those two major surgical procedures together, were far more extensive than anything that would ever be required for a single suture repair. Worse yet, he and another untested plastic surgeon did that surgery without any supervision — and that was just a few months after both of them passed their boards — that's what's so disturbing about all this. And from what I hear, McCain had previously failed his boards several times."

"Damn it," Bill whispered — stopping to stare at Mary, with his eyebrows raised in outrage. "Without a doubt, those two major procedures should've required an unbiased second opinion from a qualified surgeon. And we both know that all newly boarded surgeons are required to work under supervision for at least the first year."

"Another thing I've found is Doctor McGrath had never been granted research privileges by the Board of Directors. He'd requested them, but they were denied."

"For God's sake, we both know that when someone conducts research in a private hospital, the requirements are very stringent — documentation, purpose, and results have to all be tracked very closely. Even the Food and Drug Laws require the hospital to track every patient with written reports to them. Damn it, our standards are going to hell with all these new money making schemes."

"Bill, I could find no record of any research approval" she shrugged, as if mystified by it all. "And from Veronica's medical record, it shows her heart stopped when they started the second major Sub-orbital Reconstruction. In fact, it wasn't until then that the student administering the anesthesia called in a boarded anesthesiologist to help him resuscitate the patient, while McGrath and Allen hurriedly closed the incision without even putting the skull bones back in place. And worse yet, they made no effort to freeze the infants skull bones so they could be used later."

"That's unreal," Bill sneered.

"That's why Veronica had to undergo two more surgeries later, when another surgeon had to remove several of her ribs and split them in half to help construct an improvised skullcap. Then later, McGrath suggested that the cardiac arrest was due to her heart condition, saying the Cardiologist should've warned him prior to giving him the go ahead for surgery."

"Boy! Doesn't that sound familiar — these sociopaths always want to point the finger, don't they? I don't suppose he's even thought that this whole damned fiasco could have been avoided if he'd made a proper diagnosis in the first place."

"Bill, you need to meet with Doctor Wilson. He's a neurosurgeon on the faculty at the Medical School, and I think he'd be able to provide some real insight into the problem — and I believe you'll at least find him ethical."

As they stopped in front of Mary's house, Bill smiled, looking into her remarkable blue eyes. "How'd you like to take a ride to the top of

Pikes Peak? Let's go view this area we're living in from fourteen thousand feet."

"I thought you'd never ask." Mary chuckled.

Chapter 4

The Interviews

Early Monday, Bill left for his meeting at Mrs. Keppler's home, which was on the outskirts of Denver. During his trip, he kept thinking of how great it was to have Mary working with him again. *We both seem to need each other*, he thought, parking in front of the Keppler home. After meeting Mrs. Keppler, he asked, "Mrs. Keppler, how's Veronica doing?"

"Please call me Linda," she explained. "No one wants to make a prognosis, but she's certainly has a lot of problems that she has to live with the rest of her life. As you probably know, the surgery made her blind, and her cognitive skills are lagging. I guess you'd say she's retarded, and nobody wants to try and predict just how long she'll survive. To put it bluntly, we've all been devastated by this ridiculous surgery."

Bill could see that she was physically drained and her sunken eyes appeared almost haunted. It was obvious that her burden had long ago taken its toll, and even her marriage hadn't survived as a result of McGrath's incompetence, leaving her all alone to carry this overwhelming burden. Watching Veronica play quietly under the supervision of a therapist, Bill noticed she had many of her mother's facial features.

"I'm aware that you've recently filed a lawsuit against both the hospital and Doctor McGrath and you need to know that I'm not involved in that lawsuit. I'm only seeking the facts of what happened, so I can provide an unbiased professional opinion of what can be done to prevent a reoccurrence. And to accomplish that I need you to tell me your side of the story," he whispered, sitting down next to her on their well-worn sofa.

"I understood that from your phone call — and as I told you, I'll try to help if I can."

Bill nodded. "All right, why don't you just start at the beginning?"

With that Linda's shoulders kind of slumped forward, folding both hands in her lap.

"Let's see, where should I begin? — I guess I'll start by telling you Veronica was born on March 10, three years ago. Before her surgery she was a very active baby, doing things like trying to crawl and roll over, and even raising her head at this very early age — but her pediatrician, for some strange reason, seemed concerned during her three-month check up. He mentioned there was a sign of CS, and he'd like Doctor McGrath to check that out. That was the first time we'd ever heard the term CS, and we certainly had no idea what it meant. Worse yet, we hadn't even suspected that something was wrong," she chocked. "Then after McGrath looked at her X-rays, he immediately told us Veronica had CS — casually describing what he termed a *Total Calvarial Reconstruction* as the surgical procedure that would be required to correct the problem. He also advised us that it would be best to do the surgery before Veronica was six months old. When we asked what would happen if we decided not to go ahead with the surgery, he told us she'd most likely experience pressure to the brain, and a severe deformity of the skull. He even said she could possibly have brain damage, or die. When we attempted to question him about it, he suggested we talk with Doctor Allen, a plastic surgeon."

"When did you find out that Doctor Allen assisted McGrath with most of his surgeries?"

"We really didn't find that out until later, in fact we thought Allen was going to give us a second opinion, and at that time we had no idea the two of them collaborated in their surgeries. Then later we also found that McGrath used the same radiologist to interpret all his CS X-rays. But worse yet, we were never informed that there were many other options for treatment. Now that I've learned the facts, I know we should have seen some other unbiased physician who wouldn't have terrified us into proceeding with such a radical procedure."

Bill tried not to show his visceral disgust saying, "Yes, I understand."

"Here's the hard part for me to understand," she gasped, sucking in a quick breath. "Those physicians received upwards of fifty thousand dollars for that procedure, when a lesser procedure could have sufficed — and perhaps surgery wasn't even necessary. Can you explain that to me?"

"So he never explained any other options to you?"

"Hell no!" she shouted. "But now that the damage is done, he's telling our attorney that he never heard of anyone dying from CS, whether they went treated or untreated. In retrospect — time could've resolved many things, but we weren't given adequate time to decide. And we were given no other option than a Total Calvarial Reconstruction."

Bill's mind was spinning, realizing for the first time that things were far worse than he'd even imagined.

"There's something else I need to tell you," she blurted out. "Veronica was diagnosed as having a minor heart defect, and her cardiologist was considering heart surgery, but he wisely delayed that procedure so he could observe that problem a little longer. In the mean time, McGrath pressured our cardiologist into orally approving what he called a simple cosmetic procedure, without ever obtaining a proper written consultation from him. In fact our cardiologist was never told they intended to do two major surgical procedures. In retrospect, I guess it's our own fault — I don't know how we ever allowed him to proceed with such a gruesome procedure, when our daughter appeared perfectly normal to us." With that, tears of guilt filled her eyes. "I'm sorry, but I can't talk about this without crying. You'll just have to forgive me," she explained, burying her face in her trembling hands.

"Linda, we can stop if you wish?" Bill said. "I'm really sorry to upset you."

As Bill tried to comfort her, she raised one hand, which was now shaking uncontrollably.

"That's all right — I go through this every day, whether you're here or not," she sobbed, gasping between each word. "It's always on my mind. No, I'll continue," she muttered, "Just give me a moment." Then after taking a deep breath she finally added, "As I look back, it's like we were pushed into this whole damned thing, and we certainly weren't given any other options."

Bill nodded, not wanting to interrupt her outpouring of emotions.

"I don't know how to explain it, but we were terrified not to cooperate with this man. In fact, my husband and I were so traumatized we didn't even think about going somewhere else, or seeing another doctor — yet I don't know why we didn't. Now we know all about the other options — right down to the Arizona group that solves the same problem by using rubber bands around the skull to remold its shape. I guess it was that deadline he gave us. You'd think you could trust a doctor. How were we to know he was just after money?"

Bill nodded. *Thank God she's willing to tell her story,* he thought. *Maybe her venting will help rid some of this horrible guilt she's carrying — it's certainly apparent what she's been through.*

"What you've told me is very helpful," Bill said, reaching out to softly touch her hand. "And I can certainly understand why you feel violated," he continued, rotating his neck a bit to ease his tension. "Linda, do you recall if he ever did any measurements or comparative analysis that might have documented the progression of CS?"

"I remember he took some measurements, but we weren't given enough time for him to do any comparative measurements — and to be very honest, we felt like we were being rushed into surgery in order to prevent brain damage."

Bill nodded, noticing the deep lines that had already been permanently etched in her forehead.

"Perhaps I'll have more questions on the workup later, but let me ask you about her surgery," he said, changing the subject.

"Sure," Linda said, stretching both legs out as she leaned forward and pressed both hands against her knees, knowing this was going to be the tough part. "I remember when that clerk asked my husband to sign that surgical consent. He just signed it — ignoring all the fine print. She couldn't have answered our questions anyway. If you've ever signed one of those things it's kind of like jumping off a cliff. You've already placed your total blind faith in a physician you know little about, and even though he hasn't explained things very well, you place your child's life in this individual's hands. Talk about blind subservience."

With that she pressed her fingers tightly over her lips, holding back another sob — and then shaking her head from side to side as tears once again flowed freely.

"There's no turning back, you just roll the dice," she chocked. "You'd never even think they'd take advantage of you."

God all Friday, Bill thought, *she'll never recover from this.*

"Then when your daughter goes to surgery, you sit where they tell you to sit and wait for someone to tell you what's happening. You helplessly place your total trust in everyone and anyone," she groaned, awkwardly wiping away each tear with the back of her hand. "Then after three or four hours, Doctor McGrath came out with our daughter's blood spattered all over his scrub gown and explained that Doctor Allen had just started to reshape her eye orbits."

"Why don't you go and have lunch in the hospital cafeteria, it's going to take several more hours," he'd said.

"Then, no sooner did we arrive in the cafeteria than my husband and I were paged and informed that Veronica had gone into a full blown cardiac arrest. We were told she was still alive, but she had to be resuscitated — and that they'd stopped the surgery. We demanded to see her, but it was a full hour before they permitted us to go into the Intensive Care Unit where they'd taken her. It was all such a nightmare." Gasping between sobs, she again held her hand over her mouth for a moment as she stared at the wall, unable to continue. Both eyes were now red and swollen.

"That was the tough part," she mumbled. "I saw her tiny little face peeking out from all those bandages, and tubes and wires seemed to be running everywhere. On top of all that, those damned machines wouldn't stop beeping as we watched our little girl struggle to stay alive." As she pressed both clenched fists against her eyes she choked. "Her little face was so swollen I couldn't even recognize her. I just wanted to grab her and run. I wanted to take her home where she'd be safe — but it was too late."

Bill patted her shoulder, asking they take a break since this was far too much for her to bear. As she scurried out of the room, he walked over to a table where there was a wedding picture of Linda and her husband, showing a vibrant and beautiful bride full of hopes and dreams — obviously looking forward to a wonderful life. There was also another picture of her holding her newborn daughter, and it tore at his heart to feel the destruction she and her daughter had endured.

This case needs to set an example, so it will never happen again, he thought. *People need to know what's going on with this ridiculous marketing of our sick and disabled.*

When she returned, Bill could see that she'd washed her face and had regained some composure before sitting down to continue. "That's the hardest part for me to talk about," she whispered. "Needless to say, it seemed like she was in ICU forever, but when we were finally able to take her home, it was only a couple days later when we could tell that Veronica was unable to see. Her eyes were open, but they just weren't focusing. It was as if she was staring into space. Of course she was too young to measure her vision loss, but she did seem to recognize bright colors. Surprisingly, she was trying to pick up larger objects, which she could better focus on. Later, when she began to take her first few steps, she was trying to touch and identify everything. If she couldn't tell what it was with her hands, she'd touch it to her face or her mouth." With that, Linda slumped forward, exhausted. "She's been very difficult," she whispered, again shaking her head in disgust — "and justifiably so." Then as a second thought she added — "She requires constant therapy." After she blew her nose, she inhaled deeply, trying to relax. "Doctor McGrath told us we'd find gaps in her skull, and he assured us they'd all grow back together eventually. 'Gaps hell' — my God she had no skull at all — there was nothing there to grow back."

Bill was astounded at this, and had to stand up and walk so she wouldn't see his agitation.

"As I've already told you, recent tests indicate her motor skills are abnormal, and she's almost totally blind — but surprisingly, her speech is close to normal. The worst part has been comparing her with other infants. It's so frightening to see how Veronica could have been — but now that's all changed."

As Bill stared at her, he realized it was time to stop this nightmare. *Her life will be hell if she doesn't get some financial assistance,* he thought.

"Linda, you've been very kind to tell me about Veronica," he said, reaching out to give her an affectionate hug. After they chatted a few more minutes, he took one last glance at those pictures of happier days as they walked toward the door. Before he left, he turned and asked. "Would you be available for me to call if I have any further questions?"

"Certainly," she replied, slowly closing the door behind him.

* * * * *

As Bill drove away, he could only think of the hell this young family had endured. These thoughts continued through lunch and remained with him until he reached the Denver Airport, where he was scheduled to fly to Columbia, South Carolina. In Columbia, he planned to meet with Doctor Rahn, who was the resident that blew the whistle on these CS surgeries. Doctor Rahn was waiting in the airport dinning room when Bill arrived.

"Doctor Rahn?" Bill asked.

"Yes sir, that's me."

He was a tall man with pitch black hair that was combed straight back. His skin was olive colored, and as he rose to shake Bill's hand his broad shoulders and strong handshake indicated he was not a man to be taken lightly.

No wonder he had no fear in exposing McGrath, Bill thought to himself.

"I really appreciate your meeting with me," Bill said, sitting across from him in a booth that was far too small for the both of them.

Once again Bill briefly reviewed his role with the Harrington Associates and how he was only seeking an unbiased review of the CS surgery that was going on at that hospital. He also knew it would be very unlikely that Doctor Rahn would openly criticize a fellow physician, so he asked him about his residency first.

"I was accepted into a pediatric neurosurgery residency right after my internship," he replied. "It was a three year program, and the surgeons I worked with were all very capable."

"I believe Doctor McGrath arrived about the time you were a second-year resident, am I right?" Bill asked.

"Yes, I was just finishing my second year, and Doctor McGrath and Doctor Hanes had some type of arrangement with the school, where their patients were available to the residents."

"So you must've scrubbed on their CS cases?"

"Oh yes — but during the first year, you're usually an observer. Then during the second and third year you get to assist a little, under supervision."

"Did you scrub with both Hanes and McGrath?"

"No, I just scrubbed with Doctor Hanes."

"As I understand it, you had some difficulty your third year. Could you tell me about that?"

Doctor Rahn looked away for a moment, clearly debating how he should respond.

"That was the year things began to fall apart. I guess I felt there were just too many CS surgeries going on," he finally blurted out.

"What do you mean by too many?"

"Well, you know, the resident always does all the *scut* work the night before surgery, like doing the pre-op history and physical. And when I'd ask the parents what abnormalities they'd noticed about their child, they'd usually respond, we haven't noticed anything." When I questioned them further, I found that they almost always had been pressured by either McGrath or Hanes — to immediately do the surgery. Disturbingly, they'd say that Hanes or McGrath had told them that unless they had the surgery, they couldn't say how their child would turn out. Why those kids' families didn't get a second opinion — I'll never know. In any event, that bothered me because I had children myself, and if somebody was going to take my child's skullcap off, I'd damn well get a second opinion. Hell, I'd probably get three or four."

"I agree," Bill nodded. "Do you feel the parents were at fault?"

"Hell, there was plenty of blame for what was going on there. Yes, in a lot of ways it was the parents' fault. I suppose it was even the hospital's and the referring doctor's fault. I guess you can't say it was entirely Hanes or McGrath's fault, but that doesn't make it right."

"Did you talk to anyone about that?"

"I sure as hell did — and that's why you're here talking to me now. I went to the Head of the Department of Neurosurgery at the Medical School and told him there were just too many CS surgeries going on, and not enough evidence supporting what they were doing." With that he took a sip of coffee, finally relaxing a bit. "And I told him I wasn't happy about it." Looking away, he rubbed the back of his neck, clearly agitated. "I also talked to several of the professors, and I told them I didn't think things were on the up and up, and that it just wasn't the way professionals should do things."

That was all Bill had to hear. As they continued to visit, Bill's mind was wandering — he'd heard all he had to hear. Then suddenly his attention was refocused when he heard Doctor Rahn say how McGrath had even diagnosed his newborn son Johnny with CS, and recommended surgery for him.

"I took little Johnny, that's my now healthy son, to a neurosurgeon that I knew I could trust, and he told us they were crazy to even suggest surgery.   That's when I went to the Head of the Department and complained. You know, if it could happen to me, it could happen to anybody."

Good-grief, Bill thought to himself. He'd already been overwhelmed by all the fraud he'd heard that day, and although they continued to chitchat a little longer, he'd certainly heard enough for one day. Returning Rahn's strong handshake, he thanked him and said good-bye, and as he sat down by his gate, waiting for his flight home, he thought to himself. *More than a thousand infants have received major skull surgery at that hospital, and I wonder just how many of those tiny little lives have been pointlessly disrupted by these money hungry bastards.*

* * * * *

With the time change, it was only nine in the evening when Bill arrived back in Colorado, and on his way home he stopped to see Mary because he'd been thinking of her, and he needed to talk to someone about his horrible day.

"I just got home," Mary said, kicking off her shoes and flopping into a comfortable lounge chair with a freshly made sandwich in hand. "I just had a meeting with the Administrator and Dr. Dante the Medical Director, and apparently they're expecting this CS story to hit the press on Sunday. And guess what — we've all been instructed not to make any comments to the press — whatsoever," she scowled, indicating quote marks with her free hand. "And in my opinion, these guys need to get their act together. Their trying to pull as many strings as they can, but it's very unlikely they'll be able to tone things down before this whole thing hits the national news." Leaning forward to get more comfortable she took a big bite of her sandwich. "Excuse me," she mumbled with a full mouth, "would you like something to eat?"

"No thank you," Bill chuckled. "I'm still full of that airline food."

"Two of the reporters have apparently been working on this CS story for some time," she went on, holding her hand over her mouth while she chewed between her words. Finally she took a big swig of milk to wash things down. "And from what I've heard — they've really done their homework."

"That's interesting," Bill said. "Mary, I don't mean to change the subject, but do you know who the previous Medical Director was, or where he is now?"

"I believe his name is Doctor Taber, and I think he took a job somewhere in Texas," she mumbled, still trying to finish her sandwich as she drew her legs up under her to get more comfortable. "I can find out for you, if you want me to?"

"Would you? I think he might be able to shed some light on this thing. It sounds like there's a lot more people than I ever realized who've left the ship because of this fiasco."

"I think you're probably right on that."

After Mary finished eating, she was completely absorbed by what Bill told her about his meetings.

"It's beyond me how one of the better hospitals in this country can let that type of crap go on right under their nose," she grumbled. "Its sure beginning to look bad for them — isn't it?"

"I'll say, and I'll bet there's much more to this than meets the eye," Bill added, standing up to leave. "Only time will tell, but eventually it will all come out in the wash."

Mary quickly got up and blocked his path. "Say, I talked with Doctor Wilson today and he said he'd be happy to visit with you anytime. He said you should just give him a call."

"That's great. I'll call him in the morning," Bill said.

"Hey, you can't leave already, you just got here — why don't you stay and watch a movie with me? I've had a pretty hectic day myself, and it sounds like we both need to relax and talk about something besides that damned hospital," she whispered, pulling him toward the living room.

* * * * *

The next morning, Bill called Doctor Keith Wilson, and he told him to come right over. Bill had never been in the Medical School before and he was relieved to find Doctor Wilson at his desk. Wilson was rather short with uncombed brown hair that was scattered every which way. He wore thick horn-rimmed glasses, and his white coat was worn and un-pressed. Earlier in his career, he'd served as an Associate Professor of Neurosurgery at the Medical School, and now was a full professor and Director of the Pediatric Neurosurgery Department. Since pediatric neurosurgery was only a sub-service, his office was small with only one window, and his desk was scattered with all kinds of folders and books.

"Doctor, do you hold any appointments at the hospital?" Bill asked as he sat down.

"No I don't," he frowned, knowing exactly where Bill was heading with that type of question. *That penetrating stare suggests he's not going to be very cooperative*, Bill thought.

"You might as well know right off that I don't intend to express my opinions on the standards of care provided by either Doctor Hanes or Doctor McGrath."

"I understand," Bill replied, quickly changing the subject.

"You're currently treating Veronica Keppler aren't you?"

"Yes I am," he said, his scowl only deepening.

"Mrs. Keppler has told me that she asked you to take over as the treating neurosurgeon because her daughter suffered so many complications."

"Yes, that's correct."

Bill could see he was still uncomfortable, so once again he changed the subject. Looking to his notes, as if he was searching for something important, he asked. "How long have you lived in Colorado?"

"I moved here several years ago, but I'd been here prior to that for my residency training."

With that, Bill felt a little more comfortable — *at least he said more than two words.* "Did you train at this hospital back then?"

"Yes, I spent three months in General Surgery."

"Why did you decide to move back here?"

"There were several reasons. I'd worked in Boston for almost ten years, and originally I'd only planned to stay there for a short time, but I liked the man I worked for, so I just continued until he retired. That's when I decided to look for a new location. In that we were familiar with Colorado, we decided to move back here. My wife also felt it would be good place to raise our children."

Again Bill looked to his notes. "Did the Head of the Department ever discuss why your position was open?"

Finally Wilson smiled. "I don't remember, but he did tell me"— then suddenly he stopped — "I guess the answer to your question is yes."

"What did he tell you?"

"He told me he'd just taken all his residents out of that private hospital and he needed a good pediatric neurosurgeon to head up that department before he'd continue with any more hospital residencies." With that Wilson shifted in his chair, to get a little more comfortable. "I can't remember the exact words, but that's about what he said."

"Did he explain the questionable status of this teaching program?"

"Oh yah, he sure did."

"Can you recall what he said?"

Wilson paused, as if debating how he should respond.

"My hesitation is because I just don't recall. I know we talked about the residents' complaints, and I remember that it was very important for him to change what was going on."

"But didn't you say that when you first started, the residents weren't seeing hospital patients?"

"Yes, that's correct."

"Can you tell me why?"

"Well, let me think a moment. I guess he did tell me that some of the residents were upset, and had talked to him about their concern over there being too much CS surgery."

Bill could see he was still uncomfortable, but he pressed on. "What was their concern?"

"Well, I guess it wasn't just the residents. He'd also received some sort of message, I can't recall if it was written or not, but it was from the National Neurosurgery Association. The message indicated there urgently had to be some changes."

"What kind of changes were they talking about?"

"You'd have to ask him, but I could sense there'd been a great deal of pressure on him to change things right away."

"Did they want someone new to come in to run the department?"

"Yes, they wanted someone to make a fresh start."

Bill paused because his next question was extremely important.

"Do you think that was because they were doing this unusual major CS surgery?"

"That's what I understood."

Good, Bill thought — *at least he's not going to hide the issue.*

"Do you remember if Doctor McGrath was holding a faculty appointment with the Medical School at that time?"

"I don't recall, but I think that whatever status he'd held, it had expired."

"At the time you arrived, was Doctor McGrath training any residents?"

"No, the residents were only working at the medical school."

"Well then you must have been aware that the Health Department was investigating the CS surgeries at Children's?"

"Not when I first arrived."

"Were you aware the Centers for Disease Control in Atlanta, was also investigating things?"

"I just don't remember when I first learned that," he mumbled, staring out the window. "I think I was told that just before I arrived here," he said, rubbing at his unshaved chin.

"Did you ever receive that CDC report?"

"Oh yes, in fact I received several copies."

"So the head of the department had discussed the high incidence of CS with you?"

"Oh yes — and it was disturbingly high. He told me it was higher than any other place in the world, and that's exactly what the residents had been concerned about. In fact, the Center for Disease Control termed it an epidemic." With that he grimaced, kind of clearing his throat. "I'm no epidemiologist, but if you need to know, the CDC could tell you if it was ever classified as an epidemic."

Bill nodded, making a note before he casually got up and walked toward the window.

"Doctor, you're familiar with the Total Calvarial and Facial Reconstruction that Doctor McGrath performed on Veronica, aren't you?"

"Yes, I'm familiar with those operations."

Bill noticed he seemed more relaxed, so he decided to come right to the point.

"When did you first become aware that Total Calvarial Reconstructions were being done for non-symptomatic infants?"

That brought a sour look to his face. "I really can't answer that," he mumbled.

"Alright, what do you think was done surgically for Veronica?"

"Well, I can only describe what normally takes place with that procedure."

"That's fine. Tell me what you think normally takes place."

"All right," he said, pausing a moment to rethink the procedure. "Well, first of all the patient is placed in a semi upright position and the surgeon makes an incision from ear to ear across the top of the skull, pushing the scalp forward to the eye orbits and backward to the base of the skull. The skull is then cut around the entire circumference of the head, just above the ears, so that the total skullcap can be removed. On the back of the head, they'll cut just about a centimeter above the Foramen Magnum, the opening at the base of the skull. And then they cut the skull around to just above the supra-orbital rim at the base of the forehead." As he spoke, he pointed to his own head, his hands tracing forward around the sides of his skull to just above the eyebrows. Then pausing a moment, he thoughtfully bit at his lower lip. "That's always a very delicate and risky procedure, due to the nerves and major blood vessels that can be damaged. Then once the skull cap is successfully removed, it's taken to another part of the operating room where it's reshaped by sawing all the boney plates into numerous loosely floating sections that are wired together to reshape the skull. Because all the blood vessels between the skull and the brain can easily be severed, removal of the entire skullcap can result in an enormous amount of blood loss, which isn't the case with other more common CS procedures." Once again he paused. "And since this procedure is still being researched, it should only be attempted when there's no other alternative."

"Let me ask you," Bill said, looking confused. "When they remove or reconstruct more than the skull cap, let's say the facial bones, that's termed Craniofacial Reconstruction, isn't it? — Isn't that an entirely different procedure?"

"Yes, you're correct."

"I just read your article *Craniosynostosis Misconceptions.* Is that what exists at this hospital?"

"You know, the Health Department asked me to write that article, but they didn't publish it until much later. Probably because the article disagreed with what the locals were doing."

"Do you think the problem you wrote about exists at this hospital?"

"Yes. It certainly does."

"In your article, you indicated you wouldn't perform that extensive of a procedure on a child less than twelve months of age?"

"That's correct — and I wouldn't."

"Is that why the residents were upset, or should I say up in arms?"

"Well, let me put it another way. The Medical School faculty was not of the same opinion as McGrath or Hanes." With that he puffed out both cheeks, blowing the air out slowly as if he was frustrated by the direction their conversation had taken. Glaring up at the ceiling he ran his fingers through his bushy hair.

Bill noticed his frustration but continued. "In your article, you said there are relatively few serious problems associated with CS."

"Yes, and I believe that."

"So with Veronica Keppler, would you say it was a simple form of CS from your standpoint?"

"Yes — in fact I'd classify it as the simplest."

"You also indicated that the fusion of a single sagittal suture in an infant is generally a simple cosmetic problem, and then you go on to say that the surgery should require only the simplest invasive procedure?"

"Exactly, and that's what I tell the infant's parents."

"Do you tell them the child is having intracranial pressure?"

Wilson stared at Bill, startled by his question.

"Do I? — Hell no! — I don't think that's ever been an issue," he shrugged. Holding up both hands he went on to explain, "There are some reports in the literature about pressure being a little elevated, but it's impossible to interpret those reports."

Bill frowned, "Meaning what?"

"That most reports don't measure normal pressure in an infant in any way that's meaningful in my opinion. The only way you might determine that would be to drill a hole in a normal infant's skull."

With that he pointed his index finger at his fist as if he was drilling a hole in some child's skull.

"Then you wait maybe twenty-four hours while you monitor the pressure. And during that entire time the infant is required to be lying quietly on their back, which is impossible. Worse yet, you can't use any medication or sedation if you want an accurate measurement of cerebrospinal pressure. I'm not saying that in trauma cases, or in intracranial surgical cases it's not vital to monitor post surgical intracranial pressure, or ICP, because that can alert you to a serious pressure build up — but there is just not a lot of accurate data available on what might be a normal pressure range in infants."

"So you really don't know what pressure is normal in infants?"

"Exactly — and even if we could measure a build up we still don't know what is normal, or if it even varies from one infant to another. And no responsible parent is going to say hey, you can drill a hole in my normal child's head and stick a pressure monitor in there for twenty-four hours. That's pure research, and it's still not clear to me if an elevated intracranial pressure in an infant is even meaningful. I'd never even bring it up to parents with a child that has a single Sagittal Synostosis."

"What about the danger of blindness? Would you discuss that?"

"It's not been my practice to do so. Again, it's never been a problem with my surgeries."

"What about retardation, or developmental delays?"

Wilson pursed his lips. "No, but I do mention there is a possibility of brain injury during surgery."

"Would you describe the operation you do?"

"You have to realize there are at least a dozen operative procedures for Sagittal Synostosis — maybe more! What I do is I cut the bone along both sides of the Sagittal Suture, which runs along the center of the head" — once again pointing to the top of his own skull. "And then I remove that strip and take a high speed cutting tool, and cut into the remaining bone surrounding the Sagittal strip that I just removed. That's called morcellation. It all sounds kind of crude, but what remains is a lot of loose pieces of skull that are still attached on their under surface. Then I put a drain in so the blood will not collect, and sew the scalp back. In about a month or two, most of the bone grows back together, but in an eight month old infant it may take longer, because bone isn't replaced as fast."

"How long does your procedure take?"

"Well, let me think," he said, leaning back and unconsciously scratching his head. "I'd say it takes around an hour from the time I make my first incision to the time I bandage — approximately an hour, though I'm sure I've done it in less."

"Could you tell me, just as an estimate, what the average range of blood loss would be?"

He paused, starring out the window. "Perhaps eighty milliliters, but it could range higher. In fact, many of my patients lose almost no blood. You never really can anticipate what the blood loss is going to be."

"That's considerably less blood loss than in a *Total Calvarial Reconstruction* isn't it?"

"Of course, and that's why I don't like to do that procedure. When you remove the skull there's just too many complications and way too much hemorrhaging involved. I accomplish the same thing without removing the skull. But that's what this whole controversy's all about."

Bill seemed satisfied with his description and quickly changed the subject.

"When you first came here, did you understand that you were to be the Head of the Department at the hospital?"

"Yes, that's what I was told."

"But that never occurred — right?"

"You have to understand there was a lot of resentment when I arrived, and that was because the Medical School had just removed their Residents from the hospital."

"Had you been appointed Chief of that Service at the hospital, you'd have had responsibility for both Hanes and McGrath, wouldn't you?"

"Yes — that's normally the way it's done," he smirked, placing both elbows on the desk and pressing both index fingers against his lower lip. "That's the way most of the other services function at the hospital."

Bill sat quietly, waiting for him to continue.

"When I first came out here and looked at the job, I talked with Hanes over lunch, or dinner — or somewhere — and he assured me there would be no conflict in my appointment as the Head of the Department at the hospital."

"Wasn't Hanes the Chief at that time?"

"I believe his title was Interim Chief."

"Doctor, you seem very cautious about discussing this situation."

"That's because I just don't feel free to do so."

"Why is that?" Bill asked.

"Doctor McCualey, the hospital's Chief of Surgery suggested I be quiet about it. He told me there is nothing to be gained by taking a position. In other words, I'm not supposed to discuss it. It's that same old code of silence crap we all live with everyday."

Bill nodded, letting him know he understood.

"Who conducts the 'M' and 'M' meetings for Neurosurgery at the hospital?"

"You mean the Morbidity and Mortality meetings?"

"Yes. And if they have them, would you describe just what's involved?"

"In that we still have residents training at the Medical School, I call those meetings every month to review all the deaths and complications on my service, which is required by the Joint Commission, as well as the residency program."

"So it appears you're doing the monthly case audit on the neuro-surgery patients, and then conducting an educational meeting — do either Hanes or McGrath attend your meetings?" Bill asked.

"We invite them, but I don't believe they've ever attended a meeting."

"Aren't staff members required to attend at least seventy-five percent of their M and M meetings to maintain their Active Staff privileges?"

"Yes, but we never review the cases of Doctor Hanes or Doctor McGrath."

"Why don't you?"

"They do their own review of their own cases."

"Hey — that's not an unbiased review," Bill growled.

"You don't seem to understand. Those guys set their own standards. They could care less about what the Joint Commission or anyone else requires."

Finally Bill felt he'd penetrated his protective cover. From all his years of experience, he was well aware that doctors inherently protect one another, but Wilson was now speaking freely and his emotions were finally out on the table. Bill could see a light sweat on his forehead but this only prompted him to continue even more aggressively.

"Look, Doctor, just what the hell's going on here?" Bill scowled. "Either the hospital's in charge or they're not. Just how do those two get off ignoring hospital standards?"

"All right, I'll give it to you straight," he snarled — his jaw now very rigid. "Hanes and McGrath are members of the open staff. They could care less about a faculty appointment. They're too busy making big bucks for their noble gentry to worry about a Medical School stipend. When you mix a corporate medical staff that competes on the open market with a closed professional faculty that's paid a professional stipend — standards and regulations go out the window and you've got a big problem. And that's what I've run into here."

"I understand," Bill nodded, not wanting to say anything that would stop Wilson from continuing. "The hospital's not going to act on the appointment of a new Medical School Chief, when their CEO has all that CS money rolling in. Hell, those two brought in millions of dollars to that hospital last year. That's what counts. It doesn't matter if you mistreat the uninformed patient a little bit. I couldn't bring in half the income those guys do. That's where the power is. But at least I can sleep nights."

"If I understand you correctly, this problem started by mixing a professional faculty with an entrepreneurial staff — am I right?" Bill glared at Wilson, waiting for his answer.

"Now you got it," Wilson said, nodding his head several times. "And, as a result, the Medical School is embroiled in an all out battle with that damned hospital's *Dinosaur Club*."

"What do you mean, *The Dinosaur Club*?" Bill asked — shocked by what he'd just said.

"We've identified a group of more than twenty private practicing physicians that intend to destroy our standards and control the practice of medicine at this hospital. And the new head of that organization is none other than Doctor McGrath — and he's just been playing games with my appointment. Worse yet, he has that Administrator in his pocket, and when the time is ripe, their wealthy banker friends will probably own that damned hospital also. These guys are out to protect their turf, and to hell with any regulated community hospital or some damned nonprofit service that benefits humankind."

The Dinosaur Club! My God there everywhere! Bill thought to himself.

"If I didn't feel I could trust you, I'd have chased you out of here when you first walked through that door," Wilson said, "but Mary told me you were one of the few people fighting for ethics in healthcare, and perhaps you are for real. In any event, I hope I've been of some help to you — but if I'm going to remain in medicine, you better not tell anyone what I've just told you. At least you now know there are a few other people beside yourself that have had their tails burnt. I'd like to read some of your work, when you get it published," he grinned, abruptly standing up to let Bill know the meeting was over. As they moved toward the door he made one last comment. "I'd recommend you talk to Doctor David Taber, the former Medical Director at that hospital. He's another ethical physician that was chased out by the *Dinosaurs*, and he just may have some interesting things to tell you."

Bill was in a state of shock as he walked out of the Medical School, realizing he was right back in that same old battle with the same old nemesis that had murdered his wife. He also realized he'd misjudged Doctor Wilson — in fact, he was clearly one of those few remaining physicians with real honest to goodness ethics.

Chapter 5

Under Public Scrutiny

Bill and Mary sat at their favorite table at the Hatch Cover, each intently scanning a section of the Sunday newspaper. In large black headline print on the front page was the lead article, *The Epidemic*. The sub heading said, *Fear fades under scrutiny*, and a second front-page title said, *Lives Upset*. As they paged through the paper, there were two more full pages of pictures and diagrams describing CS surgery, showing pictures of deformed skulls from CS surgery, along with several separate articles describing the major events surrounding what was initially identified as an epidemic. At the bottom of still another page was a picture of the two infamous neurosurgeons and their closely associated plastic surgeon.

"I don't think there's another newspaper anywhere in the United States that would have the guts to expose this type of incompetence," Mary said in amazement.

"Those two reporters should receive a Pulitzer," Bill smirked. "They sure as hell have done their homework — haven't they?"

"I'll say they have." Mary whistled softly. "And this story should be published nationwide with all the corporate greed and corruption we're seeing today. And after watching you fight this same dishonesty in North Dakota, I'm beginning to wonder if there's any ethics left in this country. Why don't we just pack our bags and head for Mexico. I hear you can live there for one third of what it costs here, and those beaches near Vera Cruz are rather inviting."

Bill laughed, pouring himself some fresh coffee. "No, I still love this country and I'm going to fight to get it back — lets go get some breakfast," he said, folding his section of the newspaper and walking toward the brunch table.

For some reason, neither Mary nor Bill had much of an appetite as they read and reread selected paragraphs to each other.

Finally they both put their paper down.

"How did you like Doctor Wilson?" Mary asked.

"He sure as hell doesn't pull any punches," Bill smiled, pushing his chair back so he could stretch into a more comfortable position. Then after pulling himself back to the table he looked intently into Mary's eyes, obviously very concerned.

"Mary, Wilson told me something that's really been bothering me."

"What's that?" She asked, knowing he'd been preoccupied about something all morning.

"Have you heard the hospital has an informal group of doctors called the *Dinosaurs*?"

"*The Dinosaurs*? You've got to be kidding. No I certainly haven't," she gasped, returning his stare. "That sounds like shades of old. My God, tell me more."

"Doctor Wilson talked about an organization of private practicing physicians that are attempting to ban with that wealthy banking Oligarchy and take over your hospital, and their HMO. He referred to Bakencamp as their pawn, and who do you suppose is their leader?"

"Don't tell me," she scoffed — "McGrath?"

"None other," he stared coldly back at her. "Sound familiar?"

"I'll say — you don't think its part of that same Mafia we were fighting in North Dakota — do you?"

"It could well be. You remember Doc saying Colorado was one of the states in Lanin's group."

"You don't suppose Lanin's in Colorado somewhere?"

Bill looked around to see that nobody was listening before he leaned closer to her, like he was about to share a secret. Then he suddenly changed his mind.

"What's wrong?" Mary asked, "What were you going to tell me?"

Bill pursed his lips. "It's nothing."

"Hey! I've trusted you — and now you're going to clam up on me. What's going on — you can talk to me!"

Bill glanced briefly out the window at their Scrub Jay poking at a pinecone, and after a long pause he looked back at Mary.

"All right — I'm going to trust you with something that's going to blow your mind — but you need to know right up front that it must be kept completely confidential. I'm trying very hard to put things behind me, and I just can't dig up the past any longer."

"Bill, you have my word!"

As he leaned forward he whispered — "Lanin's dead."

Mary gasped, "What do you mean? — I thought you told me the FBI was still looking for that bunch of hoodlums."

"They are — but I saw him die. I saw his car, and him slip off a cliff after they tried to kill me." Bill took a deep breath and then exhaled deeply, like he'd just gone to confession. "It all happened on my way back to Colorado."

"And you've told nobody — not even the FBI?"

"That's right. And what's even worse is your friend Red Hinckley was killed with them."

"Bill, you've got to be kidding! — I can't believe what I'm hearing." Mary just sat there stunned, staring dumbfounded at him. "I just can't believe this. That's just not like you."

For what seemed like an eternity they both looked intently at each other without saying a word. Finally Mary said, "Lets get out of here," pushing her plate away and once again looking around the room to be sure nobody had been eaves dropping. "We need to talk — but not here."

* * * * *

After they reached Mary's home, Bill decided to tell her all the gory details of his secret, which he'd previously vowed never to tell anyone — risking the possibility that she'd never talk to him again.

"Mary, I'm going to tell you everything, but after you hear what I have to say, you cannot share this with anyone — do you understand?"

It was obvious that the initial shock had disturbed Mary deeply, as she nervously and perhaps unwillingly shook her head yes, based solely on their previous respect and trust they held for each other for so many years

Then after taking a deep breath, Bill began to explain what had happened.

"Mary, you remember I had to fire our controller Collier for cause, and get rid of the board chairman Lanin when I found they were stealing huge sums of money from the hospital. Then after I moved to Denver to manage all the Sister's hospitals from their Provincialate headquarters, Collier was persuaded to file a law suite for age discrimination against the Sisters. I guess he felt that since I was no longer at that hospital, I wouldn't be involved — and perhaps he could tap the poor sisters for even more than the estimated three million he and Doctor Lanin had already stolen from them. Fortunately I'd kept a confidential file regarding his termination, and after I'd reviewed this information with the hospital attorney and Sister Gerome, the attorney said, 'We don't have a thing to worry about, as long as your there to testify.' Later, Sister Gerome and I had dinner with that attorney, and Sister described the terrible problems the Lanin *Dinosaurs* had created for us. And when she was finished, she demanded he help us stop them at all cost."

The attorney replied, "I think you should file a counter suite against both Collier and Lanin — as well as that Nashville corporation that's behind all this." Mary, I just stared at the attorney. My mind had been drifting back to Susan's murder much of the night anyway, and all I could think of was revenge. To be honest I actually had thought about killing both Lanin and Collier, but I also had to remain focused on protecting the Sisters so they wouldn't lose another hospital to those vultures. Mary, a lawsuit would have only diverted our efforts, so I gave it no credence whatsoever. And as you well know, the local judges had a history of always settling in the physician's favor, right or wrong. But our attorney was smart enough to request a trial by jury for the Collier law suite, and he even suggested the possibility of a change of venue."

With that Bill paused — again nervously sucking in another breath. "In fact, I told Sister Gerome I wanted to leave this new job, as soon as we settled the Collier trial — and to be very honest, I was actually thinking about how I'd seek revenge on all these murders by myself. I can remember Sister Gerome telling me, 'Bill, this country just can't afford to lose people like you. When I think of what you've done for us,

I think of the morning star. You've been our sign of hope in the darkness. You've been our promise of a dawn. Bill, you've maintained the highest of standards in healthcare, and it saddens me to see men like you hurt by such corruption. I now know what happens to people who attempt to confront corruption, and you need to promise me that someday you'll write about all this. Others need to benefit by your experience,' she said, grasping both of my hands as she openly prayed to the Lord that I not leave them.

"As a result, I promised her that I would write about this, but I also told her it was time for me to leave and let the dust settle."

"We can never repay you for what you've done for us, and you'll remain eternally in our prayers," she finally said, "and I pray that God will somehow bless you."

"Mary, the FBI didn't like the idea of my going back to North Dakota for that trial, but I had to testify or Collier might have won the damned case — so the FBI agreed to send an agent with me. But I really didn't think I needed that type of protection any longer — so at five in the morning I decided to quietly sneak out of town on my own. *They certainly hadn't protected Susan or my daughter, and I doubted very much that they could protect me,* I'd thought to myself. And as you know, March weather is torturous in North Dakota, and to make it even worse I decided to drive the back roads. I'd traded in the car that Susan was killed in, because the memories were still way too close to the surface, and before I left I'd placed a loaded rifle on the seat beside me, just in case that God damned torpedo was following me. Since Lanin was obviously going to serve as a witness for Collier, I kept reminding myself that it would be unwise to show the least bit of contempt for him in the courtroom — but as I drove the cold lonely miles, my mind kept thinking of how I was going to kill that bastard — on the highway, in his office, or where he parked his car at the hospital. Mary, I bet I planned his demise over and over a hundred times, until I finally reached the outskirts of town. It was almost nine in the evening when I drove into the parking lot at the Hilton Inn. I knew the desk clerk, and after he greeted me he handed me a key for one of their better rooms, saying he was sorry to hear about Susan, and that her death was a shock to the whole community. After we visited a bit, I asked him to schedule a wake-up call for seven in the morning and as I reached down to grab my bag, he said, 'Oh — I almost forgot. Sister

Janice left a message for you to call her as soon as you arrive. Here's where you can reach her,' he smiled — handing me a slip of paper with her telephone number on it. So as soon as I got settled in my room, I called her."

"Hello Doctor Warner," Sister Janice said, "we've been meeting with the attorneys and Collier, and now that they know you're going to be here, they're talking about a settlement with us. I wanted to let you know, that if we do agree on a settlement tonight, I'll call you right away."

Damn it, a settlement will only make them look like saints — *I've just been on the road for fourteen hours, and now I may not even see those bastards,* I thought to myself. Then I remember staring out the window where I'd parked so I could see any fresh footprints in the snow, should someone try to fool around with my car. *That damned Lanin's killing off my family one by one, and the FBI hasn't done a damned thing. Well, we'll see about that. Two can play this game,* I thought, even though I had no idea of what I was actually going to do. *If they're going to kill me, now will be the time. But they'll never expect me to attack them* — *and that'll be my strategy. Attack them before they attack me,* I finally decided.

Although I was physically and mentally exhausted, my mind kept running over the different ways that I could force Lanin into a conflict. As a result, I hadn't paid any attention to the news, or that a major snow storm was heading into the Dakotas. I remember how disoriented I was when the phone rang. I had been dreaming Susan was alive, and she was trying to warn me to get out of town. As I picked up the phone, I expected to hear her, and it took several seconds for me to realize it was Sister Janice.

"Doctor Warner," she said, "I have good news. We've settled and agreed to end it all and go home. They knew they didn't have a case with you here."

"Who are they, I asked?"

"Both Doctor Lanin and Collier are here with their attorney," she said. "We have some agreements to prepare and sign, and it will be all over."

"Where are you meeting?" I asked.

"At the hospital," she replied.

"Although I was still foggy from my deep sleep, my mind was now racing. In fact I hardly heard Sister Janice say," 'So you can sleep late in the morning. Are you planning to head back home tomorrow, after you've rested up from that long drive?' She asked."

"I remember saying, 'Yes, I'll be leaving first thing in the morning, so I probably won't see you.'"

"Well I want to thank you for being here — it made all the difference in the world."

"It took me only minutes to get my things together, and since the room was prepaid, I just left my key on the dresser before quietly leaving through the rear exit. As I walked out into the cold night, it was already snowing heavily, and I could now see fresh tire tracks where a car had pulled in next to mine, but there were no footprints. For a moment I just sat there with the car window open, looking to see if anyone was watching, but there were no suspicious cars and everything seemed deathly quiet. Sitting for a moment, I tried to clear my head as the snowflakes melted on my face. Finally I drove out of the lot with both windows wide open."

The parking ramp will be the best place to confront that bastard face to face. He'll be the only one using that door this late at night, and the security guard won't make his round until well after midnight, I thought.

"I remember looking at my watch and it was almost eleven-thirty — and my body still ached from my long drive. Then as I turned into the ramp my heart raced as I spotted Lanin's powder blue Cadillac. *There it is,* I whispered too myself, stopping right behind his car while I let my eyes adjust to the dimly lit parking ramp. *He'll be all alone,* I figured, parking only a few spaces away. *I want to look squarely into his eyes when I grab that son-of-a-bitch by the throat.* Although I wanted to strangle him, I was still unsure of what I was capable of. *Somehow I'm going to make him squirm for the rest of his short life,* I thought to myself, as I hunched down in the seat so I wouldn't be noticed."

"It was only a few minutes later when I heard the hospital security lock push open from the inside, and I could hear leather heels echoing through the empty ramp."

"So he's staying at the Hilton," I heard Lanin say, apparently talking on his cell phone.

That's why there were tire tracks next to my car. I probably would've never left that motel alive, if I'd waited until morning, I thought.

"Hey, those Colorado license plates must have been easy for your torpedo to spot," I shouted, quickly stepping out of my car. "Are you looking for me?" I growled, ready to pounce on him if he made the slightest attempt to run.

"Paralyzed, he froze in his tracks."

"If I were you, I wouldn't be so eager to find me," I snarled. "Then grabbing his neck and shoving him into a cement pillar. Gasping for air, he looked petrified, and the terror on his face gave me more satisfaction than I could have ever hoped for. Then with an added surge of adrenaline, I lifted him off the ground by the neck, jamming his shoulders into the cement so hard his head bounced back and his cell phone flew out of his claw shaped hand."

"I remember his eyes were almost totally pinched closed, and his face was beet red. Then for some reason I suddenly released my grip, growling, 'The only reason I'm not going to kill you is I want you to think about me for a while!'"

"Mary, I had no control over what I was saying or doing as I shoved him to the concrete floor and kicked him so hard he squealed like a pig trying to escape the slaughter."

"You'd better be looking for me because I'm taking both you and Collier down," I growled — "glaring at him with such a hatred inside that I could never describe it to anyone. Then suddenly I just turned and walked to my car, as if nothing had happened."

"I've decided to head south on highway eighty-five, if you have the guts to come after me. And if you do, I'll be looking for you and your torpedo," I shouted.

"Starting my car, I almost backed over him as I snarled, 'If you don't come after me, remember — I'll be back — we've got a date with destiny you sleazy son-of-a-bitch.' As I drove off, I looked back one last time to check that no one had witnessed what had just taken place."

Mary looked at Bill, petrified at what she was hearing.

"Mary, I remember it was exactly midnight and my body was shaking so uncontrollably I could hardly drive those slippery back streets. But somehow I unconsciously wove my way to the outskirts of town — all the time damning myself for not having the guts to have killed him right there.   Finally I reached Highway 85,   and although the streets were totally empty — I kept nervously looking to see if anyone might be following, all the time checking and rechecking to be sure my rifle was within reach. In fact, I even awkwardly practiced holding the barrel out the window several times to be sure I could shoot the damned thing if I had to."

I'll be prepared if they try to follow me, I thought.

"Then after driving only a short while, I experienced an almost euphoric feeling by the very fact that I'd just scared the hell out of that untouchable. But then as always my thoughts quickly returned to Susan and Kate — and once again I found myself grieving. Mary my emotions were going up and down like a yo – yo on a string."

I should've killed the bastard right there, when I had the chance, I kept repeating over and over. "But finally I had to admit I was incapable of killing anyone. And as I stared at the empty road, I still was discouraged by what I'd failed to do. Mary, that feeling of revenge that had been welling-up in me for so long, had been so overpowering that it actually frightened me more than I'd like to admit."

I guess I just don't have the killer instinct, or maybe I'm just now beginning to understand these horrible emotions for the first time, I thought.

"Yet, when I think about what they did to Susan and Kate, I still want revenge, but I now know these feelings were far too close to the surface, to be normal. I remember opening the car window to suck in the cold outside air, and moving my head in circles to try to relax my neck and shoulders, which were tighter than a snare drum — just like two steel bands ready to snap."

"Then suddenly I noticed the distant headlights of a car following me. I'd set my speed at fifty-five miles per hour, and increased it to sixty-five to see if they'd still gain on me. And although the car appeared to be several miles back, it just seemed to keep pace with me no matter what speed I went."

They wouldn't have the guts to come after me, I thought, *but if they did, it would probably be his damned hired gun.*

"It was now twelve-thirty, and I decided to turn off the highway, on that same road Susan and I took to get to your boat that time."

If they're following me, they'd have to turn, I thought, *and if not, I'll go back and follow them.*

"After I turned I almost stopped to wait and see if they would continue on Highway 85, but then I thought better of that. Then as they reached the turn off, their headlights clearly turned to follow me, and with that my adrenaline surged."

"All right you bastard, come and get it," I shouted.

"Once again they kept pace with me, and it was now obvious that Lanin had taken me up on my challenge, since few cars would ever drive this remote country road after midnight."

Now what am I going to do? What if they all decided to come after me? I thought.

"Once again my mind was racing. Quickly I checked to see that I'd fully loaded my gun chamber, as I awkwardly steered the car with my knees."

I'll have to stop eventually, but where? I asked myself. *That spot that Susan and I'd turned to get to your boat dock was one place, but that was a dead end. I might be able to handle one person there, but if there were more than one, my chances wouldn't be so good. Everything will be closed up in New Town, and the constable is probably in bed,* I decided. *If I could make it to the bridge, I could turn into that park that overlooked Lake Sakakawea, where Susan and I once stopped to have a cup of coffee,* I thought.

"You remember that's where Doc pointed out that cliff to me on the boat trip we took with you. But I still had an eerie feeling about that place and the scary unprotected cliff you had to drive near."

The only positive thing about that place was it had an entrance and an exit, and I might be able to stop them near that cliff, if I can get in there and block that road. They'd hardly have enough room to get out of the car. That's what I'll do. They may not even realize they're sitting next to a hundred foot drop-off, in this storm, but I'd better keep enough distance so I'll have time to get in there and turn around, I thought to myself.

"As I approached New Town, the other car had noticeably closed the gap, and ignoring all stop signs I raced through the small town's crooked streets, hoping the Constable would stop me for speeding. Reaching Highway twenty-two, I skidded out of control, sliding into a huge snow drift, which brought me to an abrupt halt. As I gunned the engine, the wheels spun hopelessly as I frantically put the car in reverse, rocking it back and forth until the wheels miraculously grabbed hold. Slowly the car moved back onto the highway as I once again floored the accelerator.

Unconsciously I turned on the wipers and opened the windows so I wouldn't miss the park's entrance. The dirt road was covered with several inches of snow, but I somehow remembered everything about that eerie place as I drove carefully along the cliff, totally unable to see the drop off that I knew was only a few feet away. Finally I reached the open area, where I turned off my headlights and spun the car around so I could stop the other car on the unprotected cliff."

Mary just starred at Bill, totally unable to comprehend the fear he must have had.

"Stepping out of the car, my hands were quivering uncontrollably as I fumbled to release the safety on my gun. Reaching through the window so I could quickly switch on the headlights, with my gun ready, my teeth began chattering uncontrollably — and my whole body was now shaking violently, which was more from fear than the cold blistering snow that was swirling around me in almost every direction."

Mary just sat frozen in place at what Bill was telling her, unable to respond.

"In only seconds, their headlights reflected off the snow as they turned into the Park, and it was obvious they had no idea they were driving way too fast along a treacherous cliff as they blindly followed my tire tracks. And just as their headlight came into view, I switched on my bright's. Instantly I recognized Collier behind the wheel, and Lanin blindly wincing in the seat next to him. The two men in the back seat instinctively crouched down so I couldn't see them."

"Yah," I screamed at the top of my voice, "It's me!"

"Collier reacted by sharply turning the steering wheel, causing the left front of the car to slip over the edge, freezing the car to a halt on its frame. Perched precariously on the edge of a cliff, it soon became apparent to all of them that if they opened either door on the driver's side, they'd step out into space."

"Get out of the car, one at a time, with your hands above you head," I shouted as I shot out their front tire — "or I'll shoot you right where you are."

"Oh my God, we're on a God-damn cliff, and we need to get out the hell out of here," Red Hinckley screamed as he crouched down behind Collier in the back seat.

"Listen to me, or I'll blast you into kingdom come." I screamed even louder. "I want that torpedo in the back seat to get out first, with his hands where I can see them."

"As he moved to open the door I could see he was trying to get his gun into position where he'd have a clear shot at me. Without thinking I dropped the rifle, and raced at him, driving my shoulder into the partly open car door. My feet were slipping in every direction as my body hit the car with ever ounce of strength that remained in me, crushing his wrist as the revolver flew across the trunk of the car and disappeared into space. Grabbing his arm, he fell backward against Red, screaming in pain — and with that sudden shift in weight came a loud scraping noise, just as Lanin opened his door, scrambling for safety."

At this, Mary just covered her face with both hands.

"I can still see Lanin watching in terror as his side of the car lifted and suddenly slipped off the cliff. Then in only seconds the entire car was gone. Staring into space, I found myself crouched on my knees, watching the car's headlights swirl in every direction across the black sky. I could also hear the screams inside, as they plummeted hundreds of feet before crashing through the ice and floating like a sinking ship in the open water."

As Mary stared at Bill she just shook her head in disbelief.

"As I turned to look at Lanin, he was struggling to reach my rifle, his feet slipping from under him as he tried to stand up. In only seconds I was able to drive him back into the stone wall where I was able to throw a shiver into his jaw with the butt of the rifle, which he was trying to point in my direction. Then roughly I jerked the gun from him as I threw him around and back onto the road, his legs hanging over the cliff, with his fingers frantically scratching to grasp at the ice covered ground."

"Don't kill me," Lanin slurred through his shattered jaw that was spurting blood in every direction.

"Mary, that's what I now dream about. His bloody fingers' scratching frantically to pull himself to safety. As I stared at him, gasping for air, I was totally in shock by what had just taken place."

"God almighty, I'm slipping," he screamed.

"Grabbing hold of a small shrub near the edge of the cliff, I cautiously reached out toward him, just as he grabbed at my hand. And all I can now remember over and over is his evil eyes and his entire face taking on a terrified contortion as both his hands thrashed violently at nothing but empty space. I made one last frantic grab, but I was too late. And as I watched him fall, I can still hear his petrifying screams creating a horrible eerie like decrescendo of sounds echoing over the lake as he plummeted to his death."

"Mary, I'll never forget that face or those horrible sounds."

"Then as I looked down, I saw his body crash into the bottom of the car, which was still floating on the surface with its headlights reflecting a ghostly halo of light around the car. As I sat quivering on the edge of the cliff, I watched their car began to slowly sink with its lights flickering on and off, creating a sinister like image around Lanin's spread-eagle silhouette, which was slowly being sucked into what looked like a black hole of hell."

"Mary, I don't know why, but I recalled how Doc had said they had no idea how deep the lake was there, which made me think, there's no chance anyone would see the wheels of that car in the morning, like they found the two sister's car. And the water would certainly freeze over and be covered by snow before dawn. So it was obvious to me that I could never clearly describe what had taken place that night, and there would always be doubt in that I was the sole survivor who put a bullet hole in their front tire."

Mary just shook her head, still disagreeing with Bill.

"As you can imagine I was shaking and exhausted, and as I strained to stand up I sucked in as much air as I could, before cautiously moving away from the edge of that horrible cliff."

I guess the Sister's prayers have finally been answered, I thought to myself.

"Picking up my gun, which I now knew I could never have used to shoot anyone, I awkwardly opened the car door with my numb hands still shaking uncontrollably. Unconsciously I backed the car away from the cliff, and slowly drove back toward the highway."

Perhaps the Lord does work in strange ways, I thought. *They chased me, and tried to kill me, but it all backfired on them — they killed themselves. I see no reason why I should tell anyone what happened here tonight. Why should I risk being caught up in some politically controlled hearing with these corrupt and powerful Dinosaurs, or put the government through all kinds of expense. Worse yet, those corrupt politicians would probably put me in jail! Lanin's bloated body will eventually sink before the ice thaws, and the other bodies will be entombed forever in Collier's new Cadillac — and they'll probably never be found. And if they are, they brought it on themselves. Yes, all those deaths have finally been avenged, for whatever good that does,* I thought to myself.

"Mary, as I drove home I sobbed for miles, until the tension finally faded a little, but I can honestly say that after hours of incoherent driving, I was finally at peace with myself."

"But Bill, don't you see, you have to tell the FBI about all this."

With that Bill exploded. "Look, God damn it, that son-of-a-bitch murdered six people including my wife and my daughter. And I believe he even tried to kill my youngest daughter. That God damned FBI had more than enough info to arrest all of them, but they didn't, or couldn't for some damned reason. And then these bastards finally tried to shoot me! For God's sakes they were murdering people, don't you get it? Thank God I carried a gun with me just like the FBI told me to do — but for some unknown reason, I didn't have the guts to pull the trigger when I should have. So I did the next best thing, I fought back when their hired gun was going to shoot me. Then Lanin even tried to shoot me — with my own gun! And yes, I just stood there paralyzed and watched him slip to his death. Hell I was so terrified I couldn't move. Now how do I explain that it was self defense, without any witnesses? They brought it on themselves! They came after me! And I decided it was less expensive to leave the scene since no one was around to support my story, and no one but me will ever know what actually happened. So that's what I'm going to live with — and I still think I made the right decision. The damned FBI wanted more facts before they arrested them, so they'd have an air tight case, and here people were dying while they kept looking for more evidence."

Mary grabbed Bill by the shoulders. "Of course you're right — but why do you think they won't believe you?"

"I didn't say the FBI won't believe me, but the politicians in Washington are totally controlled by these God damned corrupt corporate lobbyists. They've all received untold amounts of brown bags and briefcases filled with hard cash from those *Dinosaurs*. Hell, they could accuse me of anything, and make it stick. You remember Doctor Heustes, the head of the NIH, trying to warn you to never trust them when you made those tapes for him. Do you think he was lying?"

"All right, I understand what you're saying, but I —"

"Listen to me," Bill cried, again refusing to ever discuss what happened that night with the FBI. "I had no idea there was the slightest possibility I could ever become involved again with this same corrupt organization, or I'd of never agreed to take this job. And if the *Dinosaurs* even thought for a second that we were both involved in this thing, they'd come after you, just as they did Susan — and I'm not going to let that happen. Maybe we better not see each other any more."

"Hey, will you just wait a minute. It was my decision to move here. I did that because I wanted to work with you, and I'll stand by you whatever you decide." Her face was now livid as she fiercely stood her ground. "But I sure as hell don't like what I'm hearing, and I'm not going to turn tail and run."

With that, Bill started pacing the floor, trying to calm things down.

"I just don't know what to do. Maybe we need to let it go," he said.

"No! No!" Mary shouted over and over. "We can outsmart them. Look, I can take a week off around Christmas, and we can fly down to my home in Florida where we can relax and plan just as we always have. You're the best damn planner on earth, and if we can put our ducks in order, we'll get through this just fine. By December they'll have finished painting my boat and we can spend some quiet time out on the Gulf, all by ourselves."

"Maybe that's an answer, but I suggest we be cautious as hell from now on. In fact, we better keep our distance just to be on the safe side — at least until we can find out what's really going on in Colorado."

With that Bill rubbed both hands over his face showing his frustration with this whole mess.

"Another thing that concerns me is you apparently told Doctor Wilson I was one of the good guys. Dave told me when I took this assignment, I wouldn't have to take sides, and I'm certainly not going to ask you to run interference for me. And if we go to Florida, I'm going to see if Doctor Heustes will meet with us. He needs to hear about McGrath's *Dinosaurs*, and what's going on here."

As Bill was getting ready to leave, Mary handed him a slip of paper with the name and address of their previous Medical Director.

Doctor David Taber at the Anderson Cancer Center
1515 Holcombe Blvd., Houston, Texas.

Grabbing Bill's arm, she hugged him tightly. "Bill, you know I'm with you all the way, and you can take that to the bank, but I need to tell you something else that concerns me. Next week, I'm meeting with our Medical Director, Doctor Dante. He's a physician who serves as our in-house attorney for McGrath's Dinosaurs. In fact, my nursing assistant tells me he was once legal counsel for that huge Tennessee outfit that now controls all those hospitals in Denver. Until recently, I thought he was personally interested in me, because he's constantly coming into my office to visit, but it's possible he's just watching every move I make."

"Now don't get paranoid!" Bill whispered.

"No," she replied rather embarrassed at Bill's quick response, "but as I think about it, McGrath had a lot to do with Dante's appointment. Rumor has it that Dante got rid of Doctor Taber at McGrath's request. He may be a nice guy — but he's constantly poking his nose into what I'm doing. Bill, I think you should meet with Taber, and find out why they fired him."

"I will, but you should also try to find out as much as you can from Dante. He just may provide us some clues. Remember, it wasn't until your husband told me about Lanin, that I knew what I was really dealing with."

Her thoughtful nod told Bill she understood and agreed.

"But I wouldn't confide in him, or even let him think we know each other."

"I understand," Mary whispered.

* * * * *

First thing Monday morning, Bill made his appointments for the week, first calling Doctor Belky, the former Chief of Surgery; and then Doctor Taber in Houston.

Doctor Belky suggested they meet at his office at about noon on Tuesday. No sooner did they sit down in his conference room than the office nurse brought in two roast beef sandwiches wrapped in plastic, asking what they'd like to drink.

"Thank you," Bill said. "I certainly didn't expect you to provide lunch, but I do appreciate it."

"It's much easier this way, where I can stay close to my patients and get a quick start on my afternoon appointments," Belky explained.

Belky was bald with a small rim of gray hair circling his head. His smile was infectious and Bill liked him immediately. He wasn't a tall man, but he appeared in good physical shape, even though he was obviously tired from the morning surgery. Bill guessed him to be in his late sixties, and his crisply starched three quarter length unbuttoned white coat was spotlessly clean. Although he was no longer a member of the Medical School Faculty, or Chief of Service at the hospital, he was obviously still heavily involved in private practice.

"Doctor, I appreciate your taking the time to visit with me. I've been hired to try and make recommendations on this CS problem in neurosurgery." Shifting uncomfortably, Bill turned so he could face him directly. "Since you were once the Chief of Staff, perhaps you can tell me some of the hospital history, so I can have a better understanding of how things work at this hospital."

"That's a tall order," he chuckled, leaning back in his chair and smiling. "I'm not sure you'll ever find a solution to how things work here anymore."

"You're probably right," Bill replied, not surprised by his comment.

"I don't mean to discourage you, but organized medicine is changing so radically I personally think we're in for some very difficult times. In fact, it's probably going to get a lot worse before it ever gets any better," he explained, leaning forward to take a bite of his sandwich. "I guess I'm from the old school — I haven't yet caught up with all those managed care monopolies, or these new aristocratic practitioners," he scoffed, laying his sandwich back on the plastic plate. "I came into medicine almost thirty years ago, when we were still trying to help the patient, whether they could pay or not. I guess that's why I'm seriously thinking of retirement."

Pausing a moment, he sipped cautiously at his hot coffee.

"Okay, what's on your mind?" he asked, finally swallowing a bite of sandwich.

"I have some questions about the hospital's standards that existed when you were the Chief of Surgery, and I'd also like to discuss the relationship that previously existed with the Medical School."

"Fire away, I'll see if I can be of any help."

"All right," Bill said, shuffling through a few notes. "I've never experienced a situation where an open medical staff could function compatibly with a professional closed medical school faculty that's paid a stipend. Since you were the Head of the Department for almost ten years, maybe you can tell me how that worked back then."

"Well, it used to be that the Chief of Service always was qualified to also serve on the Medical School Faculty as the Head of the Department. They would then receive a stipend from the college, like so many thousand a year, and they were permitted to take on a limited number of private patients that could also be used as teaching patients," he explained, wiping his mouth with his napkin. "The Department Head also assumed all the management responsibilities at the hospital in addition to the teaching responsibilities. In any event, his private practice income was not to exceed his stipend, and any excess income was used to help defer the cost of care for the financially indigent patients — kind of like a free bed fund. It was a professional gratuity that nobody ever questioned or complained about. You also have to understand however, that back then, there were only a handful of physicians at the teaching hospital who were solely in private practice, and received no stipend. And as I recall, that didn't present too much of a problem — back then."

"I take it that doesn't exist today?"

"Well, not since these HMO's and this young McGrath came on board. He's made almost no attempt to become professionally boarded, and yet he wants to be the Head of the Department, with no limits on his income. And he and Haines have been making so much income for the hospital and themselves, that they no longer recognize the faculty as professionals. In fact, they've kind of thrown our professional standards out the window, just like most of the corporations today. Faculty status or what I call professionalism no longer means anything to these managed care monopolies. In fact, they've now deregulated almost everything. They measure performance solely by profit, and laugh at that free bed fund I donated to for so many years."

"I thought Doctor Hanes agreed with Doctor Wilson's appointment as the Head of Neurosurgery?"

"He did originally, but that was before McGrath's private group of physicians took over. McGrath now has so much financial clout that he just sits back and laughs at Wilson's feeble attempt to take over the Chief's position."

"As I understand it, McGrath went a long time without ever passing his Boards, and he's never really been under any kind of supervision — is that right? Bill asked"

"That's right. But try to tell him that. Even Doctor McCauly, the current Chief of Surgery has given up on that."

"When you referred to that group of private physicians, was that the same group they now call *The Dinosaurs?*"

"Oh — I'm surprised you know about them. That's what we call them behind closed doors, and their membership seems to be growing by dimensions. In fact, they've become a very powerful informal organization in medicine today."

"Just what is it that makes them so powerful?"

"Money is power, and you've heard talk about these new managed care monopolies. Well, that's exactly what they are, monopolies. It's nothing more than a group of corrupt entrepreneurs who no longer believe in standards or the individual practice of medicine. They support corporate control and the total deregulation of America, just like it was back in the 1800's. They also want total control over all healthcare insurance, and if that isn't a monopoly, I don't know what is. It's all bound to catch up with them someday, and then we can all kiss our professionalism good-bye. In fact, they actually believe they will someday shut down Medicare and Medicaid, and prevent any future single nonprofit prepayment system from ever replacing their profit insurance scam, which keeps both the doctor and the patient confused. In fact, we're the only country in the world that doesn't have a manageable single nonprofit prepayment system."

"I guess they are powerful — if they can do all that?"

"Let me assure you they are. They demand I donate to their cause every year, so they can keep their favorite Senators paid off."

"Isn't that a pretty strong accusation?"

"Oh to hell with it all — I'm going to retire. It's getting too big for me to fight anymore and I'm tired of talking about it. But that's what's behind all these managed care organizations — it's all about greed. Standards and our Hippocratic Oath have gone out the window."

"I take it that's what's driving up our healthcare costs so dramatically?"

"You damned right it is, and it all started with this profit insurance. I remember when Congress first pushed through the McCarran Ferguson Act right after Roosevelt died. We all knew it was a mistake to let profit insurance compete with our once successful prepayment system, but none of us did a damned thing about it. And now we're in a hell of a mess."

"If I understand you correctly, you feel the private open staff at this hospital is fighting your closed faculty at the medical school, and the underlying problem is profit incentive versus professionalism? And as a result, your traditional Medical Staff standards are being ignored. In other words, you're in a battle for control."

"I think its a little more complex than that in that this hospital administrator is completely under the thumb of these *Dinosaurs* — and these unprofessional doctors are now in bed with all these powerful international bankers and corporations, who's sole purpose is to make big bucks off the sick and disabled of this country. So I guess you could say we've lost our ethics as well as the professional standards and reputation we were once so proud of. I believe this damned globalization they seek will someday destroy this country."

"Is that why McGrath is doing his own audit, and supposedly conducting his own monthly Morbidity and Mortality meetings?"

"You got that right," Belky chuckled, "and that's why all these CS accidents are happening. On the flip side, the hospital won't refuse him because he's making too damned much money for them. Recently, these *Dinosaurs* all threatened to take their patients to one of the other hospitals if they appointed Wilson Chief of Neurosurgery — and yet he's the only one qualified to serve as the Chief. That's an illegal boycott, and that's what's wrong with these God damned money seeking bastards."

"So the formal Medical Staff isn't even functioning anymore. It's all controlled by McGrath's *Dinosaurs Club*?"

Belky's nurse opened the door. "I have Mrs. Donner in room one, Doctor — whenever you're ready."

"Well, I have to go," Belky said. "Yes, I think you got the picture he smiled," standing up to leave. "I hope I've been of some help."

"Doctor, it makes my job easy when someone gets right to the point. Yes, you've been a big help. Let's hope I can be of some help in turning things around here. Then maybe you'll reconsider your retirement."

* * * * *

The Houston airport was crowded, as usual, and although Bill had only flown into Houston a few times before, he could see the airport was still in a perpetual state of reconstruction — and he was pleased that Doctor Taber had agreed to meet him for a late lunch at a restaurant near the airport.

The airport would have been a jungle had we decided to meet here, Bill thought, as he hailed a cab to take him to the restaurant. It was only a few minutes before the hostess pointed Dr. Taber in his direction, and Bill studied him as he walked toward their table. He could see he was rather tall, about six feet, with long grayish brown hair that hung almost to his shoulders. As he came closer, Bill could see he had a noticeable limp and a large scar on his forehead, just above the right eye. Later, he would find out that these injuries were the result of a very serious motorcycle accident in which he'd almost lost his life. He was also dressed casually, typical of a research faculty member, and when he reached out to shake Bill's hand — it suggested his interview was going to be friendly.

As they sat down, Taber spoke first, "I hear the CS issue is going to be aired on 20/20 tonight. I'll be anxious to see what they have to say."

"I bet you are," Bill laughed, patting both hands lightly on the table. "I suppose you still have some fond memories of that place — have any of those reporters tried to contact you?"

"Oh God no — thank God for that," he laughed.

He must be about my age, Bill thought, *and he appears sincere, which should prove helpful — particularly on a Friday night.*

"Weren't you a graduate of the Michigan Medical School?"

"Yes, I graduated from there almost twenty years ago, and then stayed on to do my residency in pediatrics — that was before I went in service."

"I spent five years in Lansing," Bill said, "and I still remember that intense rivalry between Michigan State and the University of Michigan."

"Oh yes, that's something to behold. I've cheered for Michigan many times."

"What branch of the service were you in?"

"I was in the Air Force, stationed in the Pacific for three years."

"Michigan wasn't the extent of your formal education, was it?"

"Oh no — I also trained at the Oschner Clinic, where I studied pathology for two years," and then later I returned to Michigan to complete a fellowship in pediatric oncology.

"When did you first come to Colorado?"

"Back when I accepted my first pediatric appointment at that Medical School." As Taber spoke, he studied Bill. "I was in that position for five years, and it wasn't until I was appointed an Associate Professor that I did any private practice at the hospital. Then when I became a full professor and was appointed Associate Dean at the Health Sciences Center, the hospital asked me to serve as their Medical Director — which was a big mistake!"

"Why was that?"

"Well, that's a long story."

Bill could feel his reluctance to continue so he asked, "It didn't have anything to do with the *Dinosaur's Club*, did it?"

With that, he stared at Bill, totally surprised. Finally grinning, he answered — "If you know about the *Dinosaur's Club*, I guess I can speak candidly. They're the ones that booted my ass out of there."

"Doctor Taber, you need to know I'm well aware of the infighting that's going on between the faculty, and this open staff takeover."

"Well, that's nice to know.   I think I can really level with you then," he smiled, picking up a table knife and polishing it with his napkin. "So then you know that Doctor Hanes was responsible for bringing in their Administrator — and that's when the split between the open staff and the faculty first started"

"Tell me about that, if you will."

"That's quite simple. The faculty was a closed staff that worked primarily for a stipend with limited income from their private practice, and each faculty member could only privately practice at that teaching hospital — while the non-teaching staff could practice at four or five hospitals — with no limit on income and no stipend. So to answer your question, it was entirely a money issue."

88

Pouring their ice water, their waitress interrupted, asking if they were ready to order.

"Yes, let's order," Bill said, picking up the menu. After the waitress left, Bill said, "Why don't you just pick up where you left off."

"Let's see, where was I? Oh yes — you see, what happens when you belong to too many hospitals, you begin to have no loyalty to any one, and as a result, you pay less attention to each hospital. Then if you own or participate in a Managed Care Unit, a PPO, an HMO, or a PPI or whatever acronym you want to hang on it, you then become competitive with the hospitals. If you can remember, we were all once individually licensed to make clinical decisions — and once you lose that professional independence, you become competitive and have to compete for income — like the *Dinosaurs*. And that's what's haywire with healthcare today. Profit insurance tells the doctor how to practice and now they make all the decisions for us, just so they can make those huge profits from our sick and disabled."

Bill could now see where there conversation was heading. *I'm glad I met with this guy — he at least seems to have his head on straight*, he thought.

"McGrath and his clique now set their own charges, and then turn around and pay themselves through their own profit centered HMO, which is nothing more than a good old fashioned monopoly. And on top of all that, they're also accepting these huge kickbacks from all these powerful Pharmaceutical Corporations. You can't tell me the well being of the patient is the primary purpose under that type of system."

"You're absolutely right," Bill scowled. "But isn't that against our Hippocratic Oath and the 1910 Flexner Report that helped us to establish the AMA's Principles of Medical Ethics. Wasn't the Sherman Antitrust Act to prevent that type of monopoly from ever happening?"

"Not really, that never did work in medicine, and that's because profit insurance is completely free of any government regulation under the McCarran Ferguson Act. So if you can persuade some Senator by giving him or her a few bucks under the table, it becomes a relatively simple matter to delay any healthcare legislation that could break up their sweetheart deal."

With that he paused to pour himself a cup of coffee.

"If you understand who the *Dinosaurs* really are, you'll also understand why they've become such a power over the private practice of medicine in this once sovereign nation — and that's not good! But the sad thing about this subtle power grab is that a *Wealthy Oligarchic* group of bankers is behind all this globalization and unregulated corporate crap, and these powerful bankers plan to someday own and control the entire world market, not just healthcare. And their New World Order they talk about building is much more than just a monopoly, it's actually a *Dictatorship* that involves the total control over an enormous amount of money. Hell these guys actually own and operate this country's Federal Reserve." Setting down the coffee pot, he scowled. "The flip side of this whole thing is it's destroyed the professional practice of medicine, our standards, and our once number one rated nonprofit healthcare system. Bill, these entrepreneurs are far more concerned about making money than taking care of patients, or professionalism. You know, it's kind of hard to pay attention to the sick and disabled when your primary concern is to become wealthy."

"You're absolutely right," Bill nodded. "But so far these international bankers only control the NATO nations and Japan, and the UN they created as their front — and China, Russia, India and the middle East are all having little to do with them, which means we've probably sailed our ship with the wrong crew. But tell me, why did the hospital get rid of you?"

"That was easy. Hanes hired McGrath just after I accepted the position. Then they both refused to attend meetings or participate in audits or educational conferences, and they challenged me to do something about it."

"So you knew they were violating the hospital's rules and regulations?"

"Oh, God yes, absolutely."

"And the Administrator and the Board did nothing about that?"

"The Administrator was in their hip pocket. Hell, they hired him. If they said jump, he jumped."

"What about the Joint Commission?"

"The JC never even suspected what was going on."

"What you're telling me is that the Board never did assume their responsibility for running that hospital?"

Taber, laughed. "Let me assure you, the *Dinosaurs* are running that hospital."

Oh shit, Bill said to himself — taking a quick swig of coffee, "Excuse me — I'm diverting you with all my questions, please continue."

"Okay, let me think a minute," he said, putting one finger over his lips.

"I remember when Keith Wilson was first appointed as the Neurosurgical Head at the Medical School. That was just after I was appointed Medical Director at the hospital. I remember the Dean of the Medical School had just asked the Chief of Staff at the hospital to appoint Wilson as their Chief of Neurosurgery. And because Wilson was very well qualified, McGrath could do nothing but agree with his appointment, since he still wasn't even boarded himself. But in the end, that didn't matter. The *Dinosaurs* still elected McGrath as their interim Neurosurgery Chief in direct opposition to the hospital's written requirements. In response to that, I hired a nationally recognized consultant from the east coast to come in and make recommendations, naively thinking that would resolve the situation."

"But apparently it didn't?" Bill interjected.

"To say the least." he scowled. "This consultant was well respected nationally, and in his report he recommended that Wilson be appointed the head of the Pediatric Neurosurgery Service at the hospital. He also recommended that Doctor McGrath work under Wilson until he was properly prepared for his oral board examination if he desired to further develop his academic career."

"It doesn't appear he or the *Dinosaurs* bought that?"

"No, the *Dinosaurs* just ignored his recommendations, even though McGrath pretended he was actually interested in a long term faculty appointment with the Medical School. Then later, when he finally passed his boards, he embarrassed the school when he told them their recommended faculty stipend wouldn't even begin to be adequate. Hell, he scoffed at them, as if the entire faculty were peasants working for peanuts."

"But Wilson moved here with the understanding he was to be the Chief of that service at the hospital?"

"Of course — But you need to understand that there wasn't a chance in hell of the hospital medical staff buying that."

Bill almost choked, wiping his mouth with his napkin. "In other words they lied to him, and the hospital's word meant nothing?"

"You got that right!"

"Tell me Doctor Taber, as Medical Director, did you ever tell either Hanes or McGrath that their CS cases required an unbiased monthly audit?"

"All the time — that's why they replaced me with McGrath's friend, Doctor Dante, the attorney."

"Did you ever attempt to revoke McGrath's Active Staff membership because he failed to meet the attendance requirements?"

"That was the Chief's job, and when Belky challenged them, he was also voted out."

"Why didn't you tell the Joint Commission about that?"

"Only Bakencamp and Dante were allowed to meet with the Joint Commission."

Bill leaned back in his chair. "Tell me, when did you leave Children's?"

"I left two years ago, totally frustrated by it all, and that's when the M.D. Anderson Hospital sought me out — and I've been here ever since."

"Has that left you with any opinions you'd be willing to share with me?"

"I've given that a lot of thought, and yes I've formed some opinions. I think quality assurance in medicine is falling apart as we decentralize healthcare into all these competing and insurance controlled businesses. And I feel things need to change or we're going to totally destroy the level of healthcare we provide in this country."

Even though it had been frustrating for Taber to discuss his previous job in Colorado, he sat back with a pleasant smile, casually pushing his plate off to the side as he continued to express his opinions.

"I think societal greed has played an important role in influencing today's physician to become far more entrepreneurial, and yet you and I know many of us didn't enter medicine solely to become wealthy — although I have to admit, today's physician is moving strongly in that direction. But that's also just a sign of our times.

After moving his cup in front of him he poured some fresh coffee, asking, "Would you like more?"

Bill nodded.

I guess we're all expected to be much more than we really are. In fact, our society has inadvertently placed the physician in a very tenuous position in my judgment, and as a result we've all become far too concerned with our status in society. And in so doing, we've become far more defensive — and I'm even beginning to realize there is no future in the practice of medicine, considering the direction it's currently heading."

"You can't be serious?" Bill asked.

"I'm very serious!"

Bill stared at him, honestly doubting what he had just heard. "Tell me about that," Bill scowled.

"You have to appreciate I come from an academic background, and I'm just making some hypothetical observations — which I feel are inevitable.

"That's interesting," Bill said, prodding him to continue.

"I believe the Internet will someday replace the family practitioner as the primary authority in medicine. It already has the ability to call up every drug known to man, along with a list of diagnostic treatments for almost every disease. And in the not to distant future, anyone will be able to look up what drug reactions are common or uncommon. They'll also be able to reference all the drug incompatibilities such as drug to drug, or drug to test, and the hundreds of other incompatibilities that exist. What I'm saying is every patient will someday be able to make a knowledgeable decision that will eventually eliminate the need for some magician to guess at a diagnosis."

"I guess I have to agree with you on that." Bill said.

"And now, even the insurance companies tell the physicians what they can or can't do," he scoffed. "Someday a patient will be able to enter, and retrieve their own history on their own personal computer, and their confidential database will be made available to only those that the patient chooses to release the information to. Just consider how ridiculous and expensive it is for a patient to repeat that information every time they see a new doctor. Today, patients repeatedly provide every physician they see with both vital and sometimes inaccurate information, that's then perpetually hidden in some office or hospital paper file. And doctors would like you to believe that they protect the confidentiality, but what they're really doing is suppressing knowledge because they can then be in control, just like these two pediatric neurosurgeons at that damn hospital."

"Nodding," Bill thought to himself, *how true*.

"Why can't the patient maintain their own printout of all their previous medical problems on their own computer? All they need is the software to do it. Some day, these patients will be able to interrogate a disease index with a library of all the related symptoms and characteristics for every disease. That type of software will eventually allow the consumer to compare their symptoms with the various conditions or diseases they most likely have, all ranked by order of highest priority. Just think, no more waiting in some general practitioner's office. You'll only meet with a specialist to do surgery or treat the ailment after they confirm the appropriate diagnosis."

"Had the parents of those infants had that type of information before they did this CS surgery, they may have headed off the horrible con-job McGrath and Haines pulled on them," Bill snarled, agreeing with the database concept Taber had just described.

"That type of crime should have never happened," he grimaced, leaning forward to share a few final thoughts.

"Much more importantly, genetics and gene therapy, or gene engineering as I call it will eventually eliminate over eighty percent of the current diseases known to man. And things like this ridiculous CS procedure these characters are doing will no longer be required or even allowed. Hell, we'll be able to eliminate any premature fusing of skull cartilage. What we'll do is correctly engineer the genes and maintain the patient in a healthy state, that's if these bought off politicians ever get their priorities in order."

With that he stopped — taking a last sip of his coffee.

"Bill, we're getting very close to that, if the *Dinosaurs* don't fight too hard to protect their turf. In fact, these guys are now intentionally decentralizing healthcare into competitive units with the hope of delaying any type of database system."

"Doctor Taber, I'm very impressed with you, and the hospital was very foolish to ever let you go." Then looking at his watch, Bill said, "I guess Id better catch my plane home if I'm going to see McGrath's TV debut on 20/20 tonight. But if possible, I'd like to visit with you again sometime about some of my medical record research. I found your comments to be very stimulating and I'd certainly like to hear more."

Chapter 6

Challenging Dante

Dante was a tall slender man with a full black beard. Mary had asked to meet with him to discuss their hospital standards, hoping she could persuade him to start enforcing some of these standards as they were written, but as she sat down his eyes were busy scanning the work on his desk, and they made no contact. After he signed several documents, he threw them into his out box without saying a word.

Finally Mary interrupted.

"I'd like to discuss the CS problem, and the Medical Staff's standards, bylaws, and the rules and regulations."

"If you've read them, there's really not that much to discuss," he smirked, anticipating why she asked to see him. Then quickly retrieving the material he'd just thrown in the out box, he casually walking toward his secretary's office. "Janice," he shouted, "will you get these out today?"

Mary was unable to respond because he'd completely left the room, and when he finally reappeared he casually walked over and looked out the window.

"The bylaws are really quite straight-forward," he explained, his back toward Mary. Then after briefly glancing at her over his shoulder he walked to the bookshelf where he pulled a large leather three ring binder off the shelf.

"Here's a copy of the regulations and bylaws. What is it you'd like to know about them?" he asked with a smart ass grin, intentionally dropping the book in front of her so the noise echoed throughout the room.

What the hell is wrong with this guy? Mary gasped. *I thought he liked me — and I can't even get him to pause long enough to look at me.*

Slowly Mary pulled the book in front of her as if she was going to open it, and then with her hands on the cover she just stood and stared at him until he finally looked at her.

"Doctor, I've read the bylaws and the rules and regulations several times, but I still need you to explain how you implement them. And what I particularly need to know is if they are enforced as they're written. I'm really not that interested in the bylaws, just the rules and regulations."

Avoiding her intense stare he looked straight through her before he turned and walked over to his chair and sat down,

Well, at least he finally sat down, Mary thought, deciding to change her approach.

"How long have you worked here?" She asked.

"I've been Medical Director for almost two years now, but I also served as their legal council several years ago."

"Oh yes, you're both an attorney and a physician aren't you?"

"Yes, that's right. After I became a physician, I decided to go back to school and earn a law degree."

"Did you ever practice medicine?"

"I practiced only a couple years, and then opened a private law practice — and eventually I was hired full time to help Denver start their PPO."

So he did work with that Nashville Preferred Provider Organization that took over all those hospitals in Denver, she thought to herself.

"You came to Children's Hospital about the same time as Doctor McGrath, didn't you?"

"Yes, in fact Larry was very instrumental in hiring me. He and Bakencamp had become very frustrated with a fellow by the name of Taber, who held that position before I came on the scene."

"Why was that?" Mary frowned.

"He was more a faculty member at the Medical School than a private practitioner. He just wasn't up to the times. To be very honest, we had to get rid of him," he whispered, cupping his hand over the side of his mouth, as if he was sharing a big secret.

"I see," Mary nodded. "Just what does your job as a Medical Director entail?"

"That's about as good as it gets," he laughed.

"Aren't you responsible for the medical staff and the clinical departments?"

"Oh sure, and I'm also responsible for the laboratory, X-ray, and most of the ancillary departments."

"Don't the Chiefs of Service report to you?"

"No, they report directly to Bakencamp, but I do work with them, even though I don't have a lot to say."

"I thought you supervised the medical staff activities and were responsible for auditing their credentials and attendance at meetings. At least that's what it says in the rules and regulations."

"Oh sure, but I don't really have control over any physicians' independent clinical practice."

"Okay," Mary smiled. At *least he's responding,* she thought, finally deciding to try and again ask some questions about the rules and regulations.

"Dr. Dante, in the hospital's rules they outline many committees that all deal with the quality of care in the hospital. And in these rules it indicates that the Medical Staff must accept and discharge their responsibilities subject to the ultimate authority of the hospital's Board of Directors. It also states that the management programs must be maintained in compliance with the Joint Commission and other regulatory agency standards, like the American Hospital Association, and the American Medical Association. And as I understand it, the Administrator, the Medical Director, and the Chiefs of the various medical services are all required to comply with all of these responsibilities."

Mary hadn't even looked at the big book he'd dropped in front of her, but she now had his attention.

"Yes," he replied a little more cautiously, his face clearly defensive.

"In fact, you and the Chief of each department have the responsibility to recommend and approve privileges for staff members and evaluate each of the member's credentials, don't you?"

"Yes, that's what it says," he replied, fidgeting a little more uneasily in his chair.

"Then wouldn't you say the hospital has a responsibility for controlling the quality of care the physicians provide when they practice at this hospital?"

"We try to separate the physician from the hospital so they can exercise their independent judgment."

"Certainly you want them to use their independent judgment, but that doesn't relieve the hospital of its responsibility, or its supervision — does it?" Mary glared at him, waiting for his answer.

"No — I guess not, according to the rules and regulations."

"Which way does it work at this hospital?" She asked.

"I guess I have to admit that the rules and regulations are correct."

"Is that the way it works?"

"I guess it works that way most of the time, but not always."

"Well, we both know that the hospital is accredited by the Joint Commission, and we're a member of the American Hospital Association, aren't we?"

"Oh yes — of course," he scowled, showing a little more agitation.

As she pushed the big book back at him she abruptly stood up. Glaring angrily she placed both hands on his desk.

"I'd like to get down to the real issues. We've had one infant die from CS surgery. Veronica Keppler has been permanently disabled from what was clearly a research procedure. And another patient was recently paralyzed, after receiving a plastic implant that was taken off the market. The Denver Post just professionally blasted us out of the water, and we're now about to gain national notoriety on TV," she grimaced, "and it's now becoming obvious that a dozen more cases are lining up in the wings to launch enough lawsuits against this hospital to close us down, and nobody seems to give a damn." Fiercely upset, she flopped back in her chair totally disgusted by the mess they were in. "I'd like to know what the hell is going on here, and can we just please cut the bull-shit!"

Dante's face turned beet red, completely taken back by her angry attack.

"What I'd like to know is why we aren't in compliance with our own regulations?" Pointing at the big book she'd just shoved in front of him, she snarled. "We don't have to beat around the bush. Its better I know the facts up front than listen to a bunch of bull shit." With that she took a deep breath. "I'd like to ask you some questions, and I need some honest answers if I'm to adequately manage the nursing care in this hospital."

With that Dante's mouth dropped open, as he sputtered back, "Alright, I'm listening," he said, trying to regain some control over where things were heading.

Again Mary stood up, but this time pacing the floor as she talked.

"I found no second opinion or even a consult by a qualified and unbiased pediatric neurosurgeon on any of McGrath's cases."

Leaning over the desk she quickly opened the large book and once again pushed it directly in front of him.

"Article fifteen, section 1514.3 states:"

When any unusual or unconventional drug, therapeutic intervention or major surgical procedure is to be employed which might risk life or future function, consultation is mandatory.

Mary glared at him, pointing at the paragraph to emphasize what she was reading. "Does that hit home?"

Then moving her finger to paragraph 1512.3 she continued.

"It says here,"

The attending physician must be responsible for ordering consultations, contacting consultants and formally indicating the desired nature of the consultant's involvement with the patient — providing a written and signed opinion on the appropriate consultation form.

Quickly her finger moved down the page.

The consultant must be qualified by training to give an unbiased opinion in the field in which his or her opinions are sought.

With that, Mary turned and paced back and forth before she again stopped to glare at him.

"I could not find anything in any of the patients' medical records that even remotely suggests these things were done."

"I haven't checked that out yet," Dante replied in his own defense.

"Why haven't you, isn't that your job?"

"I haven't had time."

"Well, someone better take the time. If there isn't a written consult on the appropriate form, we're in violation of your own rules and regulations."

"I understand that," he growled, nervously biting at his upper lip.

"Do you have a recent copy of the Patient's Rights, published by the American Hospital Association?"

"I'm sure we have it somewhere, but I can't just put my hands on it right now."

Mary reached into her folder and pulled out a copy.

"Let me read what it says.

The patient has the right to and is encouraged to obtain from the physician and other direct caregivers relevant, current, and understandable information concerning diagnosis, treatment, and prognosis.

Again she sat down shoving the document in front of him and pointing her finger at the text she was reading from.

"It says right here," *The patient is entitled to the opportunity to discuss and request information related to the specific procedures and/or treatments, the risks involved, and the possible length of recuperation.*

"And over here it says," she continued loudly with the same tinge of sarcasm, *the medically reasonable alternatives and their accompanying risks and benefits.*

With that, Mary stared up at the ceiling for a moment before she once again stared at him.

"Several patients have stated to me that they weren't even made aware there were any other alternatives than a *Total Calvarial Remodeling.* They told me they were deceived by McGrath saying they were told their child might be retarded or even go blind if they didn't have this CS surgery. Are you going to be able to justify that position in front of a jury?"

Dante flinched as she shook one finger squarely in his face.

Again she pushed the Patient's Rights sheet in front of him, pointing at number ten.

The patient has the right to consent to or decline to participate in proposed research studies or human experimentation affecting care and treatment or requiring direct patient involvement, and to have those studies fully explained prior to consent.

With this she paused, lowering her voice to a whisper.

"For God's sake — McGrath's drilling holes in normal infants' heads, just to measure the pressure inside their skull. Just what the hell are we doing here," she yelled, turning away and then turning back and shouting. "That's research. What are his privileges? Just what does his application for Medical Staff say?"

"Let me pull his file," Dante said, calling out for Janice to come in right away.

After they looked at McGrath's application, Mary continued.

"It says right here in his application that he requested research privileges, but the board didn't grant them — and it doesn't say why. They granted him class IV staff privileges, which are described in the rules and regulations, but there's not even a mention of his *Total Calvarial Remodeling* procedure as a proper treatment for the fusion of a single sagittal suture. As I understand it, even the National Neurosurgical Board hasn't sanctioned that type of procedure for a single suture repair. According to his application, he just passed his Boards three months prior to doing the Veronica Keppler case. And as I recall the Keppler case, as well as all his other surgeries, they were all done without any form of supervision. Even the Joint Commission requires a recently boarded physician to be under some form of supervision for at least the first year. Just what's going on in this hospital?"

Mary's face was now plum red with anger.

"Even your own rules require a staff member to exercise only those clinical privileges specifically granted. The plaintiff's attorneys are going to have a field day with this one — but of course you're well aware of those things since you're an attorney."

"You may be right on that. But that's privileged information, and in Colorado that information will not be made available to the plaintiffs' attorneys."

"You can bet your sweet ass it'll come out into the open by testimony somehow," Mary shouted. "Hell, it's already all over the newspaper. And you'd better be prepared to answer some of these ridiculous violations."

Mary could see that he was now visibly unhinged, so she sat down to tone things down a bit. "Didn't we just pass Joint Commission Accreditation?"

"Yes, we sure did, and with flying colors."

"Well, I can't see how. If you look at Doctor McGrath's Medical Staff attendance records I see no attendance information even recorded. There's not one shred of information that shows he attended any staff meetings. Doesn't the Joint Commission require each physician have a seventy-five percent attendance record to serve as an Active Staff member, just as stated in Article thirteen of our own bylaws. Can you tell me if the Neurosurgical Service even holds monthly meetings at all?"

"You mean service meetings?

"Yes — service meetings."

"Doctor McGrath reviews his own charts."

"That's not an unbiased audit. Reviewing your own charts is as biased as you can get. You know that the Joint Commission would never allow that. The Neurosurgery Service is required to review deaths, complications, infections, transfusions and every randomly selected fifth chart every month."

"I know that the Surgery Service, under the Chief of Surgery, Doctor McCauly is doing that. But Doctor McGrath reviews his own charts because he's the interim Chief of Neurosurgery."

"Damn it, you know you can't audit your own charts. No wonder the Medical School pulled its residents out of here. How can they conduct productive Morbidity and Mortality Educational Conferences without total staff participation? It appears that McGrath doesn't feel like he has to report to anyone — and that's why we're now having all this malpractice notoriety."

Dante stood up, nervously trying to explain. "If we attempt to challenge McGrath, he's going to pull his patients out of this hospital, and we just can't afford that. Worse yet, there are other physicians who'll follow him"

"That's an illegal boycott. I don't see how you can afford not to challenge them. If we don't get our butt in gear, there won't be a hospital left to work in," Mary shouted. "And if I'm going to start enforcing standards, I need your cooperation — and I hope I'm going to get it," she said as she gruffly turned and walked out of his office, completely upset and frustrated by his total ineptness.

This God damned Dante has to be behind much of the problem, she thought to herself as she made her way back to her office.

* * * * *

It was almost seven thirty when Bill arrived home from Houston, and he was just about ready to give up trying to reach Mary by phone when he heard the doorbell ring.

"I've got to talk to you," Mary said, quickly brushing past him.

"I walked over so no one would see my car in your driveway."

"What's up?" Bill asked, surprised by her excitement.

"Oh boy, I just had my meeting with Dante, and I really upset him."

"Well good for you, it's about time someone upsets somebody over there."

"Oh, my God," Mary said, rolling her eyes and giggling out loud. "I left him stark raving mad. I've got so much to tell you, it's unbelievable and you have no idea what I did to that man."

"Perhaps not, but I'm sure he deserved everything you did, and then some."

As Mary followed Bill into the kitchen, she explained how she challenged him on the hospital standards.

"That's wonderful," Bill grinned. "How can they argue with their own written standards?"

"They can't." Mary laughed. "But there's so much more to tell you, I don't know where to begin."

"Well, fire away. I don't think I've seen you this excited about your work since you moved here."

After she told Bill about her meeting with Dante she said, "No sooner did I leave Dante's office than McGrath and Bakencamp met with him in the conference room, which is right next to my office. If I stand by the air duct, I can hear almost every word that's said in that room. Since everyone in our office had left for the day, I just closed my door and stood like a church mouse and listened."

"Didn't anyone even check on you?"

"No, I'm there all hours of the day and night, and I know it sounds devious, but after my disgusting meeting with Dante, I had to listen."

As Bill searched the refrigerator for some snacks, Mary sat down on a foot stool, pressing both elbows against her knees. "Just listen to what they said," she whispered, as if she was about to share a huge secret. "Dante told them almost everything I challenged him on, but he embellished it even more. I could hardly keep from laughing out loud. To hear him talk, you'd think I really nailed the poor little thing to a cross."

"I bet you were far kinder than you should have been with that devious jerk."

"But you gotta hear what the man on the white horse had to say. McGrath told them they needed to find out more about me, and if I keep it up, they'll fire me. *Agree with everything she says, but just ignore her*, he said. That seemed to pacify Dante, and he finally toned down and became the same pompous ass he's always been."

"You didn't expect to change his stripes, did you?" Bill laughed.

"No — but here is the juicy part," she grinned. "Apparently the Dinosaurs have paid a well known Senator a bundle of money to look after their interests. I didn't quite hear his name, and I'm too new to the area to even guess if it was one of the Colorado Senators, but I heard enough to know the good Senator is promoting these managed care monopolies. They talked about how they're all going to eventually get very rich from all this and I swear it's just one big con job. They discussed how they're going to eventually kill all the federally supported healthcare programs, and how they intend to first control all healthcare in Colorado."

"That sounds familiar." Bill said.

"Bill, those *Dinosaurs* actually believe they can some day acquire all the nonprofit hospitals, and they're planning to set a low valuation on this hospital before they acquire it. Then they're going to turn around and pay themselves and a few favored board members a huge bonus after the property is revalued."

"You mean kick-backs, don't you?" Bill interrupted.

"Yes, that's what they said. In fact they've already persuaded the City Council on the benefits of privatization, and how much cheaper it will be for a profit centered corporation to run this place, if you can believe that!"

"And I suppose they're also going to give a few of the council members a piece of that pie. Boy, the public loses at both ends, don't they?" Bill smirked. "Not only do they lose their past investments in their community, but they lose control. Apparently they intend to make their noble gentry a lot wealthier, or should I say healthier. I'm afraid that's the only kind of health improvement this poor town is going to see."

Mary nodded. "You know what? I think I've finally figured out what you've been trying to tell me all along. I guess I didn't really get the big picture until I heard these weasels plotting our future. Bill, its all just one big rip off — these guys are actually intending to rape and pillage the poor sick and disabled."

After Bill handed Mary a plate of snacks, he explained, "Mary, I don't think we're ever going solve this problem. I tried that before, and you know where it got me. The only thing that'll stop these crooks is if ordinary people have enough stamina to stand up and be counted. And I guess that won't happen until they're hurting so badly they can't take it anymore, or they refuse to pay these crooked vultures that are picking their pockets."

With that Bill walked across the room and stared out the window. Finally he turned and said — "Mary, after my meeting with Mrs. Keppler, I feel we somehow have to see that the parents of those infants get a fair shake legally."

"I agree, and perhaps we should persuade Dr. Heustes and the government to go after these guys," Mary sighed — "but you're right — it's in the judicial system where we can hurt them the most."

As she picked at a piece of cheese she added. "Oh yes — another thing. It even sounds like they already have several Judges in their pocket, and they talked about how the *Dinosaurs* could confuse this CS issue, if it does go to court. What they plan to do is parade ten or more specialists in front of the judge, all prepared to lie if the plaintiff's attorney attempts to establish cause for any malpractice that involves either the hospital or McGrath. They'll say whatever they have to — whether their under oath or not."

"Boy, that's just the kind of ethics we need in our medical profession. And Mary, that's exactly why I decided to clam up about Lanin's death."

"Yes, and I now agree with you entirely. Bill I think I finally understand," she said nodding, as she bit on a piece of cold meat. "They even said that if this CS thing begins to lose any more public support, they're going to go after the news media. In fact, they've already influenced one of the principle owners of the paper to fire the Managing Editor that broke the CS story. Apparently some guy from Chicago has already been hired to replace him. They said he'll calm the waters when this thing eventually tones down a bit. All I can say is their con job is much bigger and corrupt than I could ever have imagined."

"You've got to be careful," Bill cautioned. "You've seen firsthand what can happen to do-gooder's, and I can tell you from experience, it's no fun fighting this type of corruption — that's unless you want to leave this earth at an early age."

"Oh, I think I'm still safe as long as they feel they can ignore what I have to say. I don't think they'd ever go as far as Lanin did — do you?"

"I have my doubts, but we both know that money produces strange bedfellows, and I think we've already found that greed has no limit."

"Bill, we really need to start thinking about how long we're going to stay here — don't we?"

As she stood up and walked over to him, her arms encircled his waist, pulling him closer. "What ever happened to all those Americans that use to fight for freedom and equality?" She asked.

"I'm afraid those days are gone. But I can tell you this, this nation is doomed if we don't stand up for the working class that built this democracy. And Mary, I think the most we can do here is to help those poor infants and their parents receive some type of compensation. But I also agree — we do need to think about when we're going to leave this job gracefully — and soon."

"And you and I need to think about our future." Mary said, giving him a quick hug that suggested far more than just ending their relationship.

"Mary, it's the same damn thing all over again," Bill snarled. "It's all the same, the boycotts, the monopolies, just like we fought in North Dakota. Hell, they probably trained Larry McGrath and his two henchmen, Dante and Bakencamp. And I bet many of the hospital board members don't even have a clue of what's really going on."

"Oh my God, I forgot, tonight 20/20's airing the CS epidemic. What time is it?" Mary interrupted, running to turn on the TV.

Chapter 7

Time to Think

On Saturday morning, Bill returned home after shopping for some groceries, to find several messages. Dave Nelson was in town and wanted to meet him at the Broadmoor. Since Dave was going to be busy all day, he said he'd call later and confirm an evening dinner reservation.

Bill tried to reach Mary, but she wasn't home, and it was almost six that evening before she returned his call.

"I've been at the hospital all day, and that place was a madhouse. You wouldn't believe the response they've had to last night's TV expose. People are calling in from all over the country, wondering just what's going on."

"Are their comments favorable or unfavorable?" Bill asked.

"Mostly very unfavorable — and we had every available operator trying to classify the calls and route them to the person who could best respond to their questions. Some were worried mothers or fathers who've been treated by McGrath. Some were the news media, but most were just people expressing their anger. At least the three main culprits are damned concerned about it now. Bakencamp, McGrath, and Dante have been in conference all day. They were still at the hospital when I left, and I noticed your friend Dave Nelson has been meeting with them."

"It sounds like everybody was watching television last night."

"Yes, I guess they were. In fact, my whole nursing staff has been up in arms, and I've been there since seven this morning trying to calm the waters. Many of them were not even aware it was being aired on national TV. They all wanted to know if that could really happen at our hospital."

"I can understand that," Bill said. "And it's probably only going to get worse, until they limit that butcher's privileges. Now that it's out in the open, it'll probably remain under public scrutiny for some time, and eventually someone's going to hopefully demand answers."

"I believe you're right on that. The news media has been trying to meet with Bakencamp all day, but he's just not making himself available. All three of them are parking their cars behind the boiler plant and walking to the hospital through the tunnel. I guess they don't want to try and answer any questions until they all get their stories straight. I'm not sure that's the best way to handle it, but if you don't have answers, I suppose the next best thing is to avoid the questions."

"Mary, the reason I called is Dave Nelson left a message that he wants to meet me for dinner, and I'd like you to go with."

"I'd love to — I never turn down a free meal."

"Well, I'll call you after I know when and where."

No sooner did Bill hang up than the phone rang, and it was Dave confirming an eight o'clock dinner. "Let's meet at the Tavern again," he'd said.

* * * * *

As Mary and Bill entered the restaurant, Dave waved them over to his table.

"This is a surprise," Bill said. What brings you back to Colorado? I couldn't possibly guess what it might be!"

Dave laughed. "I wish it was your smiling face, but I'm not so lucky. No, the shit hit the fan today."

As they sat down Bill said, "Mary tells me you've been kind of busy."

"That's putting it mildly," Dave grinned, shaking his head in disgust. "Bill, before I get into this thing any deeper, I need to see if you've found anything that suggests we shouldn't be associated with this bunch."

"You bet I have," Bill said guardedly. "Dave, we're fighting that same damned clique we fought in the Dakotas, only this one's probably better financed — and if you decide to side with McGrath's *Dinosaurs*, you're in big trouble."

"Oh shit," Dave muttered under his breath. "I knew it," he scoffed, bringing one fist firmly down on the table. "I had a gut feeling about this whole damned thing — but I guess that's why I asked you to get involved."

As the waiter passed them their menus, Dave ordered almost immediately.

"God damn it," he snarled, "this thing's like a cancer — it's crawling all over us."

Quickly Bill pulled his notes from his briefcase and laid them on the table. "I was going to prepare a written report and call you on Monday, but I'd prefer giving you an oral report since I want you to keep my comments to your self."

"An oral report will be fine," Dave said not knowing what to expect. "And if as you say, the *Dinosaur's* are really involved, it's best I not have it in writing anyway," he mumbled, anticipating the worst.

"Let me first assure you that *The Dinosaur Club* is clearly involved in this fiasco, and McGrath is the head honcho in Colorado — and he's still wet behind the ears, which is even worse."

With that, Bill looked at Mary. "Tell Dave what you overheard in your office after your meeting with Dante, when you challenged him on hospital standards."

When she was finished, Bill continued. "From what I've found, here is what's going on. Hanes was the past President of the *Colorado Dinosaur Club*, and he's in the process of retiring to Texas, with several million dollars in his pocket. He was sharp enough to realize the Health Department and the CDC were about to blow the whistle on his con game, so he got out while he could still sell his practice to his young resident. That way he could earn a few hundred thousand a year from McGrath, after he built up his ego."

"And McGrath actually believes he's the savior of all those infants who'd have become retarded without his divine intervention," Mary interrupted.

Dave looked at Mary and just shook his head.

"Prior to Hanes departure, he appointed McGrath as President of the *Dinosaurs*," Bill continued, "which I'm absolutely sure is an extension of that Lanin bunch. And this Colorado group includes about twenty private practicing physicians that threaten to boycott this hospital every time they're asked to obey the hospital's rules and regulations."

"Damn it Bill, these organizations are spreading so fast you can't keep up with them," Dave snarled, throwing his napkin on the table. "That God damned Lanin really started something."

"More important," Bill continued. "Bakencamp and Dante were actually hired by Hanes and McGrath, and neither one of them would dare to cross McGrath or they'd be out on their ass in five minutes. And Dave, this all happened after they booted out two of the finest physicians you could ever find in Doctor Belky and Doctor Taber." Bill paused a moment to clear his throat with a sip of water. "And the current split between the closed faculty at the medical school and the private open staff is about as bad as I've ever seen. This open staff actually scoffs at the faculty as if they're a bunch of peons working for peanuts."

"God all Friday, this has really gotten ugly." Dave whispered, shocked by what Bill was saying.

"Hell, I'm just getting started," Bill explained. "Dante also started the first managed care system in Colorado. He's both a physician and an attorney and has jumped around from job to job like a Jack Rabbit. Worse yet, this bunch of thieves are the majority shareholders of the local profit oriented HMO, which is nothing more than a monopoly. They set their own fees, and then turn around and make payments to themselves."

"That sounds familiar. It's beyond me how the State Insurance Commissioner can let that go on," Dave growled.

"Dave, you know the private insurance lobby was smart enough to eliminate all the state regulations when they lobbied the McCarran Ferguson Act back in 1945, and now the insurance commissioner has nothing to say about regulating anything in healthcare. That's what allowed the *Dakota Dinosaurs* to grease the skids for their hospital take-over's — and from what Mary just overheard, this Colorado bunch plans to eventually own this hospital. As she told you, Bakencamp and a few of his close Board Members are apparently going to set a ridiculously low value on the hospital, and then they'll acquire it for a song. That way they'll triple their equity overnight, and you know damned well that Bakencamp and a few of his cronies will receive one hell of a big pay-off from all that. And the myopic public, as usual, won't even know what happened to their once tax supported community hospitals."

"Oh shit," Dave said, rubbing his forehead.

"Let's look at another problem," Bill said, pushing his chair back. "As far as we can determine, McGrath never did a *Total Calvarial Reconstruction* before he arrived in Colorado. And as you already know, that procedure should never be used for a single suture repair. Worse yet, he was only boarded in neurosurgery just three months before he performed that gruesome surgery on the Keppler child, which was done without any supervision. Mary and I've found so many violations of the Joint Commission Standards and their own hospital's rules and regulations, it's unbelievable. And now there are approximately a dozen or more parents, at last count, that are planning to sue Hanes, McGrath and the hospital. And in my judgment, the only way to fight that type of corruption will be through the courts. Maybe that way the parents can at least get a little retribution," Bill snarled in disgust. "Dave, you know full well what happens when do-gooders like me try to single handedly challenge this corrupt group of vipers."

With that, Dave whistled softly. "Those bastards will kill you, this time."

"That could be, but murdering me becomes a little more difficult if their under open public scrutiny, and public scrutiny is what it's going to take before these rats will be forced back into their rat-hole."

"I understand," Dave nodded.

After Bill scraped the last bit of food from his plate, he pushed himself back from the table. "I should also tell you there are some very fine physicians trying to fight this clique, but they're going to lose big time — I can tell you that right up front. And Dave, you'd be a damn fool to help these shysters polish their image."

"I agree," Dave grunted in disgust. "And I wish I'd never asked you and Mary to become involved, but I honestly thought Mary could help them get their standards back in place."

"I agree," Mary smiled, "but none of us knew who we were fighting at that time."

Bill looked over his shoulder to be sure no one could overhear.

"You know, if we were really smart, we'd all walk away from this whole damned mess."

"I agree, and you should," Dave, interrupted.

"In any event, I recommend you kick them in the ass before your consulting firm gets tarnished, and Mary and I'll handle things our own way before we leave this hell hole."

After desert, they continued to visit with Dave until late that evening, and as they finally got up to leave, Dave reached out and said, "Thanks Bill. What you've done for us is worth a lot to me, and we're definitely going to bow out on this one."

Before they parted, Dave stared at both of them and smiled. "You two have a great Christmas vacation and I hope you both have a much better New Year — and let's keep in touch."

As he started to leave, he suddenly turned back and grinned.

"You know what? You both make a great team. Maybe I can take some credit for at least getting you back together."

* * * * *

Bill rolled and tossed most of the night, thinking about the mess he'd gotten Mary into. At the crack of dawn, he finally got up and loaded his camp stove and a picnic basket into his car. Driving to an all-night supermarket, he picked up some breakfast items and when he arrived at Mary's he realized it was just getting light, but he rang the doorbell anyway. It took several minutes before he heard Mary whisper, "Who's there?"

"It's your friendly neighbor, picking you up for breakfast."

He could hear Mary grown, as the dead-bolt lock snapped open.

"What in the hell are you doing? — It's still the middle of the night! Don't you realize Sunday is the only day I can sleep late," she mumbled incoherently, looking at her watch as she reluctantly stepped back and let him in. "We don't meet for breakfast for another three hours!"

"It'll be three hours before you can get dressed, and drive to the Eleven Mile Canyon with me. There's still no snow in the mountains and its going to be a perfect day — and it's time you and I relax a little," Bill laughed. "I'm going to show you what a real breakfast tastes like."

It was indeed a perfect day, and after Mary got over the initial trauma she was glad Bill had changed her Sunday routine. After a little less than an hour's drive, they finally reached Lake George, some twenty-five miles west of Colorado Springs. Mary hadn't really had a chance to see much of Colorado, and as they turned into the canyon she was overwhelmed at its beauty. The cliffs towered a good hundred feet above them and the canyon seemed void of all humanity, until they finally spotted a lone trout fisherman casting upstream as he waded in the beautiful cascading creek. Seven miles and two tunnels further, they finally reached Bill's favorite spot.

Awkwardly carrying their supplies, they crossed a very well built footbridge. "This is gorgeous," Mary said, all the time gazing at the stream and the cliffs surrounding them. Dropping what she was carrying on a picnic table beside the stream she sighed, "This is absolutely fabulous."

The smell from the giant ponderosa pines and the soothing melody of the stream surging over the worn down boulders had provided the exact reprieve Mary needed.

"Why haven't you told me about this place before?"

"Mary, it was one of Susan's favorite spots. I'm not filling a void in my life — I just wanted to share this wonderful place with you."

"Well I can certainly see why she liked it, and I can see why it would be one of your most favorite spots in the world. Thank you for including me in on it."

"Mary, I'd love to include you in a lot more of my life," Bill said, as they kissed and then walked arm and arm to gaze into the crystal clear stream gushing by them.

"I love you," Mary whispered, turning slowly and starring into his eyes." Then suddenly they were interrupted by a thrashing in the water just a few feet downstream where they saw a Dipper bird feeding off the bottom, and as it dove under the water, they both laughed at its antics.

Finally, Bill whispered, "I bet you're famished?"

Mary nodded somewhat reluctantly.

"Alright — lets eat," he shouted, and together they started to prepare breakfast. When they finally sat down it was almost nine o'clock.

"How is that for timing?" Bill asked.

"I don't think I've ever been so hungry in all my life," Mary cried out as she poured maple syrup over a huge stack of pancakes that were all ready drowning in butter, while chewing on a piece of hot thick bacon.

"That's what the outdoors does for you," Bill mumbled, pouring their coffee from his old fire stained pot that had just boiled over.

"I don't think I've ever tasted anything better," Mary said, looking up at the blue sky. "And I've never seen such a blue sky before — I think I've died and gone to heaven."

Even a large Steller Jay swooped down from the pines, making their Sunday brunch complete, just as a chipmunk scurried for safety in the rocks.

After eating way too much, and taking one last swallow of coffee, Bill turned to look at Mary.

"Now that Dave has decided to pull out of this inferno, it looks like I'm out of a job."

"I suspected as much," she said, kind of curling the corner of her mouth. "But I think you have some interesting stories to write about, and the parents of these poor children could sure use your help if they ever expect to recover from this tragedy."

"Yah, something has been telling me that," Bill scowled. "I don't think it's any type of divine intervention, but I believe the courts are the only way to ever get these scoundrels to face up to their crimes." Bill turned and scraped his plate for the Chipmunks and the birds — even thought that was a no-no. Thoughtfully he stared at the ground before finally saying, "Mary, after failing to protect my family from Lanin, I still have a great deal of vengeance in my heart, and it's going to be very difficult for me to remain unbiased in any court room. But I guess that feeling isn't going to fade until someone steps in and stops all these transgressions against these poor sick and disabled victims."

"You're absolutely right, and I want to be a part of that," Mary said. "Bill, I believe I can improve this hospital's standards, even though these scumbags will probably fight me every step of the way. And although I've never fought an administrator, or the Medical Staff before, I think I see a way this can be accomplished."

"And I want you to do just that," Bill whispered. "But I don't want you to risk your life if things are going to explode in our face."

"I understand," she said, reaching out to squeeze his hand tightly.

"Maybe we should just start out fresh, without any more *Dinosaurs* in our lives, Bill whispered."

"I'll buy that, but I also think we still should finish what we started — that's if it doesn't take too long," she added as an after thought. "But if it's going to take forever, perhaps we should quit right now! Bill, I have all the money we'll ever need, and we can do whatever we want, or go wherever we want."

"That's the other thing we need to discuss. Mary, I need to prove to myself that I can write. Why? — Because I've got a lot to write about, and so much to share with the world. But I also need to carry my own weight financially, if I ever want to be happy with myself."

"I understand." Mary said.

"I also think my research on the medical record database will someday improve healthcare, and I really need to also write about that. That's if I can ever quit fighting with all these scoundrels. I wish you could of heard Doctor Taber talk about the future of medicine — it was like a breath of fresh air. I want to meet with him again someday to discuss my research and the future of the database system in medicine — but I guess we've got this bigger problem right now." With that, Bill looked into Mary's crystal blue eyes. "Do you understand what I'm saying?"

"Yes, I certainly do — and I want to be there this time to help you accomplish those goals," she smiled. "Bill, as Dave said, I believe we're going to make one hell of a team, particularly if you can cook like you just did today," she giggled.

Bill looked smugly back at her. "All right, so we're going to stay and finish what we started."

"Yes," Mary shouted. "But I also need your help. That's why I'm making arrangements for us to fly to Florida right after Christmas, where we can have some quiet time to discuss how we plan to make this damned hospital a better place, without hurting any more patients — cause if they don't have our support, they're going to lose big time."

* * * * *

During their flight to Orlando, Mary's head rested on Bill's shoulder as she tried to catch up on some sleep. They were both anxious to get away, and Bill had made arrangements for Doctor Heustes to meet them while they were on Mary's boat. When they arrived in Florida, the Orlando airport was filled with holiday tourists, and they had to wait for almost an hour before they could finally pick up a rental car. It was then another hour's drive to Highway 75 before they finally headed south to

Fort Myers. When at long last they crossed the bridge near Mary's boat dock, the late afternoon sun was reflecting off the water and they could hardly recognize her boat as they stared into the bright sunset.

"There it is," she yelled, "and it looks like they've finished the paint job. Oh Bill, I like those dark blue strips on the hull, they look great, don't they?"

"They sure do," Bill smiled.

As Mary stepped out of the car, a friendly voice yelled, "Mrs. Swanson, we've been waiting for you," as they both turned to see a tall gangly man with a big smile hurriedly walking toward them.

"We just got it out of dry dock yesterday, and everything's working great. When do you plan to take her out?"

"Hey Matthew," how are you? Mary replied, giving him a big hug.

After she introduced Bill, she continued. "We're going out first thing in the morning, and before I forget, we have a visitor by the name of Doctor Heustes, the head of the NIH, who'll be trying to find us on the twenty-ninth. And I might as well tell you right now, we'll be anchored on the leeward side of La Costa, and you'll have to tell him how to find us."

"Okay, I can do that for you," he smiled, "by the way, Snapper and Sea Trout are filling out regularly, and you shouldn't have trouble catching fish." As they checked out the boat, the smell of fresh paint was hardly distinguishable and having been on their boat before, Bill could sense they were in for a fun time, which they both needed desperately.

Their first order of business was to shop for groceries, and after they finally loaded everything into the galley, they left for Mary's house. That evening they decided to eat at one of Mary's favorite seafood restaurants, ordering what she described as the best soft shell crab on the entire west coast of Florida. Then later, when they arrived home, Mary grabbed Bill's hand and directed him toward her bedroom. "I've wanted to make love to you far to long," she whispered, slipping both hands under his shirt.

Bill responded immediately unbuttoning her blouse. Once they were completely undressed, Mary turned and walked to the bed, pulling back the covers.

"Come over here," she said, reaching out to him.

The soft curves of her body were flawless, as Bill absorbed her complete nakedness for the first time.

"You're beautiful," he whispered, touching her shapely breasts.

Pulling him closer she cried, "Oh God, you feel so good."

Her words echoed in Bill's head as memories of Susan flooded his mind. That was exactly what Susan would have said, he thought. Chills of excitement were already sweeping over Mary when suddenly his hardness disappeared and it took several moments for her to realize what was happening. It was like she was in the midst of a storm and all of a sudden everything stopped. As she lay there confused, she looked to him for an answer.

"What's wrong?" she whispered.

Bill was obviously upset with himself as he rolled to his back. "I desire you more than anything," he sighed. "It's Susan — I'm so sorry."

Mary pulled him back into her arms saying — "Its okay, I understand."

As Bill kissed her softly, hoping his excitement would return, he whispered, "I've never had this problem before. I don't know what to say."

Finally he looked at Mary. "You know my feelings for you are sincere — don't you?"

"I understand — its okay," she repeated, holding him closely as she reached down to touch him. "We'll just wait a minute," she said. "I have the same fears you do."

As she began to kiss his chest and his stomach, his desire was finally rekindled and this time their satisfaction was complete, and they both fell exhausted into a deep sleep.

As the morning sun slowly peaked through the window, they found themselves still in each other's arms. Mary raised her head, murmuring softly. "You were wonderful, and to think I'm going to spend the rest of my life with you."

They both moved closer for a moment before Mary suddenly sat up and shouted, "Oh my God, I told Matt we'd be there first thing in the morning — he's probably waiting for us right now. Damn it, I guess we'll have to wait until we're anchored in Charlotte Harbor," she smirked, quickly jumping out of bed.

"Hey, I'm as anxious as you are to get on that boat?" Bill laughed as they both scrambled for the shower, where the warm water helped regenerated their tired bodies.

The morning wind was brisk but not threatening, and after Matt cast the last mooring line to Mary, Bill powered up both diesels. "Try to avoid any wake until you reach the harbor," Matt yelled, as Bill slowly pulled back on the throttle, gradually moving away from the dock at a snail's pace. Once Mary had secured the lines, she made her way next to Bill in the Captain's tower.

"It looks like a great day doesn't it?" she shouted. "I can't tell you how much I've looked forward to this."

"Me too," Bill yelled over the diesels as he turned the boat into the wind.

"I'm going to get into my swim suit and get rid of this anemia," Mary said, gawking grotesquely at her white skin.

As Mary reached for the hand rail, Bill shouted, "You look great!"

By the time Mary returned, Bill had increased the speed, and was now heading out into the open water. Quickly glancing over his shoulder, he could see she was wearing that same tiny bikini, remembering the first time he saw in anything other than a white starched nursing uniform. "God you're beautiful," he shouted, turning so he could once again fully appreciate the view. "You're absolutely gorgeous. You don't have a flaw anywhere," he said, studying her closely and giving a long prolific whistle. "How long before I can park this boat and untie those two strings?"

Mary coquettishly smiled as she curtsied gratuitously. "We've got a good hour before we'll reach the place I want to anchor. You'll need to point us exactly northwest once you get around that point by that beacon," Mary yelled, raising one finger and pointing at a small spit of land on the horizon.

Once Bill confirmed the direction, he set course.

"I'm going to lie in the sun," she said, opening the door to the top deck. As Bill watched the wind trying to blow the towel from her hands, it was obvious she'd done this many times before and in only moments she had the towel skillfully stretched over the deck. Bill had to adjust the direction several times until he was finally accustomed to looking at her almost totally nude backside, and then no sooner would he get the boat back on course than she'd change position.

Just think, we've got a full week together," he thought to himself.

After the boat rounded the point, he had far more trouble keeping a steady course because of the wind, which was much stronger in the open harbor. Off in the distance he could see a thin line of islands on the horizon, and he yelled for Mary to once again confirm his direction.

"Yes, that looks right, but it'll take a good hour before we get there," she shouted over the diesels that were now running wide open. As Bill challenged the rough waves, she yelled, "It looks like we're going to have a bumpy ride until we reach those islands. In about a mile, you'll be able to pick up the main channel markers, and they'll take us close to where we'll anchor."

"I see a marker now," Bill shouted.

As the boat finally approached the calm side of La Costa Island, Mary made her way down to the bow to help guide him to the exact spot she wanted to anchor, which was only a short distance from the white sand beach. The boat could actually land on the beach, but Mary preferred the privacy of the open water, using their small dingy to get to the shore or fish. Finally she signaled for Bill to cut the speed as she dropped the bow anchor over the side. Then as soon as the first anchor caught hold, she dropped a second one from the stern of the boat, which kept boat from swinging every time the wind changed direction.

"Eureka!" she yelled. "We're finally here."

As Bill shut down the diesels, they both suddenly became aware of how quiet it was, and at last they were completely alone. As their eyes scanned this beautiful paradise, a cooling gust of wind blew a lock of hair over Mary's face. Kissing, they walked toward the bedroom. "Now, I'm going to change into my swimming suit," Bill chuckled.

"I don't think you're going to want your swim suit just yet," she laughed.

* * * * *

The following morning, they were up at the crack of dawn and after a brisk hike on the Gulf side of the white sand beach, they returned to their small boat to try some early morning drift fishing. Matthew had filled their bait tank with fresh shrimp, giving them the added assurance they'd catch fish if artificial bait didn't work. The wind was perfect for drift fishing, and they both had seen several Red Snapper breaking the water earlier. Since Bill had fished Reds and Sea Trout before, he suggested they cast popping corks ahead of them using live shrimp, while drifting in about three to five feet of water.

"Just cast as far ahead as you can," Bill said, throwing his line out to show her what he meant. "Then every few seconds you just give the line a jerk so the sinker rattles against the cork, like this," he said, popping the cork in the water. "For some reason the fish are attracted by that popping noise, and if they strike, be prepared — because you'll have a real fight on your hands."

"All right," Mary laughed, "I'm ready."

"Before you cast, you want to see if a fish breaks the water, and then try to throw the bait a few yards past him."

Mary kind of mumbled to herself. "Hell, I'll be happy if I get it out of the boat," she cursed, trying to untangle her line after her first try. It only took a few more tries before she was casting like a pro, and before the sun was too high on the horizon she had her first strike.

"Good for you, Bill shouted. "Keep that line tight."

As she raised both arms high into the air, the line suddenly went slack.

"It must be a trout," Bill yelled. "He's coming straight at you. Crank in some line."

No sooner did she get the line cranked in than it surged straight out again, only now the pole bent toward the other side of the boat.

"Oh my God," Mary screamed. "What should I do?"

"Just keep the tip of the pole up and the line tight," Bill calmly said, trying to calm her down. "Just play him."

Mary's arms were going every which way as the line would first thread out rapidly and then she'd crank it back in. Every so often she let out a squeal or a profanity to let the fish know she was still in charge, but at times Bill could only wonder.

After a long fierce battle, Bill said, "I think you've finally worn him out. Why don't you bring him up to the side of the boat, and I'll try to land him. That may be our dinner for tonight," he explained, as he netted a huge Sea Trout.

Putting the fish on a stringer, they both laughed with excitement as Mary described her battle over and over, before they finally had a moment where they could sit peacefully and discuss their plans for the future.

"When I was down here all alone," Mary said, "I was so lonely I hated it. Your call was a blessing. I never liked being alone, and I needed to find something meaningful to do with my life, and your call gave me that new lease on life."

Bill smiled. "It was the same with me," he admitted.

As they began to feel the hot midday sun, they both put some lotion on, trying to head off the inevitable sunburn.

"And I couldn't do what I'm doing if I didn't feel I was helping people," she continued. "But, deceiving patients just isn't my cup of tea, and I'm having a lot of internal turmoil working for Bakencamp."

"That's why you must establish higher goals that improve the quality of care, even if it's in direct opposition to those *Dinosaurs*."

"I understand," she frowned, turning her head to stare at Bill.

"But I also want a future with you."

Bill turned, and looked at her. Mary, we've worked together for many years now, and I can say with all assurance you're a remarkable woman. And I love you."

Slowly Bill laid down his fishing pole and adjusted his position so he could hold her hand. "We've both been through a lot, and it would be a simple solution to stay right here and enjoy life, just like we're doing today, but you and I are goal oriented people. We're at our best when we're doing something meaningful."

"I know that!" she nodded.

"And that's why we need to expel these *Dinosaurs*," Bill said, his jaw determined. "So, I'm going to write about what's been happening with the hope that I can help expose these horrible crimes against humanity. But if I'm going to do that properly, I really need to first get these culprits into a court room."

"Yes, you do," Mary, agreed.

"You also need to understand that I could never live with myself if I was responsible for something happening to you," he added, staring into her eyes. "Those bastards would kill you, just like Susan if they even suspected you're working against them — so you'll need to keep the faith with your employer."

"But that doesn't mean I can't help you. Eventually we'll all benefit from what we're both trying to do."

"Yes, but we can't mix my fighting them and you educating them. Those two things just don't mix. You can see that, can't you?"

"Yes, but I'll tell you right up front, you're far more important to me than those damned *Dinosaurs*." Mary became choked-up as she looked away, once again hiding her emotions. After a short pause she looked back at Bill, agreeing with him, but not happy about it. "All right — let's work in our separate camps until you satisfy that inner need of yours — and then I'm bringing you back here, and I'll make you write every time you try to make love to me."

"But I'll need a break from writing now and then," Bill laughed.

"I think we might be able to arrange that," Mary said, slyly curling her lips into an impish smile.

No sooner had they formalized their agreement with a kiss, than Bill's fishing rod went flying out of the boat. They both turned and watched in astonishment as the rod sank in the water. Quickly Bill dove after it, struggling to retrieve the reel that was now bouncing along the bottom. Finally he stood up in the waist deep water and set the hook. Then after he worked his way toward the shore, he finally beached a huge Red Snapper.

That evening, Bill and Mary stayed up late, eating fresh Sea Trout, while watching the moon rise above the glow of Fort Myers.

"Let's say we leave Colorado in no more than a year," Mary said. "That way it sets a deadline for both of us to accomplish our work."

As she stood up, gathering the dishes, she continued talking.

"Boy I'd like to go for a moonlight swim, but for some reason I'm terrified of the ocean at night. I have that weird feeling that something might swim up and take a bite out of me."

"Mary, that's very possible in these waters. I remember when I was stationed at Pensacola Naval Air Station; one of the cadets had a leg taken off while he was spearing flounder at night. Later, they thought either a large Barracuda or a shark might have been attracted by the light he was shining in the water."

"You're kidding? How gross! Why in the world did you ever tell me that?"

"Well, it is dangerous out there at night, and I'd rather take a bite out of you than some damn fish."

With that, Bill picked her up and carried her toward the bedroom. "Let's do the dishes in the morning," he whispered.

Chapter 8

The Democracy Hypocrisy

A U.S. Coast Guard cutter met Doctor Heustes at Matt's Marina on the twenty-ninth of December, and Matt gave the Captain directions to where Bill and Mary could be found. It was midmorning before Bill and Mary noticed their boat heading towards them.

As they approached, their Captain indicated over the loudspeaker they'd be boarding on the port side. Bill waved back to let them know he understood, and in only a matter of minutes Hugh was on board, along with a man by the name of Ted, who quickly scurried off to inspect Mary's boat. When Ted returned, he signaled everything was okay for the cutter to leave.

"It's good seeing you two again," Heustes said, finally explaining that Ted was his new security guard. Ted was a huge ruddy-faced redhead with a crew cut, and his handshake felt like a vice as he crushed Bill's hand, and smiled. Bill had been working with a committee to develop the Diagnostic Related Groupings for Medicare with Doctor Heustes during much of his tenure as head of the NIH, and it was a surprise for him to see the good doctor dressed in an immaculately clean white sport shirt and white shorts, which made his already thin legs look even longer.

"I'm impressed," Heustes explained. "They had no trouble finding you whatsoever. Those guys sure know what they're doing — I bet they could find a needle in a haystack if they had to. Did you have a nice holiday?"

"We arrived the day after Christmas, so we just skipped Christmas this year," Mary replied. "But yes, we've been having a great time Doctor Heustes."

"Mary, please call me Hugh," he grinned. "You certainly have a remarkable boat. What's her name?"

"I haven't decided yet, I'm in the process of renaming her."

As they walked into the main room, Mary asked Hugh, "Can I get you something refreshing to drink?"

"Yes, that would be nice."

"How about you Ted?"

"Yes please, and if you don't mind, I'd like to then take it up in that tower and leave you people to visit."

As Mary prepared drinks, Bill placed some snacks on the table.

"This is kind of a hush-hush trip," Hugh explained as he sat down at the table. "I told my new secretary I'd be with the Coast Guard most of the day, inspecting the river outlets for some of those whirling microbes that have already destroyed the fish in Chesapeake Bay. No one but the Coast Guard and Ted know I'm visiting with you."

"Hugh, there's nothing earth shaking about what we've stumbled on, but I think you need an update on the *Dinosaurs* since our last meeting when Mary secretly taped that Lanin bunch."

"You know, we've never found a scrap of evidence that would even suggest where Lanin and his cronies disappeared to. That's quite unusual, since almost every country has their description," he scowled. "We usually get some type of report, but we've heard nothing."

Bill could feel Mary's foot nudge him under the table.

"Yes, that is unusual," Bill agreed.

Hugh looked puzzled — "Anyway, you need to be aware that Doctor Oderoff has filled Lanin's shoes, and he's sicker than Lanin."

"Let me assure you he is," Bill, grumbled, quickly changing the subject. After describing how Dave had asked him to investigate the CS surgery situation, Mary described what she'd overheard between Dante, McGrath and Bakencamp.

Shocked at what they told him, he sat quietly for a moment before reacting. "Bill, you need to know that things have changed dramatically since we last talked. My long-time secretary died of cancer six months ago, and I'm lost without her. And I haven't been able to choose a proper replacement with all these Washington quotas we have to meet. It no longer seems to matter whether a person has the skills required to do the job, as long as we meet these damned quotas," he explained, shaking his head in disgust. It seems that you can't depend on anyone anymore. That's why I told my new secretary I'd be with the Coast Guard today, because I can't even trust her."

Mary got up and walked toward the Galley, returning with some sandwiches she'd made earlier. As Hugh continued, he picked up a ham and cheese and took a big bite.

"I've had an attempt on my life recently, and that's why I now have Ted at my side constantly."

"I was wondering about that," Bill said. "He's certainly a new addition. I hope you trust us?"

"Implicitly," he grinned. "But I just can't afford to take chances any longer. As a result, I'm seldom alone anymore."

"That's a terrible situation, "Bill scowled.

"To be very honest, I'm going to give it all up pretty soon."

Mary could see he looked tired. "I don't know how you put up with it all," she groaned.

"Well, it's not getting any easier. This deregulation of healthcare is destroying almost everything we've worked for, and the poor unsuspecting public hasn't a clue of where things are heading. In fact healthcare is almost one fifth of our total budget and climbing"

Bill nodded. "Hugh, I'd really be interested in what you have to say about all this, since I'm writing about this Oligarchic destruction of our healthcare system."

"Well I could bore you all day on that subject."

"Please do," Bill said seriously.

"Yes, we'd both be very interested," Mary quickly chimed in.

"You flatter me," he chuckled, sliding his chair closer to the table.

"All right, I'll tell you some of my thoughts if you're really interested," he smiled leaning forward to rest both elbows on the table.

"Do you recall the first nonprofit single prepayment system that was established back in the days of Roosevelt?"

"Yes, I certainly do," Bill said, looking at Mary.

Mary looked puzzled. "I think that's a little before my time," she snickered.

Hugh laughed. "Well anyway, that program was under state enabling legislation that declared this program could never become a profit insurance company. In other words, it was supposed to be kept under strict state regulation."

"That was the Blues, right?" Bill asked.

"Exactly, and the Blues eventually became world renowned because it was a community rated system under which everyone paid the same rate, regardless of their age, sex, where they lived, or how sick they were. And at that time healthcare cost us only four percent of our total budget. Another thing to remember was that hospitals and doctors were paid equitably for some thirty years under that program."

"I do remember my parents talking about how good Blue Cross was," Mary said. "The way they talked, it was the best program in the world — so what happened?"

"That's what we're all asking ourselves," Hugh replied, intentionally scratching at his baldhead to make the point. "Well, here's what happened," he continued, nudging his chair a bit forward so he was more comfortable. "In the mid forties, the profit oriented insurance companies wanted to get a piece of the action, but they realized they'd first have to protect themselves from any state regulations. So they greased the skids by having congress pass the McCarran Ferguson Act, which allowed profit insurance to enter the field but remain totally unregulated and exempt from all anti-trust laws. In other words, the insurance companies bought themselves a sweetheart deal, so they'd be untouchable by any state regulation. I still remember a few Senators who became very wealthy from the insurance payoffs, and that was the start of our healthcare deregulation, which is now seriously screwing up the entire system."

Mary scowled, disturbed by what she was hearing.

As Hugh looked at her, he slowly raised one hand, "And that's only part of it," he smiled. "Then in the sixties, the insurance industry began to skim selected best risk customers from the Blues, without any federal or state intervention."

"How could they do that?" Mary asked.

"It was simple. They initially offered the younger and healthier low risk clients lower group premiums in place of the single community premium."

With that Hugh raised both hands, indicating in quotation marks.

"In other words, they sold *'group'* rating as if it was *'community'* rating."

"What do you mean, community rated?" Mary asked.

"That means everyone paid the same premium," he explained. "But, under group rating, the profit insurance companies could raise the older or sicker groups' premiums. Then as they started new groups, or as individuals slowly became higher risk clients, the poor patients could no longer afford health insurance."

"That's not fair," she scoffed. "I thought insurance was to level the playing field."

"No, that really wasn't fair, but the public never realized what was happening to them," he said, picking up his glass and taking a swallow. "And ever since then we've been marketing the sick and disabled to death. Eventually the Blues were unable to compete with this type of unfair competition, because they were left with most of the sick and disabled patient's bills. And as a result, many of the Blues were eventually forced to become profit oriented group insurance companies, just in order to survive."

"Yes, I remember, and that should never have been allowed to happen," Bill interrupted with a sour look on his face.

"Of course not, but how could our Senators challenge this powerful insurance industry that had just paid them off? Allowing profit insurance into this private nonprofit healthcare arena was like letting a fox into the chicken coop."

"I don't believe I know a single nurse who understands what you've just told us, Mary whispered. It's hard to believe all that went on right under our nose."

"That ain't all," Hugh groaned, taking another quick swallow of his drink.

"Then in a feeble attempt to cover up their tracks, President Johnson signed into law an amendment to the Social Security Act, on July 30 1965, which established Medicare and Medicaid. The impetus for that program came from our own NIH survey that revealed half of the elderly in the United States could no longer afford this new profit oriented health insurance. The subtle and almost subversive thing about Medicare and Medicaid was that it was actually designed to free profit-insurance of the elderly and disabled, making this new discriminatory profit type health insurance even more profitable. Under the previous Blues prepayment program, the average annual per capita cost of healthcare was one hundred and forty-three dollars. Now, under this new profit system, it is projected to reach almost seventeen thousand dollars a year by 2015. That's kind of scary, isn't it?"

"That's ridiculous," Mary shouted. "And you're saying the public didn't realize this? They surely must have had some clue that they were all going to someday become older and poorer, and certainly less insurable under this group rated plan."

"You'd think so, but the younger uninformed public only saw the immediate savings, and now they're paying for it. On top of all that, profit insurance makes all the decisions about what they can get for their money, as they deregulate even more of the healthcare standards and regulations we all worked so hard for. And as a result they now make their decisions based on profit, not service. Worse yet, this profit seeking aristocracy has now totally deregulated almost all our infrastructure and service entities," Hugh snarled. "Lobbyist, pressuring politicians with their under the table cash pay-offs is the biggest problem I have to deal with in Washington today, and it all gained momentum under this healthcare fiasco. That's why I have a security guard hovering over me all the time, and that's why I lay awake wondering how to stop all this payola."

Mary sensed how upsetting this topic was, suggesting she'd put on some coffee.

"Hugh, I'm overwhelmed by what you've told us — please tell me more," she said as they moved to the more comfortable lounge area.

"Well, if you can take more, I'll just ramble on for a moment longer."

"Please," Bill said. "You just may be the next article I write."

"All right, let's see. The thing that scares me the most is how profit insurance has now established all these discriminatory programs that rate the policy-holders by age, sex, groups, individuals, pre-existing and prospective conditions, and secondary and primary insurers. By creating such a complex rating system, they intentionally confuse the consumer, which of course provides hundreds of loopholes to deny coverage and increase their totally unregulated profits." Stretching out his long legs, he pushed on both joints as if to loosen them up. "As a result, there are almost fifty million people who have been placed in what is called the

130

Group Rated Death Spiral. Their insurance policies are becoming so costly they can't afford to buy coverage any longer. And now there's another fifty million policy holders standing in the wings, about to lose coverage because of these new *Managed Care* monopolies," he growled, again scrawling out quotes as he spoke. "All those monopolies will eventually become nothing more than profit centered *Dinosaur Clubs*, like you just described to me. And eventually the powerful international banking industry, which currently owns our Federal Reserve and finances all these insurance scams, will own our democracy, setting their own unbelievable reserves and profits — which are huge."

Mary nearly chocked on her coffee, glaring at Hugh.

"Of course you must realize, we're the only country in the world that has allowed this type of socialized healthcare system to control us," he despairingly frowned. "I'm sorry — we've never really allowed it, our corrupt politicians have forced it upon us. So, supposedly, here is a democracy of the people that was once considered a world leader in healthcare and human services, finding their costs spiraling out of control solely to feed this corrupt and wealthy Oligarchy that totally controls Washington."

With this, he shook his finger boldly in the air.

"So with all this deregulation and competition, we've totally lost sight of our community infrastructure, our healthcare area wide planning, and any hope of ever developing a single nonprofit cost effective prepayment program that's managed cost effectively by healthcare professionals under reasonable state regulations. And worse yet, people just don't seem to understand how big a roll their tax dollar has previously played in building this country's once successful healthcare system. So now we're turning it all over to some wealthy aristocracy to skim these huge profits right off the top. Hell, the confused consumer has already paid for eighty-four percent of our hospital beds. They've supported a massive emergency center development program, and they're currently funding over eighteen federally related healthcare programs, including: Medicare, Medicaid, Maternal Health, Workman's Compensation and Disability, Veterans Care, Indian Health Services, Vocational Rehabilitation, the Veterans Administration, our prisoners, our military service, and all our federal employees including all these favored Senators and Congressmen. Isn't it time we stop and look at all this chaos they've created? And don't we even realize our salary benefit programs are currently saddled with all these new profit insurance scams. Yet, on top of all this, *We the People* still have to meet our individual deductibles and make our own private insurance payments. Doesn't that sound like these wealthy bankers want us to donate our system to them and pay them a profit for something we've already paid for? In other words, the confused consumer is being raped, and they don't even know it. And we're certainly not enjoying it."

"I can't believe what I'm hearing," Mary said, shaking her head wildly as she ran both hands through her hair.

"Worse yet, all hope of a cost effective database communication network, like Bill's researching, have been destroyed by their ridiculous decentralization and deregulation tactics. All we now see are costly advertisements bombarding us with all this *"ask your Doctor,"* crap about some drug that has so many side effects it scares the hell out of us. We use to consider pharmaceutical advertizing illegal, but now they spend more on advertizing than the drug costs to manufacture — and we're paying for all that shit."

Hugh finally stood up and walked to the window.

And now that our rich corporate executives are sending our jobs overseas to make more profit, just what are these poor sick and disabled going to do? Go to Canada or China to get their healthcare?"

"Are you serious?" Mary choked.

"You're seeing the wealthy business owners move our jobs over seas, aren't you? And you know what, eventually these money hungry *Dinosaur* are going to become totally submissive to this New World Oligarchy — and yet they would still like you to believe they are professional physicians with ethics."

"I guess you're right, that's exactly what I overheard the *Dinosaurs* planning," Mary growled.

Hugh stared at her. "Unknowingly, what they're creating is a two level system; one for the wealthy, and one for the poor — similar to what existed in the nineteenth century. If that isn't moving back in time, I don't know what is. I know it's not a Democracy."

Mary just sat there, her mouth wide open. "I've never heard anything so corrupt in all my life," she scoffed.

"If I hear you correctly, it's really the wealthy international banking system that's raping our communities?" Bill asked.

"Absolutely, but if you ask them, they're just trying to make a little profit and globalize the good old United States into their new *World Government*. That's what makes the world go round."

Slowly walking back to his chair and sitting down Hugh continued. "What's wrong with that? Well, let me tell you. If you can remember, the United States was once the single most powerful nation in the world after they won the cold war with Russia. In fact the U.S. was so powerful, these bankers needed to deflate our ego by focusing our attention on globalization and a global market, and they accomplished this by deregulating and decentralizing our infrastructure and deemphasizing the importance of this once great single nation, which they intend to someday own. And like a bunch of sheep, we took our eye off the health of our own nation, which they are intent on destroying. In other words this new world Oligarchy wants to rule the world just as so many other countries have tried over so many centuries — all ending up as a socialized system under another powerful Oligarchic dictatorship."

Bill stared at Hugh. "What can we do about all this?"

"For one thing, the consumer needs to face up to the fact that profit insurance in healthcare has failed miserably. We need to demand that the country return to a single nonprofit community rated, privately owned prepayment program that's either private or tax supported, or some combination of both. State enabling regulations need to demand community rating," he added, "not group rating." Covering his mouth, he coughed to clear his throat. "Premiums must be the same for everyone, regardless of age, sex, where one lives, or how sick one is, or has been — or whether the benefactor is a service person, a child, a woman, an elderly, or wealthy or poor. Pausing a moment he added — or even some God damned congressman. Isn't that what a democracy is all about?"

"But, we already know that isn't going to happen, unless there's a revolution," Bill added, raising his voice angrily.

"You're right on that," Hugh replied. "But you both need to understand our standards, rules, regulations and laws must be re-established and administered by professionals in the field, not some get wealthy entrepreneur that's intent on creating some powerful new world Oligarchy."

"You're absolutely right," Mary said. "And that's just what I'm trying to accomplish at this screwed up hospital right now."

Hugh nodded his agreement with her as he continued listing his solutions to the problem.

"You know, providing equitable quality healthcare that people can rely on must become our primary objective. But this international Oligarchy has us so busy arguing within our dysfunctional two party systems that we'll never get there," he raged, bringing his fist down hard on the arm of his chair. "And something that's even more important is, we need to close our Federal Reserve System, which these international bankers totally own and control — taking almost two billion dollars a day in interest payment on all the loans their individual banks make to the United States. And these guys already control far too many of the less powerful countries that are rich in natural resources, which they've financed through their many wars and their financial oppression and colonization tactics. And all that happened because they wanted to level the U.S. to that of other nations after the cold war. And whether you know it or not, they've blamelessly maneuvered this great nation into some sixteen conflicts, selecting Iraq as their most recent victim. After World War I and World War II, we all said we'd never go to war again unless we were attacked, but since then these guys have skillfully involved us in Vietnam, Cambodia, Laos, Philippines, Somalia, Haiti, Croatia, Bosnia, Chechnya, Albania, Kosovo, Serbia, Sudan, Iraq, Afghanistan, and East Timor. Why? Because they all served them well in their money making interventions and war provocations, and now they're working on still another provocation that involves a weakened U.S. Military in this perpetual religious conflict in the Middle East. Eventually this Oligarchy will destroy this once great nation, and they don't give a damn."

Mary reached over and patted Hugh's tightly closed fist, smiling at him.

"I understand you loud and clear," she nodded. "And now I understand much better why I can't even professionally audit the quality of care our physicians are providing anymore. That's the impossible job I've taken on."

"Mary, I feel just like you, but I'm going to give it up," Hugh said, looking terribly frustrated by it all. "I've been fighting this thing far too long. Hell, we've forgotten how to cooperate and work together in this country. It's all profit and competition, and it's only going to get worse. I've got so many politicians fighting to protect their own turf that I'm now afraid for my life. Someone just tried to kill me on that God damned tobacco issue," he chocked. "It's just not worth it any more, and I believe like Bill, it'll take a huge catastrophe like a revolution or a complete collapse of the system before it will ever change," he scowled, standing up to let them know he was finished complaining about the mess this country was in. "Hell, let's go catch some of those fish you told me about, and enjoy the rest of the day."

* * * * *

After they returned from fishing and walking the beach they had a delicious fish dinner, and then Hugh strolled over to the window to look for his Coast Guard cutter. Nervously he checked his watch. "They should have been here by now," he mumbled, clearly concerned over their tardiness.

Finally, about a half hour later, they heard a helicopter circling directly over the boat. "We're here to pick up Doctor Heustes," someone announced over their loudspeaker. "We'll land on the beach."

Bill ran out and waved, indicating he understood as the helicopter circled towards their landing spot.

As Hugh stood up, he looked puzzled. "I hope nothing's happened to my Coast Guard friends," he anxiously whispered under his breath.

Quickly Bill pulled the Dingy to a place where Hugh and Ted could get on board as Mary ran over to Hugh and gave him a big hug, saying, "Thanks for a memorable day. I hope you think things over before you take any drastic steps like resigning. Our country needs men like you."

Hugh smiled, returning her hug.

"We also need more nurses like you," he said, stepping into the small Dingy.

When Bill returned, they both stood and watched the helicopter fade off into the distance, heading toward Ft. Myers.

"God this whole thing scares me," Mary whispered.

"He's quite a man, isn't he?" Bill said.

"He sure is," Mary agreed, putting her arm tightly around Bill's waist. "I hope everything's all right. He seemed concerned, didn't he?"

"He sure did," Bill replied.

* * * * *

As Bill and Mary arrived back at the marina, Matthew caught their mooring lines and quickly tied them to the dock.

"Everything worked great, and we had a super time," Mary yelled as Bill shut down the diesels. Lowering her voice she continued, "But it looks like it's going to be a while before we'll be able to do it again, so it's back to dry dock."

As Bill jumped down to the dock he said, "Matt, the fishing was outstanding, but I learned that you should never lay your fishing rod down in the bottom of the boat with the lock on unless you're prepared to swim after it."

"Were you able to retrieve it?" Matt laughed. "You know, you're not the first one to do that."

As Bill described how he eventually caught the huge Red Snapper that stole his rod and reel, they all had a good laugh.

"You two couldn't have picked a better time to come down here, the weather was perfect. Normally it can be a little chilly out there this time of year, and in a few days we expect some serious rain storms off the coast."

Then all of a sudden Matthew's face grew somber.

"That's too bad about the Coast Guard. In all my years I've never seen anything like that happen before."

"What do you mean?" Mary gasped — shocked by what he'd just said. "What happened?"

"Haven't you heard? It's been on all the news stations."

"We haven't heard a thing," Bill said. "What's wrong?"

"Well, the Coast Guard picked up your friend at my dock on the twenty-ninth, just like we agreed, and that was the last anyone heard from them. I told the Coast Guard that Doctor Heustes was with you, and so they sent a helicopter out to pick him up. Apparently the Coast Guard had just completed a routine check on some boat, when they suddenly disappeared from the radar."

"You've got to be kidding," Mary gasped.

"No I'm not, and they've said very little about it on the news. They just keep saying it's being investigated."

Matt was obviously upset, as he tried to explain their strange disappearance. Finally he said, "I'd gotten to know that crew over the years, and they were as good as they come. It's a real loss to the community."

Mary and Bill asked several more questions, but there was very little Matt could tell them other than what he'd already said, and as they drove home their silence was one of fear.

"I have no idea where I can reach Hugh on a weekend," Bill explained. "But I've got to talk to him," he whispered. "I guess I'll have to try and reach him at his office on Monday, after we get back to Colorado."

* * * * *

Returning to Colorado, Bill anxiously checked his phone calls and found that a Mr. Adams, an attorney, had left several messages on his answering machine, asking him to return his call as soon as possible — but there were no messages from Hugh. After failing to reach Hugh at the only number he had, he finally returned the Adam's call.

"Mr. Adams, This is Bill Warner. I'm sorry I wasn't home when you called.

"Yes — Doctor Warner — I'm so glad you returned my call. Mrs. Keppler told me about you, and I'm wondering if you'd be available as an expert witness on her case. Right now it looks like the District Judge may throw her case out if I can't establish negligence on the part of the hospital, and I need some professional advice. I've also received a *Motion for a Summary Judgment* from the hospital, indicating we failed to validate any negligence on their part. Their saying that all physician credentialing procedures were properly followed and that a hospital cannot be held responsible for any private physician's actions. They also state that Veronica clearly had a Sagittal Synostosis that required surgery, and that all the proper consent forms were completed by the hospital prior to

137

surgery. Worse yet, the District Judge intends to respond to their motion very soon, and he's given me a deadline of two weeks to come up with my response. Do you think you could help me with this?"

"Possibly, but I'd have to review Veronica's medical record, the hospital policies, rules and regulations, and whatever else you have that might be important before I can answer your question."

"Yes, that's fine, and I'll overnight the material I have immediately. But I'd like to meet with you before you prepare any written report — that way I can at least discuss your findings before I decide to endorse you as an expert in our behalf."

"Alright, let me review your material and I'll give you a call just as soon as I have some answers."

No sooner did he hang up than he called Mary to let her know he'd been contacted by Adams and was possibly going to serve as an expert witness on the Keppler case.

"That's great," she cried. "So it looks like we're going to be in separate camps as you predicted — have you heard anything from Hugh?"

"I've tried to reach him at his office number, but there's no answer. I'll try again first thing Monday."

* * * * *

Bill had decided to sleep late Sunday morning, but the phone woke him.

"Have you seen the paper?" Mary asked.

"No! What's up?"

"I decided to go in and clear off my desk before Monday, and as I was reading the paper, I saw a small article on page two of the front section. Hugh has resigned!"

"Oh my God, he told us this but I didn't expect it this soon."

"I bet that missing Coast Guard cutter had something to do with it."

"That was probably the last straw," Bill replied.

"You better read the article," Mary said, "and I'll stop by later. I just felt you should know."

"Thanks, Mary."

No sooner did Bill step out of the shower than the phone rang again.

"Hello," Bill shouted, struggling to dry himself as he talked.

"Bill, I thought I'd better call you and let you know what's going on," Hugh said. "I thought you might have been concerned about me since that delightful day I spent with you and Mary."

"I sure have, and Mary and I've been beside our selves wondering what's happened."

"Well, I tried to reach you several times, but we just haven't been connecting, and I'm not at a place where I can be easily reached — so I didn't leave a message."

"I understand," Bill replied.

"By now you probably know I've resigned from the NIH."

"I just read that in the paper. That's a little premature, isn't it?"

"Not if I want to live out the rest of my days with my family."

"What in the world's going on?"

"Bill, this aristocracy I talked about wants me out of the picture permanently. And I've decided to step aside before they can accomplish that."

"I can't believe what I'm hearing."

"Believe me," Hugh explained nervously. "I just found out my new secretary was an illegal immigrant who could speak fluent English, and she'd somehow obtained a forged identification that was the best we've ever seen. Bill, we suspect someone helped her get into this country in return for some type of favor. We still don't know who, but we think someone pulled all the right strings so she was included in my list of candidates for the job. The scary thing is she was the only one in my office that knew I'd be on that Coast Guard cutter that day. Thank God your friend Matt knew I was with you, or they'd have thought I was dead."

"Oh my God," Bill mumbled, stunned at what Hugh was saying.

"We've not yet identified the head mechanic that orchestrated this whole thing, but they've got a good description of the man that leased the fishing boat that the Coast Guard last inspected. Last night, they found the sunken hull of that cutter within only a few hundred yards of their last reported drug inspection. And they think it was sunk by some sort of implosion device that was most likely planted on the outside of the hull."

"You're kidding," Bill said. "You mean someone intentionally blew up their boat?"

"Exactly — and since these boats are kept under the tightest of security, they probably planted that implosion device when the Coast Guard boarded that fishing vessel."

"Oh my God, wouldn't they need a highly skilled diver to pull that off?" Bill asked.

"I would think so, and that fishing boat wasn't just boarded by accident."

"*No, I guess not,*" Bill thought.

"It's a pretty good guess that the bomb was exploded by some type of remote device, after the Coast Guard moved a few hundred yards away."

"Have they found any of the crew members?"

"Yes, they found some of their remains. In any event, everything is kind of hush-hush for the moment."

"So you believe the whole thing was another attempt on your life?"

"We're absolutely sure of that, and we're holding my Secretary until we've determined exactly what her role was in this whole damned mess. Bill, she's the only lead we have right now, but we certainly know it involves someone who doesn't like what I'm doing, and that's a pretty big list to search."

"Boy, that all sounds familiar," Bill muttered, even more discouraged now.

"In any event, I've decided to turn in my badge before they get me. A change of scenery is long overdue. Bill, I'm going to let someone else fight for the glory of healthcare in America — it's just getting too tough for me to continue this way any longer. Profiting from the sick and disabled is much more than I can handle and it all seems to be mushrooming everywhere. Bill, it's no longer just your damned *Dinosaurs*, it's everywhere."

"I can tell you right now, they aren't going to find too many candidates of your caliber to fill that job." Bill said.

"So be it," he snarled. "I've just plain had it. No one is going to know where I am for a while, but I also wanted to tell you and Mary to be careful. These guys are clearly playing hard ball."

"Hugh, I know I'm losing a great friend in the NIH, but I fully agree with you — and I think you're making a wise decision."

They talked for a few more minutes before Hugh finally said, "I'll get back in touch with you once I feel a little more secure — but remember, you and Mary need to be very careful."

"Yes, I understand. You be sure and get back in touch with me after things settle down," Bill said, thoughtfully hanging up the phone.

Chapter 9

The Depositions

On Monday morning, Bill received all the material he'd requested from Adams, and after he paged through much of it, he sorted it into stacks.

My God, it's going to take me an eternity to get through all this, he thought.

In addition to all the paper, there were several videotape depositions of McGrath, Bakencamp, and a Doctor Joseph Cross, a craniofacial plastic surgeon who Adams must have hired to serve as an expert for the plaintiff.

McGrath appears older than I'd pictured him — and almost human, Bill thought as he watched his tape first. Although he intentionally combed a small tuft of hair over his receding hairline, his bald spot was very obvious and his forehead and chin had sculptured like wrinkles that appeared almost frozen in place. And amongst all these strong facial features, his large nose was even more prominent.

"Doctor, will you please state your name and your office address for the record," Adams asked. Then after several more preliminary questions he continued. *"When you arrived in Colorado, was Doctor Hanes training residents?"*

McGrath appeared confused by the question, obviously trying to determine where this might lead. As a result he responded cautiously, *"Yes, there were residents training under Doctor Hanes."*

"Were they doing CS surgery?"

"Yes."

"At what point did that all stop?" Adams asked, quickly pouring himself some ice water and leaning forward to take a sip. *"Is that correct — things did change?"*

"I don't know," he stammered. *"I was new at the time — I guess when Doctor Wilson arrived, they no longer needed our help or our patients."*

With that Adams just stared at him, waiting for him to continue. Then after rethinking what he'd said, McGrath cautiously continued, after recognizing a familiar conference brochure that Allen had just picked up off the table. *"Ah — they might have also been concerned about a presentation that Doctor Hanes and I gave at a national conference."*

Adams quickly reacted, holding up the conference brochure so McGrath could see it clearly. *"So you're saying it may have been because of your Craniosynostosis presentation at this conference?"*

McGrath was clearly taken back in that Adams had a copy of that brochure.

"I believe that had something to do with it," he mumbled, looking to his attorney for some direction — but his attorney said nothing.

"What was the controversy all about?"

"Well, it involved a group of patients that we'd been asked to evaluate," he stammered, unsure of where this would take him. — *"Who were all less than a few months old and had behavioral problem, like spitting up, or being generally fussy,"* he continued. *"In any event, we were trying to determine if there was increased pressure on their brains, which could have possibly caused such clinical symptoms. So we did intracranial pressure monitoring on them. And what we found was that many of them did have increased pressure. And since no one had studied that before, we presented our findings at that conference."*

Then after pausing to think a moment he added.

"But for some reason the other neurologists all seemed upset. They asked, 'How could they have increased pressure with little or no skull deformity?'"

With that, McGrath raised both his hands in front of him, expressing disbelief.

"Well, that was exactly what we were trying to find out."

McGrath now appeared very uneasy, but continued to justify the virtues of this research, which Bill knew they were not even qualified or authorized to perform.

That's ridiculous, Bill thought to himself, staring at the screen. *Just how the hell can any private hospital allow that type of crap to go on within its walls? Did he ask the parents to sign the appropriate research form describing his study? Had the Hospital Board approved it?* Bill stood up and paced back and forth, glaring at the TV screen. *My God, I can't believe what I'm hearing. He has no research privileges and he's conducting casual research on infants in a private hospital. Worse yet, he's cutting burr holes in infants' skulls, so he can do intracranial pressures research on normal infants. No wonder the other neurosurgeons were concerned. And now he's performing total Calvarial Reconstruction's he's really never been professionally trained in* — Bill's agitation was obvious.

"What are the symptoms of increased pressure?" Adams asked.

"Headaches and vomiting, and if the pressure keeps increasing, the patient could even become comatose. When an infant has a headache, they can't very well describe it other than having a degree of fussiness."

Hell, any three month old could have fussiness, Bill thought. *If he had a few of his own, he might understand that.*

"In your research, did you employ basic scientific methods, or use control groups that you compared those children to?" Adams asked.

Good for you, Bill whispered, *I'll need to recheck the FDA standards on research. I know the FDA and the hospital are required to approve all research.*

"Were the children anesthetized?"

"No. Well yes, they were when we drilled a hole in their skull. Then what we did was leave the pressure monitor in for a few days. We basically wanted to see what the pressures were when they were fussy, or when the nurse was holding them, or when they were in their crib."

"So for a few days you kept them in some laboratory?"

"No. They were in the ICU."

Bill made a quick note, before standing up and shutting off the TV. He then picked up the phone and called Mary at her office. He was fortunate to find her at her desk, and he spoke only briefly.

"I've been going through some unbelievable material, which I think you need to see. Can you stop by tonight?"

"I'll be there for dinner," she said, quickly hanging up the phone, which indicated someone was meeting with her.

* * * * *

That evening Bill grilled steaks for dinner, and after they ate, he started the tape at the beginning, and while Mary watched he cleared the dishes. After only a short time, she stared at Bill and said, "My God, I can't believe what I'm hearing. He has no concept of research. He actually believes he can treat private patients like they're his own private chattel. Where does he get off thinking like that? — Just who does he think he is? He's just looking for more patients!"

"Mary, It's that same old Witch Doctor voodoo that's haunted humans for centuries. We always place our trust in others when we don't understand something. You remember when the barber surgeons bled patients, or some damned herbalist fed them secret potions. Well, drilling holes in a fussy infant's head is no damned different."

"Bill, "how many tapes do you have like this?"

"I still have Bakencamp, and a Neurosurgeon, who's serving as an expert witness for Adams."

"I'd really like to watch them all — if I can? This is really revealing. But you can't be slaving over a hot grill every night, or you won't get anything done. Let's agree I bring dinner tomorrow."

* * * * *

The following day they watched the Bakencamp's deposition, and when Mary arrived she had a bag of hamburgers and French fries under her arm. Bill quickly un-wrapped a burger and gobbled it down. "I skipped lunch and I'm starved," he grinned, giving Mary a big hug to show his appreciation.

Mary nodded, unwrapping her burger and flopping into a chair where she could watch Bakencamp perform under oath for the first time.

"I've been thinking about McGrath and Hanes all day, and I've concluded that neither one of those characters should ever have been allowed to practice medicine, she snarled sarcastically. Just what type of system allows that to happen?"

"Mary, that's why it's so important to get this shyster in a courtroom, and expose his con-job — he's doing nothing but lying to patients to make big bucks. Do you think he cares about anything else? Hell no," Bill grunted, answering his own question. "Just wait until you see what he's capable of when the roof caves in on him. He'll try to persuade the entire medical staff that he's right, and that the poor parents just don't understand. After all, they're not doctors — they couldn't possibly fathom why he's performing such complex procedures."

"I know," Mary nodded. "And with all that competition and profit incentive out there, it's only going to get worse — isn't it?" she grumbled.

145

"I've heard it all too many times now." Turning, she looked at Bill. "It seems like we're just chipping at the base of a mountain. Thank God there are still a few good physicians left," she muttered as Bill started the Bakencamp tape.

This time a Mr. Hayward introduced himself as the plaintiff's attorney, identifying several defense attorneys that represented McGrath and Allen, the plastic surgeon, the anesthesiologists, as well as the hospital before the camera was finally focused on Bakencamp.

Hayward was short and frail with wire rimmed glasses, but also appeared astute and a take-charge person.

"I was really getting to like Adams. I hope this guy does as well." Bill said.

After the court reporter swore in Mr. Bakencamp, Hayward gave his usual litany of instructions, finally saying, *"If you do not understand a question, please feel free to tell me, and I'll rephrase it."*

With that Bakencamp nodded.

"It's also important that you answer verbally as opposed to nodding your head, or using huh-uh or uh-hum — that way the court reporter will be able to record the right information. And I also ask that you wait until I'm done asking a question and I'll try to wait until you're done answering; that way we won't over talk each other."

Picking up his notes he continued.

"Would you please state your name and your professional address and position?" Then after the court reporter confirmed the address, Hayward asked, *"Did you understand that more surgeries for CS were being done at Children's Hospital than any other institution in the United States?"*

"Yes."

"When did you as President learn about that?"

"I can't tell you exactly."

"Did you receive a copy of the CDC report?"

"Yes, but just their final report."

"Who provided you with that report?"

"I think it was the Health Department."

"When did you receive that report?"

"About two years ago."

"So you're telling me you never reviewed the report until two years ago?"

"I may have reviewed portions of it."

"You can see he's going to dance all over hell's half acre — isn't he?" Bill interrupted.

"Do you recall if the report said that a number of the patients treated for CS didn't in fact have the disease?"

"I was told there was a difference of opinion, and that most of our cases had been confirmed by pathological or radiologic reports."

"Boy, you can just feel he's devious," Mary smirked. "I hope Hayward makes him squirm," she snarled, crumpling her hamburger wrapper and throwing it at his face on the screen.

"You know, some people have a little more trouble facing up to the truth than others. Maybe a jury can help him resolve that issue," Bill scoffed.

"Don't you recall a specific percentage of infants that did not in fact have CS?"

"Maybe that was true, but I was also informed there were other doctors who confirmed the diagnoses."

"Do you recall that the CDC determined that your hospital had used different diagnostic criteria than was being used by other hospitals in other parts of the country?"

"No. What I remember was there was not a uniform way of diagnosing and treating patients with CS."

"Did the Board do anything to address that issue?"

Bakencamp was clearly upset at his persistence, so he intentionally stalled things by saying. *"I didn't understand your question."*

"What did your Board do if anything to address the issue of misdiagnosing CS and the high incidence of CS at your hospital? Didn't they respond to the CDC findings? If they did nothing, just go ahead and say nothing. That's all right."

Mary raised both arms. "Good for you — keep the pressure on him," she yelled.

"Alright, let me ask it another way. If a child was misdiagnosed and surgery was recommended, and if the parents then gave their consent, they would be doing so while being misinformed, wouldn't they?"

"Form and foundation objection," the hospital's attorney interjected.

Immediately two other attorneys chimed in, *"Join."*

"What does that mean?" Bakencamp asked, still trying to slow things down.

"Let me explain. We have to make a record. Because there is no Judge here that can rule on an objection. If objections are made we're simply required by our rules to

make those contemporaneous objections. That's done so if the other side tries to use that testimony at the time of trial, the District Judge can pass on the objection. A form objection means there is some legal defect in the question. Foundation objection means there is some part missing. You need not be concerned, but you do need to allow time for the attorneys to make their statements. Their comments are just being reserved for ruling at a later point. Anyway, you can go ahead and answer the question."

After an hour of questioning Mary scowled. "This is ridiculous, I don't think we're going to learn much from this screwball," she growled with a sour smirk on her face.

"I agree, he's an embarrassment," Bill added.

After a few more questions, Bakencamp's attorney interrupted to say they'd only scheduled Mr. Bakencamp for two hours, and since his schedule was very busy, he'd have to leave. You could tell they all wanted to get him out of there as soon as possible.

With that Hayward stood up, sternly glaring at everyone around the table.

"Gentlemen, I advised counsel earlier that two hours wasn't going to be enough time, and I'm not going to be held to any restriction in the future. From here on I'm going to require we complete all depositions." With that he turned to the court reporter and said, *"That's the end of my record."*

* * * * *

Mary called Bill at noon on Thursday.

"You've got to be suffering from cabin fever by now. Let's plan to meet for dinner at the China Doll restaurant on Star Ranch Road around five. It won't hurt you to get out of the house for a few minutes."

"All right, I'll meet you there," Bill, laughed. "Boy, you sound just like a nurse."

"No, I'm just looking after my equity — to hell with your philanthropic attitude."

It was almost five when Bill looked at his watch. *Oh my God, I'm glad the China Doll is only a short distance away,* he thought.

Mary was waiting when he arrived, and she'd already ordered the wine.

"How would you like to split an order of pea pods with beef and shrimp and cashews?" she asked.

"That sounds great," Bill nodded, quickly squeezing into the booth.

"Good, because that's what I've ordered," she laughed.

"It doesn't take you long to learn my habits, does it?"

"Well, I knew you'd be absorbed in your work and forget to look at the clock, and you've probably worked right through lunch again, so I decided I'd get things organized before you got here."

Bill looked into her eyes, which seemed even bluer if that was possible, giving her an affectionate smile.

"Every time I saw Bakencamp at work my skin began to crawl," she said, shaking as if shivers were running down her spine.

"Mary, I'm sorry, but I think it's important you see first hand what we're dealing with."

"Oh, I agree — but I'm certainly glad we don't have to watch him anymore. I hope Doctor Cross is at least a little more professional."

"You may be surprised. It just dawned on me that I'd already met Doctor Cross at the Medical School in British Columbia, where I presented a two-week seminar on the medical record. He's a Canadian who trained in plastic surgery at Toronto, where they have one of the best programs in the world. And since he's moved to Seattle, he's made quite a name for himself. In fact, he's now considered one of the world's leaders in craniofacial surgery. I think Adams was very fortunate in getting him to serve as an expert in his behalf. In fact I'm anxious to hear him, unless you'd rather get some sleep tonight?"

"Oh no, I understand how much material you've got to go through, and I definitely want to listen to him tonight — maybe he'll help me correct some of the damage our *all-stars* have done."

After they returned to Bill's home, they watched the hospital's plastic surgeon's defense attorney, a man by the name of Mr. Thomas, depose Doctor Cross. Thomas was a tall handsome man with dark brown hair, and after he swore in Doctor Cross, he asked.

"Would you state your name please?"

"Joseph Cross."

Doctor Cross had a very pleasant appearance, and he was absolutely comfortable being deposed. He was perhaps in his mid-fifties, Bill guessed, having just enough gray hair to present a scholarly appearance. His voice was loud and clear, and it was easy to accept his friendly manner. After discussing some of the ground rules, Thomas asked several more questions about his background.

"I'm a plastic and reconstructive surgeon who specializes in craniofacial surgery." Doctor Cross said.

"Have you ever had a deposition taken before?"

"Yes."

"How many times have you been deposed?"

"I would guess I've been deposed a dozen times or more."

"Have you ever testified on standards of care for craniofacial surgery?"

"Yes, many times."

"All right — are there national standards of care in craniofacial surgery?"

"Yes."

"Who sets those standards?"

"That would be our specialty board — but there are many related standards set by other regulatory agencies."

"Have you kept up with those standards?"

"Yes, but things don't really change that much."

"Where did you train?"

"My early training was under Doctor Martin, in Canada. And as you probably know, he's internationally recognized for his work in craniofacial surgery."

"Do you know Doctor Ian Jefferson?"

"Yes, I know him well. I also trained under him in England."

"Do you consider Jefferson to be competent?"

"Yes, I certainly do."

"Do you know of, or have you read his publications?"

"Yes, In fact he's helped me with my writings, and of course I've read almost all of his work."

"Do craniofacial surgeons consider him a leader in the field?"

"Definitely"

"I understand Doctor Huber is the editor of your specialty Journal. Do you know him?"

"Yes. We're a small specialty, and since there are only a few of us in the whole world, we all know each other quite well."

"Would this Journal be an authoritative publication?"

"Well, it depends. When you publish, it doesn't mean that what is published is authoritative. In fact, we're all skeptical of every article we review."

"That's for sure," Mary laughed.

"Okay, how would you define the type of surgery that McGrath and Allen performed on Veronica Keppler?"

"I'd call that a Total Calvarial Reshaping and a Bilateral Frontal Orbital Advancement and Reshaping."

"Have you ever performed that operation?"

"Yes, but you need to understand that we consider those surgeries two distinctly separate procedures."

"How many times have you performed this procedure?" He asked, ignoring his response.

"Individually — maybe a halve dozen or so — perhaps a few more."

"How many of those cases involved Sagittal Synostosis?"

"Oh boy — I'd never perform that type of procedures for a pure Sagittal Synostosis."

"Can you elaborate on that?"

"Certainly — either of those two procedures usually involves some very major deformities. For example, with a Total Calvarial Reshaping, you'd remove the entire skull, and there's a very large blood loss, which makes that procedure very dangerous."

"In that procedure, could you advance the orbits?"

"No — that's a separate procedure."

With that, Thomas appeared uncomfortable, quickly changing his line of questioning.

"What was your understanding of the diagnosis for Veronica Keppler?"

"She had a simple Sagittal Synostosis with a moderate to mild Scaphocephaly, or a boating of the skull."

"So you agreed with the diagnosis?"

"Yes."

"And do you agree that Veronica needed some surgical intervention?"

"No."

"Tell me what you mean by that."

"Well," he shook his head. *"Not all children with fused Sagittal Sutures should have surgery. Some parents just leave the children the way they are."*

"He's really good," Mary grinned. "I'm glad you persuaded me to watch this."

"In reviewing Doctor Allen's and Doctor McGrath's depositions, you must be aware that they've performed this surgery many times, and they have an excellent record. Doesn't that suggest that it would be a safe procedure in their hands?"

"No, not at all"

Mary almost fell off her chair, "He's marvelous!"

"Why do you say that?" Thomas asked, obviously taken back by his quick response.

"Well, every procedure is judged on its own merits and the risks involved. They're all uniquely dissimilar. Doing many procedures successfully doesn't make a single procedure safer."

"Wow, I love this man. At least he understands medical ethics," Mary grinned.

"Wouldn't you agree that some surgeons might elect to do procedures differently?"

"Well, I personally don't know of any other surgeon in the entire world who'd perform a Total Cranial Vault Reshaping and an Orbital Advancement on a six month old infant that only had a simple Sagittal Synostosis."

"Isn't there an advantage in doing the surgery as early as possible?"

"That depends on what sutures are fused."

"What if it was a Sagittal Suture?"

"The Sagittal Suture should be done as early as possible, if the parents want surgery. But you should also inform the parents of all the surgical options available, as well as the risks. That's called informed consent."

"If Doctor McGrath seldom performs any other procedure, wouldn't it be best not to offer the other option to the parents?"

"Doctor McGrath certainly doesn't have to offer it as an option, but he's required to review all the other options available to them."

"Do you feel Doctor Allen or Doctor McGrath didn't inform the parents of their options?"

"Based on all the material I've reviewed, I couldn't see where they ever even attempted to inform them about the other procedures available. In fact, McGrath made it sound like a Total Calvarial Remodeling was the only procedure available. And another thing that concerns me is nobody seemed to take into account the infant had a congenital heart abnormality. When you have a six-month-old infant that has both CS and a cardiac problem, such a procedure has to have an increased risk. Particularly when they themselves know there is going to be an enormous amount of blood lost, and the two procedures are going to last almost eight hours."

"He's right," Bill said emphatically. "And neither one of them offered the option of no surgery."

"Did you see anything in the patient's record that suggested there was an abnormal blood loss?"

"The only thing I could determine from the patient's poorly documented record was the fact that the blood pressure kept on dropping throughout the entire procedure, and the patient's hematocrit was dangerously low. That poor little infant required almost eleven hundred ccs of blood. For God's sake, that's almost three times the amount of blood she has in her entire body," he scowled, raising both eyebrows as his eyes scanned each attorney sitting around the table. *"In fact, Doctor Allen said he saw the patient become hypotensive. That must have caused quite a stir, because the resident anesthetist asked Doctor Morris, his supervisor, to come in and take over. Even Doctor Allen admits that they had difficulty in maintaining the blood pressure and he said, 'he stopped operating to minimize the blood loss.' In other words, he knew there was a blood loss, just from dissecting the tissue around the eyes. My friends, that suggests this tiny infant was extremely fragile. Just that simple procedure had caused another hypovolemic episode and a drop in blood pressure."*

Again Cross paused to look at each one individually.

"In fact, that little baby had no reserve whatsoever." With that he leaned back in his chair, staring up at the ceiling. When he finally looked down he looked at his notes before flipping to another page. *"That's probably the most significant sign I could find, and Doctor Allen should have been asking what the reason was for this sudden drop in pressure? I would never have continued until I had that answer — talk about persistence. My God, you'd have to be blind, deaf, and totally insensitive not to have seen what was coming."*

"Are you finished?" Thomas asked — his eyes narrowing as he regrouped.

"Who's responsible for monitoring blood loss?"

"Everyone's responsible, but you must remember the surgeon is the man in charge. He's responsible to constantly check the blood loss and the hematocrit."

"Are you saying that neither Doctors Allen nor McGrath were conferring about the blood loss or the hematocrit?"

"Yes, and they themselves admit that," he explained, raising both hands hopelessly up into air. *"So we have to presume they're telling the truth — don't we? We both know they were under oath during their testimony, and they themselves say the blood loss wasn't discussed. It doesn't take a great deal of common sense to see that a six month old infant needed almost double the amount of blood she'd been given after the arrest occurred. And that was just to stabilize her and get her off the table."*

"All right, let's assuming the cardiac arrest was caused by hypovolemia, as you seem to think — do you think Doctor Allen acted below any normal standard of care?"

"Absolutely — a surgeon's required to make immediate decisions in order to prevent injury, and I feel Allen failed to do that."

"Isn't the anesthesiologist responsible for monitoring the blood loss, and isn't the surgeon dependent on what he tells him?"

"Of course, but the surgeon should be aware of all the facts. He or she has to consider the patient's diagnosis, their age, and all the underlying problems. He must be aware of how the operation is going, the blood loss, and a hundred and one other things that go on in surgery. He has total and ultimate responsibility, and he must put all that information together and make sensible decisions. In other words, he's the Captain of the ship. The anesthesiologist is just a member of the crew. He's only there to help the surgeon."

"Okay, so Doctor Allen waited until the patient stabilized, and then the patient suddenly crashed."

"Yes, but that's not what happened with this little girl. That tiny infant was going through two major surgical procedures over an eight hour period, and she was very unstable. That wasn't a sudden crash."

"Do you have any other concerns?"

"Yes I certainly do. Their failure to replace the skull bones before closing, or at least properly storing them in the freezer, concerns me deeply."

"Tell me what you're critical of?"

"When you cannot complete an operation, you either place the bones back in the skull or you freeze them. That's standard procedure."

With that he paused, his eyes once again examining each person around the table.

"As you all know, there was a considerable amount of bone that was lost, which required this tiny infant to later undergo several extensive reconstructive surgeries, using her ribs to form a new skull. Veronica's skull had to be somewhere, and yet no one knows where it went. In my judgment that's negligence!"

"But Doctor Allen had not completed the wiring of the bone."

"So what — All you have to do is take the wired bone and the unwired bone and put them back under the skin."

"But Doctor, they were concerned that the patient might die."

"Look. They either quickly put the bone back in the infant's head, or they put them in the freezer — you don't throw them away."

"Anything else?"

"Yes." Running his fingers through his hair he drew in a deep breath before pulling his chair closer to the table.

"As I go through their depositions, the more I read, the more I see how they are using wrong terms interchangeably. They keep referring to other groups doing Total Calvarial Remodeling, and you need to understand that the Calvarium is the skull. The orbits are part of the face — not the skull. I'd heard they were doing Cranial Vault Reshaping, but I didn't understand they were also cutting and moving the eye orbits."

With this he took his index finger and placed it just above his eyebrow.

"The forehead is from here up, and the orbits are from here down. CS children may have a forward bossing of the forehead, but it seldom if ever affects the shape of the eye orbits in any way."

"Are you saying she didn't need anything done to the eye orbits?"

"Exactly," he nodded, again placing his elbows on the table.

"If you're doing a procedure that involves the orbits, that's Craniofacial Remodeling."

"Anything else" Thomas asked.

"Yes. Doctor McGrath didn't obtain a proper written consultation from the patient's cardiologist. Worse yet, they didn't sit down as a team and discuss her cardiac condition, the danger of blood loss, or the size of the surgery they anticipated doing. Under those circumstances, no cardiologist could ever anticipate what's going to happen to that infant's cardiac function. They'd have to be a magician to do that."

"But you can't say that caused the cardiac arrest, can you?"

"I can't say it didn't."

"Are you finished?"

Again his finger tracked down his notes.

"I also find it very troubling that Doctor Allen does not make hospital rounds after surgery."

Both Bill and Mary had been entranced by what they'd been watching, and both had barely moved during his entire presentation. "That's another area that I need to pursue," Bill said. "That not only violates hospital and Joint Commission rules and regulations, but every attending physician should at least see the patient every twenty-four hours."

"Boy, that's an incredible statement for someone who's operated on a tiny infant with such a high risk. In my judgment, that falls way below all standards of care. I know of no surgeon who'd ever put an infant under eight hours of major surgery, with extensive blood loss, and not see the patient after surgery."

"Doctor, do you have any clinical opinion as to whether her post-operative care contributed to or caused any kind of damage?"

"No. I guess the damage was already done," he said, tensing his jaw as the room went silent.

"Had that operation been stopped at the skull, Veronica would probably be close to normal today. I feel McGrath and Allen's entire work-up of Veronica leaves much to be desired."

"What is the basis for your saying that?" Thomas asked.

"Well, you have to realize Doctor McGrath had made no comparative measurements over time, and Doctor Allen stated that he wasn't even aware they'd taken X-rays of the orbits. Normally, I'd take pictures and have a 3-D scan of the orbits before I'd ever proceed with that type of surgery."

Cross stood up and walked to the chalkboard, sketching the eye orbits and describing where the eyeball rested and how the conduits that contain the eye muscles and ligaments were attached to the orbital bone.

"I was able to take measurements of Veronica's X-rays, and I've marked those classic attachments for both eyes at 1.4 centimeters in length — which is normal."

Walking back to the table he sat down. *"Normally my team of surgeons would meet to discuss this type of detail before ever attempting an operation, and we'd review those things in detail with the parents, so they could make an informed decision. I'd also have discussed all the alternatives available, and I'd have required a second opinion by another unbiased and qualified craniofacial surgeon."*

Mary slowly nodded her head, overwhelmed by what she was hearing.

"I'd like to make one final statement" he said, as he again stood up.

"From all the depositions, records, X-rays, and everything I've reviewed, I couldn't find anything that would justify why a six-month-old infant with a mild to moderate degree of Sagittal Synostosis and a congenital heart defect would've fallen into the category of two major surgeries. Nothing even remotely suggests the patient required that much reshaping."

Chapter 10

Mr. Adams

James Adam's office was located on Broadway in the heart of downtown Denver, just a few blocks from the Capital. As Bill pulled open the glass door with James Adams and Associates printed in gold letters, he swung his heavy briefcase ahead of him. Adams was of the same height as Bill, looking younger than on the video, and his blond hair had a tinge of red, enhancing his ruddy complexion.

"I'm glad to finally meet you," Jim said, leading Bill down the hall to a large conference room. "How was the traffic this morning?"

"It was bumper to bumper for the last half hour. I'm glad I allowed some extra time."

"That Interstate never changes — you eventually adjust to it if you live here. I sure hope they complete that toll way pretty soon."

Pointing at the counter he said, "There's some fresh coffee, if you'd like a cup."

"I think I will," Bill said, walking over to poor himself a cup before sitting down.

"A lot has happened since we last visited," Jim explained, trying not to spill his own coffee as he cautiously walked to the conference table.

"You recall the hospital filed a motion for summary judgment back in December?"

"Yes, that's one of the first things I read, and I also read your response," Bill explained, paging to that exhibit in his notes. "Lets see, here it is, that was in February, right?"

"Yes, that's it. But now I've got even a bigger problem," Jim scowled, wiping a bit of spilled coffee off the table.

"As I told you on the phone, Robert Fuller, the District Judge has reviewed my response, and it looks like he's not in favor of my claim against the hospital."

"Ouch — that's not good," Bill said, razing both eyebrows.

With that he handed Bill a copy of the Judge's most recent order.

"You can take that copy with you, but look at number twelve on page four. It says *the court finds that the plaintiff must provide an expert to testify as to the hospital's standard of care.* If you look at thirteen on the same page, he's allowed me sixty days to come up with an expert to support my claims."

"Does that mean the case is already hard-wired against you?"

"If you study his full order, it looks that way," he said, fidgeting uncomfortably. "So, if I'm going to keep the hospital involved, it's going to depend on your report."

"I see," Bill frowned finally taking a sip of coffee. "What would you like me to do?"

"Well, this case will never support the type of settlement Mrs. Keppler needs if the hospital gets off Scott-free. So we have to change the Judge's mind."

"And how are you going to do that?"

"We have sixty days before he'll make his final ruling. That means we'll have his decision sometime in July. And I suspect he'll need some time to review our response. So I think it would be wise to get your report in his hands as soon as possible."

"Well, that's no problem — I can do that."

"Yes, but since I've already submitted my testimony, I don't know if your comments will support the position I've taken."

"I understand."

"Another thing, I'll need your curriculum vitae."

"Of course, I'll send that right away," Bill said, jotting a note so he wouldn't forget.

"All right, why don't we first talk through your preliminary findings to see if we're at least on the same page?"

Bill nodded, reaching for his notes.

"Do you mind if I tape you?" Jim asked.

"No, go right ahead."

"Okay," he nodded, placing his hand held recorder on the table.

"Let me see. I'd like to start by making a general statement."

As Bill talked, he spread his notes on the table.

"First of all, I feel the hospital has not carried out its responsibility for proper governance, and they've certainly not met their mission statement."

"Just ignore any exhibit material," Jim interrupted. "If I haven't already provided it to the judge, I will."

"Okay, I won't use the exhibits as I talk. That will make it a lot easier."

"That's fine," Jim agreed.

"They've also ignored many of their own medical staff bylaws and rules and regulations, which were in force at the time of the incident."

"I agree, and we can list those later." Jim interrupted.

"Oh — Okay." Quickly shuffling some papers around Bill continued. "I feel the Governing Body has completely disregarded many recommendations, reports, and concerns of key professional organizations such as the American Board of Neurologic Surgery, and the State and National Public Health Services, which includes the Center for Disease Control. They've also ignored the concerns of other health professionals throughout the nation. But most importantly, they've ignored their own patients."

Jim hurriedly began jotting notes as Bill talked.

"Prior to this incident, they hired a professional consultant to advise them about a particularly hazardous situation that exists within their Medical Staff, and they then totally ignored his recommendations. I've talked with several physicians that confirmed this problem, describing boycotts, monopolies, self-referral concerns, and far too many conflict of interest problems. And then after Veronica's tragic outcome the hospital made no effort to even remedy any of these dangerous situations. Nor did the hospital's Medical Staff ever review the problem. In fact, the hospital's neurosurgical service appears to be functioning autonomously, entirely outside the hospital's mission of providing high quality patient care to the community."

Bill paused, taking another quick sip of coffee.

"That's my general statement"

Jim smiled. "Sounds fine to me, we're tracking so far."

"Next, I have four very specific areas where I found hospital negligence."

As the receptionist walked in with a tray of rolls, she smiled at Bill, "would you like a nice fresh roll?"

"How can I refuse?" Bill said, picking out one with a caramel coating.

"All right, let's now focus on what I refer to as the hospital's responsibility for governance and supervision. In my opinion, the hospital's Medical Staff is providing a substandard level of supervision over their Neurosurgical Service at this hospital. In fact, there is no supervision — it's nonexistent. All the material I've reviewed clearly shows informal open staff confrontations with the closed staff and those problems all seem to center around the neurosurgical physicians. Boycott, self-referral, monopoly, and conflicts of interest have replaced the hospital's bylaws and the Joint Commission's standards, which require proper communications at their routine monthly service meetings. They've allowed Doctors' Allen, McGrath and Hanes to control the Medical Staff by permitting them to work outside their own written bylaws. And in allowing that, the hospital has abrogated its responsibility for the quality of care they provide. In fact, they've failed to provide even reasonable staff surveillance as they allow unapproved research surgery to be performed on uninformed private patients."

Bill stopped and took a bite of his roll, licking a small piece of caramel from the tip of his finger. Jim looked up from his writing, "That's great so far."

"Now — specific to the rules and regulations, and the policies and procedures, I'll start by saying the hospital has not only violated numerous JC standards, but their own bylaws, which required Doctors McGrath and Allen to obtain an unbiased second opinion by another qualified specialist. Worse yet, the procedures they are doing are not only controversial, but their code numbers are not even properly identified or approved as an authorized neurosurgical procedure at that hospital. The patient's informed consent form was also executed in a substandard way, and they failed to properly identify and code this surgery in the patient's medical record. They listed these two distinctly separate surgical procedures as a *Total Calvarial Remodeling*. And on top of that, it appears the hospital has failed to approve, classify, review, or record several other research procedures McGrath is doing, and in all cases they're required to inform the unsuspecting public of the potential risk involved in such unproven research. Worse yet, they're marketing and advertising these research procedures as a service to the public, and these procedures have yet to be approved or accepted as routine by the Neurosurgical Association."

Jim nodded, relieved by what Bill was saying. "I'm still with you, and you're right on the money."

Bill smiled, reaching for another set of notes.

"A third area deals with the hospital's credentialing process for medical staff membership. Neither Doctor McGrath nor Allen were specifically authorized, trained or credentialed by the hospital to perform this very controversial procedure they are doing. And I suspect that few if any patients understood that this unusual procedure involved replacing more than twice the infant's total blood volume, a procedure that these two physicians noted in the record as a moderate to mild cosmetic procedure."

Jim stood up refreshing Bill's coffee and then his own. "I have one more to go," Bill said, again focusing his attention on still another set of notes.

"In my judgment, the hospital clearly failed to define or identify their research, or their unclassified neurosurgical procedures that could be considered dangerous, or not normal or routine. And because of that, a six-month-old infant was placed in a life and death situation for what would normally be a simple surgical procedure. Both physicians knew these two complex major procedures involved more than eight hours of surgery, and they anticipated a large loss of blood — while knowing the patient had been previously diagnosed with a cardiac problem. I believe Veronica's catastrophic outcome could have been avoided if the hospital had provided proper supervision, and applied normal healthcare governance rules, regulations, policies and procedures, which they themselves have in writing — and I've listed all those for your review."

With that, Bill waited for Jim's response.

"That's excellent. With that report, we just may have a chance to turn things around," Jim said enthusiastically.

"I've got what you said on tape, and I'm going to have it typed right away so you can proof it."

"You mean I don't have to type it myself?" Bill laughed.

"Absolutely not — in fact, I'm taking it to the District Judge in the morning," he grinned, hurriedly heading down the corridor.

As Bill finished eating his roll he stared at the traffic jamming the streets, and in what seemed like only moments Jim was back with a rough copy. They both proof read it for errors and it took only a few more minutes to correct the typos for Bill's signature.

As Bill was handing him the exhibits, the receptionist came in with a faxed message. When Jim finished reading it, he looked at Bill. "You need to see what their Association just sent me."

As Bill looked at the fax it read:

The following paragraph was taken from our last Board meeting:

Surgery for craniosynostosis in the above indicated hospital in Colorado Springs, Colorado has provoked much controversy. Both the Society and several agencies have expressed serious concern over this CS procedure. Therefore we have disallowed this procedure, and our Association will be prepared to become involved if required.

"Wow," Bill said. "That's the kind of ethics we need. It looks like they're no longer going to ignore the problem."

Jim was smiling from ear to ear as Bill left his office. It was obvious that his report had made his day.

* * * * *

In early July, Jim called Bill.

"Guess what?"

"You sound excited," Bill said, anticipating some good news.

"I am. The District Judge refused to dismiss the case, and I have you to thank for that."

"That's wonderful. So now you're going to trial."

"That's right, and I've got two more cases I want you to review. I'm putting them in the mail today. I think you'll find they're very similar to the Keppler case. I don't know when your local newspaper will announce this, but if the news media calls you for a comment, you should probably refer them to me."

"I understand," Bill said.

The next morning, in large print across the top of the front page, it read: *Hospital to Stand Trial*

The article covered the entire top of the front page with four more columns on page seven.

Bill skimmed to where it said; *Judge Fuller's ruling came after lawyers for Veronica filed a statement from an expert witness.*

Anxiously Bill spread the paper out on the table.

In the statement, Hospital Administration Consultant, Dr. William Warner determined that the hospital violated numerous local, state and national standards in performing the Keppler's surgery.

He states, 'They failed to provide appropriate medical staff surveillance and improperly allowed unsupervised freedom to perform limitless major neurosurgical procedures.' He indicates 'the hospital has effectively disregarded concerns and recommendations about that procedure from numerous organizations, including the American Association of Neurologic Surgery, the Medical School, and the State and National Public Health Service, including the CDC.' Warner added that 'they've failed to remedy that situation even subsequent to the infant's injury, which was never properly reviewed by the Medical Staff in the required hospital monthly primary or service meetings.'

Chapter 11

Bill's Deposition

In preparation for the Bill's deposition, he spent several days going through the volumes of exhibits he'd accumulated, and he felt confident in presenting his claim of negligence on the part of the hospital. His deposition was to be done at the Denver office of the Montague, Little and McGee law firm. After exiting the DTC turn off, he drove into the office building parking ramp, where he unload his material and then found his way to the twelfth floor.

"I'm Doctor Warner," Bill explained to the receptionist. "I have a deposition at nine o'clock."

"Yes Doctor — I'll take you right to the conference room, can I get you a cup of coffee?"

"No thanks," Bill replied, looking down at the traffic, which reminded him of blood cells trying to get through a plugged artery.

Jim Adams had also arrived early to set up his video recorder, and as Bill greeted him an attorney by the name Red McMann interrupted them. Bill reached out to shake his hand, but Red just flippantly nodded and walked away.

"Don't let that bother you, "Jim laughed — moving closer so he could whisper. "I'm sure he read your report and he's got his sights set on you today — come on, let's go talk in that little room over there where we can have some privacy." After Jim closed the sliding door he explained, "As you can see, he's going to attack you every way he can because you could seriously damage his career, but I want you to keep your cool.   Their insurance company is not the type that can lose a multimillion dollar case, and just write it off."

"I understand," Bill nodded.

"Answer his questions as briefly as possible, since he'll be trying to discredit you.   And if you wait long enough, he'll probably give you an opportunity to unload on him."

"I got you," Bill said, raising his thumb.

"Let's just stay right here until they're ready to start — that way you won't have to watch that manic character perform."

"He doesn't bother me in the least." Bill laughed. "But I like your strategy."

While they waited, Jim made a phone call to his wife, visiting until several minutes past nine, well after all the others had assembled for the deposition.

Finally they entered the room at about nine fifteen.

Red hurriedly went over the usual instructions, acting like a nervous animal about to pounce on its prey.

Finally he looked towards Bill, saying, "My name is Mr. McMann — I'm the defense attorney for the hospital.   I've read your statement, where you purport to say the hospital was negligent in the Keppler case."

Bill studied him as he spoke, noticing how he had trouble making eye contact.   McMann's hair was unmistakably dishwater blond even though they called him Red, and he appeared deceptively frail.   His gray shirt, tie, and suit enhanced the pallor of his gaunt face, making one feel almost sorry for him, which Bill knew would be a big mistake.

"Before you attempt to try and justify your remarks, perhaps you could enlighten us as to why you feel you qualify as an expert witness in healthcare.   You're not a doctor, are you?"

"Yes I am, but I don't actively practice medicine.   I'm trained in the administration of healthcare facilities, and the management of hospital medical staffs.   I've spent almost twenty years managing major healthcare facilities — consulting and advising physicians in the preparation and maintenance of high quality medical standards and medical records."

"What do you mean by high quality medical records?"

Bill could feel he was trying to upset him, so he paused, taking a deep breath before responding.

"In the medical record one must record the patient's diagnosis and the physician's orders and observations. It should also include a comprehensive patient history and physical, and much more."

"Isn't that the practice of medicine?"

"Certainly not, the practice of medicine is to simultaneously prescribe, treat and diagnose. Properly recording patient information is entirely different, and is one of the governance responsibilities of every healthcare facility."

"Just what is a Hospital Administrator?"

"Well, a Hospital Administrator usually acts as the Respondeat Superior of a hospital. In that capacity, he or she represents and acts in behalf of the Governing Board by carrying out the governance of the institution."

"Have you ever served as an expert witness before?"

If I'm going to stop these petty questions, I'd better change my approach, Bill thought.

"Have I ever is a long time," Bill responded. "During my career I've been retained as an expert on perhaps twenty or more cases."

"Would you please tell me the names of each case and what each case was about?"

Rather than look foolish and say I don't recall, Bill handed him a list of cases, and began to describe each case in detail.

After the fifth case, Red said, "That's enough."

Hopefully that will discourage any more open-ended questions about the universe, Bill thought, but it had no effect on Red at all, as he continued his abrasive line of questioning for the rest of the morning — tirelessly asking one open ended question after another about Bill's background, where he worked, what books he wrote, what salaries he'd received, and a hundred and one other personal questions that had no bearing on the case whatsoever. At one point, when he was clearly badgering Bill, Jim interrupted.

"You're intentionally badgering my expert witness, and I want it to stop."

Red snarled right back, "I don't need you to intercede in his behalf. You don't have to protect him!"

"Now you're trying to badger me," Jim yelled, as he jumped up from of his chair with his finger pointed right at Red's face. "If this continues, we're taking our material and we're walking the hell out of here, and believe me we won't be back. You haven't asked one question all morning that relates to the case, and if this continues, we're leaving."

"Just a minute," one of the senior defense attorneys interrupted. "I think it's time we take a lunch break. Perhaps we can all come back with a different attitude."

His comment seemed to cool everyone down, as they broke for lunch.

As Bill stood up, Jim whispered, "If you have anything you don't want them to see, I'd advise you to take it with you, or lock it in your case. They'll copy everything you're using as back-up while we're at lunch."

"You're kidding?"

"Oh no — you'll see when we get back."

Bill had never experienced that before, so he leaned over and casually locked his brief case.

"Its common practice for this bunch to make copies of all the material you bring with you, whether you like it or not." Jim explained.

On their way to the car, Bill shook his head. "If it continues like this all day, we'll never get to the real issues."

"All he wants is a pound of flesh." Jim replied. "He already knows what you're going to say at the trial. He's read your report and he's just softening you up for the trial."

Bill wasn't hungry, but he tried to eat as they talked about the deregulation of healthcare and the growing corruption in business in general.

"I'm planning to write a book on this case when I'm through — win, lose or draw," Adams said. "Someone needs to expose this type of corruption."

* * * * *

That afternoon, the same line of questioning continued until Jim finally asked for another break.

"I'm going to stop his nonsense by telling him I've got to finish by six p.m. You're doing fine, but I can see you're starting to unravel a bit. Be careful."

As the meeting reconvened, Jim interrupted.

"I want you to know that I've only allowed one day for Doctor Warner's deposition. I have conferences that cannot be canceled all day tomorrow, so if you desire to review Doctor Warner's position as an expert witness, you've got an hour and a half left to accomplish that."

"I definitely will require most of tomorrow to complete the deposition," Red snarled.

"No, that's not possible. We might as well stop now and reschedule," Jim growled. Throwing the paper he had in his hand down on the table, he swiveled his chair so his back was facing Red. When he finally turned back he continued. "I'm going to tell you right up front — my calendar is completely filled until our trial date in March. We may be able to work something out, but I wouldn't plan on it."

"Well, we'll just have to go into the evening until we're finished. I can stay up all night if we have to," Red said, curling his lips scornfully into a sly grin.

"I've already told you, I'm leaving at six-thirty, and it's impossible for me to cancel my meeting tonight." Then as his jaw tightened, he leaned forward, saying in an almost conciliatory voice, "Why don't you just get started and see how far we can get by six-thirty."

Red shuffled some papers, gathering his thoughts before finally proceeding.

"Okay, Mr. Warner. Oh that's right, you're a doctor aren't you — he snickered with that same ugly sour look on his face.

"In general terms, can you tell us where you think the hospital was negligent?"

Thank God, Bill whispered to himself. *He's finally opened the door so I can say what I came here for.*

Quickly he reached down and unlocked his briefcase and took out his notes.

"What are you reading from?" Red growled.

"My summary notes, outlining where I feel the hospital was negligent."

"I'll need a copy of that."

"Fine," *He bit on that one,* Bill thought. *Now it's a part of the record whether I finish or not.*

As they waited for copies to be made, Red asked, "Do you have any other notes that are pertinent to the trial?"

"No, I certainly don't," Bill replied, pursing his lips to show his revulsion for what had transpired much of the day.

"All right, you can proceed," Red finally said, distributing the copies of Bill's notes around the table.

Slowly Bill drew in a breath as he casually leaned forward, placing both elbows on the table, staring directly at Red.

Within moments, Red looked to his notes to avoid the intensity of Bill's stare.

"I plan to review several areas, and if you'll wait until I'm completely finished, I'll be happy to try and answer any questions you may have." Then clearing his throat, he looked at each attorney for confirmation.

"Okay, since I've heard no objections, I'd like to first make a general statement. It's my intention to refer to a specific standard, bylaw or rule and regulation of the Joint Commission or the hospital when I point out any violation of normal hospital standards. For example, all I could find in Veronica Keppler's medical record was a very minimal history and physical that clearly failed to meet standards. Therefore, I'll refer to rule 1519.2 which states:"

A complete history and physical examination shall in all cases be placed in the hospital record within twenty-four hours after admission of the patient.

"That's an exact quote of the hospital's written rule as approved by the Joint Commission."

Bill again looked to his notes before making the next point.

"Let me start by saying that Veronica Keppler underwent a sagittal suture repair, involving two very extensive major surgical procedures which included a Total Calvarial Remodeling, as well as a highly controversial Supraorbital surgery, for which both Doctors McGrath and Allen failed to record the appropriate procedure codes. In other words, they failed to refer to those two procedures by their proper name. They lumped both of those two distinctly different major surgical procedures under one term called a *Total Calvarial Reconstruction*, which is deceitfully incorrect."

Red started to interrupt, but Jim stopped him immediately.

"Please let him finish. You asked him to respond to your question, and he's doing just that. As he told you, you can ask questions when he's finished."

"Thank you," Bill said, nodding in Jim's direction.

"Dr. McGrath states in his deposition that he routinely uses this complex eight hour procedure to repair a simple cosmetic Sagittal Synostosis. However, it should be clearly understood that this type of complex surgical procedure, which removes the entire skull cap, is neither normal nor routine for a single Saggital Suture repair. And because this type of procedure is so dangerous, particularly when performed on a six month old infant, it should have been clearly classified as research. Worse yet, the parents and their cardiologist were told that this surgery was to be a simple cosmetic procedure, while the hospital was well aware that Doctors McGrath and Allen were utilizing a different surgery for those children than done anywhere else in the world, and that these two procedures not only involved over eight hours of major complex surgery, but a loss of more than two full body volumes of blood. The hospital was also well aware that this six months old infant was previously diagnosed with Pulmonary Stenosis.

Again, Red started to interrupt, but after looking at Jim, he decided to just let out a gasp and shake his head, demonstrating his agitation.

"National standards are very clear regarding that violation," Bill continued, "and the hospital rule 1522.4 also speaks to that."

A surgeon desiring to perform a new procedure, either as presented at a meeting, as described in the literature, or as a personal innovation will secure an appropriate consultation to document the indication and applicability of the operation. The local consultation will be in addition to either documentation in approved literature or a letter from the pertinent national specialty organization as to the feasibility. Consideration may be given to referring some innovative procedures to the Research Committee for discussion.

"And of course, that was not done in the Keppler case."

The room was embarrassingly silent as Bill again looked to his notes to find his next topic. Red's associate, an obnoxious looking gray haired woman had been scowling at Bill as if she was shocked at everything he was saying. Up until now, she'd been acting as Red's prop, making faces at just the right time, but Bill knew enough to wisely ignore her performance.

"The hospital also disregarded numerous publications that questioned this neurosurgical procedure. They ignored recognized standards, concerns, recommendations and reports of professional organizations, including the National Neurosurgical Specialty Organization, the Medical School, the National Public Health Service and the Center for Disease Control. Worse yet, the hospital had been informed that the CDC report had concluded that almost seventy percent of the CS X-rays were misdiagnosed. Yet, they ignored those unbiased third party's finding, and failed to determine the real reason for their extreme number of misdiagnosed X-rays. On top of all of that, they ignored an overwhelming number of concerns from patients and other health professionals. They even disregarded the professional consultant they themselves hired to recommend changes in the organization and management of their Medical Staff. From everything I've reviewed, the hospital's Neurosurgical Staff was unsupervised and totally free from any form of hospital or Medical Staff surveillance."

Pausing a moment, Bill bit at his lower lip while shaking his head over what was going on at this hospital.

"Based on all the material I've looked at, it's obvious the governance and organizational supervision in this hospital is nonexistent, in that the hospital actually allowed Doctor McGrath and Doctor Allen to influence their close clique of physicians to boycott the hospital and threaten to take their patients to other hospitals if McGrath was not appointed as Head of the Neurosurgical Department, even though he wasn't qualified for the position. In fact, threats of boycott and the huge hospital income from these procedures provided the way McGrath maintain his control over the hospital. Numerous depositions described these same informal open staff confrontations with the closed university staff members, and it's apparent that boycott, self-referral, monopoly, and conflicts of interest have usurped and replaced the hospital bylaws, as well as the Joint Commission standards.

Routine monthly Medical Staff service meetings are also required so that the Medical Staff and the Board of Directors can impartially evaluate patient deaths, complications, infections, and disease. That's written in their own bylaws as described in article eight, section two, describing department meetings. It says:"

Departments shall hold regular meetings at least monthly to review and evaluate the clinical work of staff members with privileges in the departments.

With that Bill sighed, once again looking at each attorney in the room.

"I could find no evidence that Veronica's complication or incident report were even prepared or reviewed. Doctors McGrath, Hanes, and Allen appear to be running things, rather than the hospital governing its Medical Staff."

Red looked at his associate and together they both appeared ready to pounce on Bill, but again Bill just ignored them.

"Doctor McGrath and Doctor Hanes have even refused to comply with the seventy-five percent meeting attendance standard that's required to maintain active staff membership. Deposition statements indicated they attended no more than one or two service meetings a year, if that. And I again refer you to the hospital's bylaws regarding attendance requirements for active staff, which states:"

Each member of the active staff shall be required to attend at least seventy-five percent of all medical staff standing committee and service meetings to which he/she has been appointed.

"Now, just a minute," Red yelled.

"Let him continue," Jim shouted so loudly that everyone in the room jumped.

"In fact, McGrath and Hanes audited their own charts," Bill continued, "rather than seek an unbiased department review for quality assurance. Quality assurance requires documented symptomatology be available before making an admitting diagnosis. But Doctor McGrath and Doctor Hanes didn't accept that concept of unbiased neurosurgical surveillance, even though the hospital has a duty to exercise proper supervision to prevent unjustified and dangerous surgery."

With that, Bill's finger again traced over his notes.

"The hospital even retained an expert to review those controversial Medical Staff problems, but almost twenty open staff members identified as the *Dinosaurs,* pressured the hospital to disregard the consultant's recommendations due to their inherent conflict of interest."

With that Bill held up the large notebook of depositions.

"If you've read any of the staff member's depositions, they leave little doubt as to how these *Dinosaurs* boycotted this hospital. Since the hospital was unapproachable concerning those controversial CS surgeries, the National Neurosurgical Specialty Organization contacted the Medical School, asking them to withdraw the residency-training program from the hospital, rather than risk revocation of that program. One of the residents openly questioned the marketing and misrepresentation of those needless surgeries, and as a result, the school removed Doctor McGrath and Doctor Hanes from the faculty because of their departure from national standards. But even then, the hospital didn't attempt to revise or review Doctor McGrath's privileges. That review should have been accomplished when those two surgeons first began to vary from national standards. And even after the hospital was made aware that the doctors were misrepresenting the need for that surgery, they advertised the service as shown in this Newsletter."

Bill held up the Newsletter, looking directly at Red's associate, with her eyebrows still raised as if in shock.

"The scary thing is that until just recently, the hospital continued to promote and support this surgery, even though the negative response was overwhelming. What's even worse is nothing actually changed until the public and professional outcry finally reached the national news media."

With that Bill intentionally cleared his throat to allow just enough time for his words to sink in. He could see they'd had enough, but he'd finally gotten on stage after a full day of harassment, and he was damned well going to stay there until he was finished.

"Now, here is another very important point," he added, raising one hand to emphasize his point.

"Neither the hospital nor Doctor McGrath properly inform the parents about the risk of this research procedure. And as I've already said, they also failed to require a routine standard second opinion by another unbiased and qualified specialist, which is recommended nationally on all major surgical procedures."

Again his eyes slowly scanned each individual.

"There are other numerous standards that you need to be aware of such as 1513.2 (a) which says:"

The consultant must be qualified by training to give an opinion in the field in which his opinions are sought.

"And (b) says:"

The consultant must provide a written, signed opinion, which is made part of the record.

"Number 1514.3 requires:"

Mandatory consultation for every child when any unusual or unconventional drug, therapeutic intervention or major surgical procedure is to be employed which might risk life or future function.

"Yes, a clerk did obtain a badly scribbled and incomplete consent form from the Kepplers during the traumatic time of admission, but then the hospital failed to obtain what is termed an appropriate informed consent. Let me cite a few more requirements. Rule 1519.3 (b) says:"

All operations performed shall be fully described — whether intraoperative complications or unexpected conditions or findings arose, particularly if such conditions may affect postoperative care. If not adequately dealt with elsewhere in the chart, that note should also contain a statement as to the reason for surgery and the fact that it has been discussed with the patient, or appropriate relatives in the case of children, and that those concerned understood the reasons for surgery, alternatives thereto, the nature of the operative procedure per se, and the substantial risk involved.

"That's what this hospital's own *Patients Bill of Rights* is all about, and that's also reconfirmed in the hospital's mission statement."

Bill held both hands out as he continued.

"Did those physicians inform the parents about other more sensible treatment options? Heavens no! To the contrary, they misinformed and even terrified the parents concerning the infant's prognosis if they failed to agree with these two major surgical procedures. Worse yet, they never informed the parents that they actually intended to perform two major and distinctly separate surgical procedures involving a *Total Calvarial Remodeling*, as well as the *Supraorbital Reconstruction* — which substantially increases the surgical time and risk factor. McGrath said he didn't want to confuse the parents. And then as members of the hospital's Medical Staff, they didn't even obtain a written cardiac consult and evaluation regarding the patient's pulmonary stenosis." With that, Bill grimaced, indicating the hopelessness of it all.

The group around the table now seemed resigned to the fact that Bill was going to say his piece, and everyone other than Red's associate seemed to acknowledge that.

"There's clear evidence that McGrath's surgery involved extensively more than the defined procedure that's currently accepted and coded nationally as a *Total Calvarial Remodeling*. In fact, it's now very clear that McGrath's research surgery was unnecessarily extensive, therefore subjecting this tiny little infant to extreme danger, massive blood loss, as well as considerable transfusion risk."

With that Bill looked up at the ceiling.

"Now, here is the most important factor. The hospital was unable to provide documentation that supports Doctor McGrath's credentials — such as his training, his specific procedural privileges, or any documentation that would confirm that he even passed his Specialty Boards. And on top of all that he was never authorized to perform unsupervised research."

Once again Bill held up the standards.

"According to 1522.2:"

Every surgical resident and practitioner has available the list of procedures that he has performed and that list is to be submitted for board eligibility — the department chief, should also require submission of a complete list of operative cases performed in the surgeon's training or practice. Operations may be done if there is evidence that the surgeon has previously performed or assisted at five such procedures. Certain rare operations may be performed by qualified surgeons with broad experience and depth of knowledge about the organs in question and the surgical techniques involved.

"Yes, Doctor McGrath eventually became board certified, but only a few months prior to performing Veronica's very risky procedure. Here again, the Joint Commission and the hospital's own rules and regulations recommend supervision for one year after board certification. In fact, Doctor McGrath's application for staff privileges to do research was denied," Bill scowled, holding up a letter from the hospital's Board of Directors outlining McGrath's approved privileges.

"He was also never approved to conduct the very controversial research surgery involving the drilling of burr holes in the skulls of normal infants, which he questionably diagnosed as having abnormal intracranial pressure. The hospital never even attempted to determine if he was in compliance with their approved privileges or documented education."

Bill was finally ready to stop, and before Red interrupted, he said, "Let me summarize. Here is what I think. The hospital has knowingly failed to meet its mission and governance responsibilities. They've deviated from nationally recognized standards and their agreement with the Joint Commission of Accreditation of Healthcare Organizations. They're not meeting the American Hospital Association's or the American Medical Association's guidelines. And they're just not carrying out their own documented mission, or their own Medical Staff bylaws, rules and regulations, as I've shown you. On top of all that, the hospital is performing unsanctioned and unnecessary research procedures that are subjecting patients to unnecessary risk and injury. They also ignored the report issued by the National Center for Disease Control, which established basic diagnostic criteria for CS surgeries. And the hospital ignored other healthcare agents, as well as their own concerned residents."

Bill could see the embarrassment around the table, and it was now obvious they were not about to question him any further.

"What's even worse, Mr. Bakencamp stated in his deposition, that he doesn't intend to investigate this problem, which has now reached national prominence since it's come under both public and professional scrutiny. That suggests that neither the Board of Directors nor their CEO is functioning with any degree of responsibility."

With that, Bill lowered his voice to almost a whisper. It was now time to summarize all this negligence. "I find all kinds of evidence that the hospital was aware that the defendant's research procedures were unapproved, extensive, and unnecessary. It's also apparent the hospital did nothing to prevent this dangerous surgery from being performed on their premises — in fact they promoted it. And it's even more apparent that Doctor McGrath conducted this bizarre research on private patients, without proper parental approval or understanding."

"Are you finished?" Red snarled.

Bill looked down at his notes.

"In the memo you just copied, you'll see that the hospital has recently indicated they've discontinued this very questionable surgical procedure, and I want to commend them on finally taking the first step to correct this problem."

Again Red interrupted, "Are you finished?"

Bill raised one hand.

"No, let me say one more thing. The care provided by this hospital hasn't only been sub-standard, it was also the cause of Veronica Keppler's blindness, her irreversible brain damage and the disfigurement of her skull, as well as her many developmental delays and her emotional and behavioral problems. Were it not for a very serious breach in hospital governance over this uncontrolled research, the damages and injuries to that very fragile infant could have been prevented."

Bill took one last look at Red's associate.

"Those are only a few of my comments. I certainly could go on, but in consideration of the time remaining, I'd be willing to answer any questions you may have."

Red immediately asked that they take a break.

Again Jim and Bill returned to their small room and closed the door. Jim turned and smiled. "Boy, did Red finally serve up a big white softball, and you just proceeded to hit it out of the park. They sure as hell aren't going to ask any more questions of you. And they can't afford to get anything else on the record — I can assure you of that."

After what seemed like an eternity, Red returned and announced that they'd be in touch to reschedule another time to complete Bill's deposition.

As Bill threw his two briefcases into the back seat of his car, he opened the driver's door and flopped into the front seat exhausted. Putting his head back, he mumbled, "Shit, life's too short for this kind of bull-roar. I hope that's my last case on CS with that son-of-a-bitch. But perhaps I've done a little bit to help stop those wealthy Oligarchic noblemen from deregulating our healthcare standards any more, just so they can make big bucks off our poor sick and disabled."

The traffic home was a nightmare, with one driver after another bent on committing suicide. As he finally drove up to his townhouse, he noticed the lights were on. Walking in the front door he found Mary wearing a flowered apron over her white nursing uniform.

"I thought you might need some tender loving care. How does veal stew with dumplings hit you," she smiled.

Bill's voice quivered. Putting his tired arms around her he sighed — "Oh how I love you. Please don't ever leave me."

"Not a chance," Mary said, kissing him tenderly.

* * * * *

Two days later, Bill received a call from Jim. "They've settled out of court," he cried exuberantly. "But I can't release any information on the case, so I guess I won't be able to write my book. I can tell you this however; Veronica will be well taken care of for the rest of her life."

"Well, that's what we all wanted," Bill sighed.

* * * * *

At Mary and Bill's next brunch, they discussed the Keppler settlement of some seven million, the highest ever in the state of Colorado, as Mary grinned like a Cheshire cat.

"Do you think we can leave now? I'm starting to get into trouble."

"What do you mean?" Bill asked. "You haven't been threatened, have you?"

"Not yet," she replied — realizing how she must have sounded. "No, let's just say I'm irritating the hell out of Doctor Dante." With that she paused — her face dead serious. "But I do have something else to tell you, which is very confidential."

"What's that?" Bill asked.

As he looked at her, he could see she was still debating whether she should say anything.

"Bill, I've been warned by our great leader not to breathe a word to anyone, and although I feel guilty saying this, I've decided you need to know what's going on," she whispered, rolling her tongue against the inside of her cheek.

"Hold it," Bill said. "If you're going to have guilt feelings, you don't have to tell me anything."

"Bill, if I respected the people I worked for, I'd try to maintain their trust, but this is something you need to know. Don't worry, it's all right."

Again she hesitated briefly.

"Last week, a woman was waiting outside the surgeon's locker room to hear about her son's minor surgery. She was almost certain Doctor McGrath was the only one in there, and after waiting more than an hour, and hearing them page him over and over, she finally knocked on the door and peaked in, only to see him lying on the floor with an empty syringe next to him. She immediately ran for help, grabbing the first nurse she could find."

Bill looked shocked. *Thank God that didn't happen while he was performing surgery*, he thought to himself.

"I never did find out what was in that syringe — they're keeping that quiet — but I do know the Medical Staff has temporarily suspended McGrath's privileges until they can sort things out. One of my supervising nurses, who can find out almost anything, tells me he was injecting some type of mood altering drug or speed, before his next surgery. And Bill, you should know he's been very depressed lately."

"God almighty, you don't think it was a suicide attempt?"

"Oh no, he was just trying to keep alert, and there was evidence that he'd done this before."

"That's terrible. I never thought for a moment that he was using drugs."

"I know, but that's not all. He also had a heart attack, and they just performed by-pass surgery on him on Friday. His doctor has placed him on complete bed rest and restricted all practice for at least six months, maybe longer."

"Well, that explains something."

"What's that?" Mary asked.

"Adams had shown me a memo from the American Association of Neurologic Surgery that indicated the hospital has now discontinued this major procedure for CS. The Association apparently intended to investigate the problem, and the hospital has assured them that they won't be doing that procedure in the future."

"That's nice to know. I guess I'm always the last one to hear about those things," Mary said — once again discouraged at not being informed. "No wonder Bakencamp and Dante have been walking around with their chins on the floor."

"Well, it's about time. I was beginning to doubt if we were ever going to put a dent in their armor."

"The other thing I need to tell you is Dante is really pissed at me lately. I've been enforcing standards on second opinions, signed consent forms, and checking physician's privileges with his office almost daily. Last week he told me he wants it stopped."

"Have you stopped?"

"Hell no — I told him I'm just getting started. In fact, I've got the Research Committee reviewing anything that even smells like research, and my surgical nurses are measuring blood loss and recording blood pressure on every surgery — thanks to you."

"That's great. All I can say is keep it up, but always have a written standard to back you up. They'll be hard pressed to defy their own written standards."

"You know what? My nurses have never been happier. They tell me their skin doesn't crawl anymore. They all knew it was wrong. I guess they'd just got a little careless over time."

"They'll all respect you for it in the long haul," Bill said. Then he added, "But you can't entirely ignore those damn *Dinosaurs*."

"I understand," Mary said. "Now, let's talk about when we can get out of here. You've certainly damaged McGrath's reputation and his pocketbook, as well as his physical stamina. You've also taught the hospital a lesson in ethics. And I also know you're busier than you'd like to be. And you're probably getting anxious to get back to writing — am I right?"

"Okay, let's make a deal. In six months, I'll be through most of my work, and we'll leave then," Bill replied.

"Now I've got something tangible to look forward to," she grinned.

"I guess we'd better start planning. That's not too far away." Bill explained.

"It won't be hard to plan. I can pack my bags in less than a couple hours. Just give me a few minutes warning."

Bill threw his napkin at her. "That's a deal," he laughed.

As they walked from the restaurant, Mary suddenly dropped Bill's hand and skipped out the door like a schoolgirl going on summer vacation, as Bill doubled up laughing at her.

Chapter 12

Another Death

When Bill arrived home, he found a message from Sister Janice asking him to call her.

"Doctor Warner, I have some very bad news. Sister Gerome died last Saturday. She had a surgical procedure on her hip, and died on the operating table. Our Board wants to meet with you as soon as possible in that we suspect her death wasn't an accident, and we need your advice."

* * * * *

When Bill arrived at the convent, Sister Janice greeted him, and Sister Elizabeth, Sister Maureen, and Sister Colleen were all waiting in their conference room where they could talk.

"What in the world happened?" Bill asked.

"As you know, Sister Gerome had been having trouble with her hips for some time," Janice explained, "and she finally decided to have her left hip replaced with a prosthetic at St. Paul's hospital in Denver. One of our sisters works in surgery at that hospital, and Gerome felt secure having it done there, but she mistakenly asked to have it done on a Saturday — not realizing their regular anesthesiologist wouldn't be available."

"Have they told you what the cause of her death was?" Bill asked

"The surgeon told us that she either had a massive pulmonary embolus, or an allergic reaction to heparin."

181

"You've got to be kidding. Who was this anesthesiologist?"

"His name is Doctor Hurly," Sister Janice said. "He's a new anesthesiologist in the area, and we think he usually works at one of the other hospitals, but we're not certain of that. Sister Marion was acting as the circulating nurse, and she told us that the anesthesiologist ignored hospital policy, and pressure infused her with cell-saver blood. I can get Sister Marion if you'd like to talk with her?"

"That would be helpful," Bill replied.

Sister Marion was a very quiet reserved person, and after briefly visiting with her, Bill felt certain that she'd never have taken it upon herself to tell them as much as she already had, if there hadn't been something seriously wrong with the surgery.

"Sister, before I ask you any questions, could you tell me if you thought there was anything unusual about Sister Gerome's surgery?"

"Well, I guess the thing that concerns me the most is the scrub nurse told Doctor Hurly that hospital policy doesn't allow them to use a pressure cuff to infuse blood from the Cell-Saver. But he just ignored her, and went ahead and used it anyway."

"Sister, do you know why the hospital policy requires that?"

"I think there's a danger that air can be infused into the patient."

"That's right — that's why the manufacturer provides a special reinfusion kit when pressure infusion is necessary. In fact, it's extremely dangerous to pressure infuse blood from the recovery bag without that kit. And it's hard for me to believe a qualified anesthesiologist would not know that, or would ignore the nurse's warning."

Sister Janice interrupted, "Doctor, could you tell us what a cell saver is?"

"Yes, of course. When a person has major surgery, there can be a considerable amount of blood loss. And when the surgeon anticipates that, he uses a machine called the cell-saver. The cell-saver has a suction they use to recover the patient's blood from the surgical field. That blood is then suctioned into a reservoir, where it is washed with saline solution as it spins in a self-contained centrifuge, and heparin is added to prevent the blood from clotting during the spinning process. What happens is the saline solution, the heparin, and any waste materials that may contaminate the blood spin off, leaving washed or clean blood cells, which is called heparinized blood that can be re-infused into the patient. Does that make sense?" Bill asked.

"Why don't they use blood from the blood bank?" Sister Elizabeth asked.

"Re-infusing one's own blood enhances the patient's recovery, and it minimizes the potential for an allergic reaction to blood that's been obtained from someone other than the patient," Bill explained. "But, if some remnants of heparin happen to remain, after the spin down, there can also be a danger of an allergic reaction to the heparin. And that can result in what we call an antiphylatic reaction, which can also cause death."

After Bill stopped to take a sip of coffee, he asked, "Does that all make any sense?" He asked

Yes, they all nodded.

"Then after the suctioned blood is washed, it's pumped into a recovery bag for re-infusion into the patient. That recovery bag is usually hung on an I.V. pole where it can be infused by hydrostatic pressure. By that I mean gravity. The higher they raise the pole, the faster the infusion takes place."

"Is that what happened with Sister Gerome?" Janice frowned.

"No, it's not. If that had been the case, everything probably would've been all right, but what Sister Marion has told us suggests that Doctor Hurly used a pressure cuff, which is against hospital policy, and forced the blood into the patient manually. Am I right, Sister Marion?"

"Yes you are, and that's what the scrub nurses warned him about."

"Sister Marion, do you know why he felt he needed to force the transfusion?"

Marion looked down to think a moment before answering. "Well, her record at that time indicated her blood pressure was 105 systolic over 45 diastolic, and the pulse was 90, and according to his notes she'd lost five hundred cc's of blood, and I guess he wanted to infuse five hundred cc's of blood to bring her blood back to a normal level. But to be honest, I really have no idea why he wanted to pressure infuse the cell saver blood," she said, looking puzzled. "I don't think she was in trouble at that time."

With that Bill scowled. "Sister Marion, can you tell me if the patient had both a peripheral line and a CVP, or central line?"

Again she looked away, as if to gather her thoughts.

"Yes, she had both."

As Bill looked around the table at the other nuns he explained, "They usually mix cell-saver blood with blood bank blood, or packed cells, because they seem to get the best results that way." Then turning back to Marion he asked, "Do you know if they did this with Sister Gerome?"

Marion nodded, "Yes, if I remember correctly they were giving her 300 cc's of packed cells, and 200 cc's of cell saver blood."

"Do you recall which line was receiving the packed cells?"

"I'm quite sure that it was the peripheral line to her arm. Yes, In fact I'm sure of that."

"So the yellow line from the cell saver recovery bag was hooked into the central line, or what they call the CVP."

"Yes."

"Could you see any air in the recovery bag?"

"What I remember is after he applied the pressure cuff, the bag and the line went empty." With that, Marion appeared distressed, putting one finger to her lips as if recalling the incident. "In fact, he asked me to get him a six hundred cc syringe to purge the air out of the system."

"Do you recall if he closed the main line when he noticed the bag was empty?"

"As I recall, he seemed to watch it for several moments before he closed the line, and then he purged the air out of the system," she scowled.

"Do you remember how many times he pulled the plunger on the syringe?" Bill asked, nervously biting at his lip.

"Oh, let me think — perhaps five or six times."

"Didn't Sister Gerome show some symptoms of stress by then?"

"Oh yes," she said, staring at Bill. "I remember her pressure fell to forty over eighteen, and her pulse suddenly dropped to thirty-five."

"What did he do then?"

"He ordered an X-ray stat, and administered epinephrine, one half milligram twice."

"And what was happening to Sister Gerome?"

"She was in a total cardiac collapse," she stammered, obviously upset.

Bill could feel her emotions rising, but he pursued one last question.

"So she began to have a cardiac collapse from what was clearly a pulmonary embolus?"

"Yes, I think so, because he told the surgeon he would need to close, and they quickly rolled her to a supine position and started chest compression and CPR. That's when the room filled with all the other surgeons and anesthesiologists, all trying to help." With that, tears began to fill her eyes.

Quickly Bill thanked Sister Marion for what she was able to tell them, and then asked if she could be excused. After she left, he continued. "I feel terrible about this, and I agree with you, her death appears to go beyond negligence, in fact it may well have been intentional. You definitely need to have your attorney find out more about this anesthesiologist. As you know, Sister Gerome has received threats, and Lanin's cronies had blackballed both of us." Then as an after thought he added, "I also need to tell you, in total confidence, that an attempt was recently made on my life, and I'm very fortunate to be meeting with you today."

Bill always had a difficult time lying to anyone, let alone a group of nuns, and as he looked away he thought, *I just can't tell them what has actually happened,* so he said nothing.

"You also need to be aware that the FBI was about to apprehend these men that were involved in all these deaths, but now they've all suddenly disappeared and the FBI feels that Lanin, Collier, Hinckley and their hired gun have all left the country to escape prosecution. In any event, I feel certain that those men will never return, but apparently what Lanin has started in our country remains alive and well, and I can only hope they were not involved in Sister Gerome's death."

The Sisters could see Bill's distress, and they knew enough not to pursue the threat issue any further, as they just sat and stared at him. As a feeling of guilt swept over him, there was a long pause before he continued.

"Apparently Gerome was not even safe in the hospital," he mumbled as an after thought. "And I'd suggested you contact Joel Wilson at the FBI, so he can investigate what went on here. And yes, this could be another murder," he explained, writing down Joel's phone number for them.

As Bill stood up to leave, he realized it was time to say good-bye to the Sisters once and for all — if he was ever going to rid himself of these Dinosaurs.

Chapter 13

Mary's In Trouble

Mary called late in the evening, apparently upset.

"I hate to bother you, but you made me promise I'd tell you if I sensed something was wrong."

"Absolutely," Bill said, "What's up?"

"Well, I had to drive into work several times today and each time I noticed someone was following me. I couldn't see their face, but it appeared to be the same man each time," she whispered. "And now I'm really paranoid."

"Listen, I'm coming right over and I'll stay with you tonight. I'll walk the back way, and knock on your patio door. Check that all your doors and windows are locked."

"They are and I have," she laughed.

It only took Bill a few minutes to reach her house, and Mary was anxiously waiting. "God I feel so stupid calling you, but I am concerned. I'm absolutely certain this guy was following me, but I don't have a clue as to who it might be."

"Listen, I've been down that road before, and you're doing the right thing. Let me assure you these guys know how to play hardball, and I know their mad as hell at me — and by now they've probably decided you and I are working together."

Bill gave Mary a hug, trying to relax her. "Is Dante still upset with you?"

"Well yes, in fact he's been very upset with me, but I don't think it's him. This guy appears to be a much bigger man."

"It wouldn't be him I'm worried about. It's who he'd hire."

Bill's jaw tightened. "Mary, instead of going to brunch in the morning, we'll drive to the police station and report this, so they can check things out. Did you get a license number?"

"No, he's never been that close. Maybe it's just some weirdo that noticed me in the store — or at the hospital."

"That could be, but we need to stop it — don't we?"

"Yes we do," she sighed. "But I sure hate to go to the police — yet I know what happened to your family, and I don't want to take any chances."

"That's right. And if it is that *Dinosaur Club*, we need to find that out. We can't live a life where we're afraid to walk down the street. You know — maybe it is time you get out of that nut house."

"I'm not leaving without you."

"Well, let's find out what's going on first."

After Bill rechecked all the windows and doors, they went to bed, and as he lay awake thinking about the fear he lived with in the past, he thought, *Will I ever be able to have peace again?*

Suddenly he heard a loud snapping noise. In that he wasn't that familiar with the noises in Mary's house, he looked at Mary to see if she heard the same thing — but she was already sound asleep. Not wanting to wake her, he just laid still and listened. Just about the time he decided the noise was probably the furnace or something like that, he heard what sounded like the patio door sliding open. Quickly he moved to the edge of the bed and stood up. As he walked toward the door, he remembered Mary had a fresh vase of flowers on the dresser, and he groped in the dark until his hand touched the bottom of the heavy glass vase. Slowly he lifted it up, removing the flowers before standing motionless next to the open door, where he could listen. Looking back to where Mary was he suddenly sensed something move past him, and then he saw the shadow of a huge person blocking the light from the clock radio.

My God, he's standing right at the foot of the bed, he thought to himself, *and he's gigantic.*

By now Bill's heart was pounding in his throat, as he watched this enormous shadow hover over Mary, with what looked like a knife. Quickly he swung the vase at the man's head, hearing a sickening thud.

As the intruder hit the floor, Bill pounced on top of him, water flying in every direction.

"Mary," he shouted, and as he pulled the intruder's arm up behind his back, his knife fell to the floor. Straddling him, he pinned him down as he kicked the knife out of reach. It seemed forever before he finally heard the bedside lamp click on, as Mary stared in his direction totally confused, and still half asleep.

"What is it?" she cried — "Oh my God," she screamed, starring at the blood that was spattered everywhere.

"Call 911," Bill yelled. "Tell them we need the police right away."

Mary could hear the tension in Bill's voice as her shaking hand reached for the phone.

"I need some rope or something, so we can tie him up," Bill blurted out as Mary fearfully tried to explain what had happened to the 911 operator.

As Bill re-gripped the man's arm tightly, he frantically searched his pockets with his free arm. Under his chest he could feel a gun, which he struggled with until it finally came loose. Releasing the safety he jammed the barrel into the back of the man's head, yanking up on his right arm until he finally heard a feeble groan.

As Mary rushed back into the room she had a roll of duct tape.

"Tape his ankles together good and tight, and then we'll tape his wrists. Hurry," Bill nervously shouted. "He's starting to wake up."

"The police should be here any minute," Mary whispered, as she frantically wound duct tape around both ankles.

As Bill held him down, he finally realized the massive size of the man as he stared at his dark greasy hair, which was soaked with blood.

He must weigh close to three hundred pounds, Bill thought.

As Mary furiously cut the tape free, she yelled, "I can't believe I didn't hear him. Thank God I called you," she cried — tears now flowing freely.

The groans were now coming more rapidly and as he began to regain consciousness Bill pulled up even harder on his arm.

"All right you bastard, you're going to tell me who sent you, or I'm going to put a bullet in your skull."

Again he groaned, but there was still no answer.

"Did you hear me?" Bill screamed, violently pulling his arm higher.

Finally he mumbled what sounded like, "I don't know." Then after sucking in a deep breath, he again slurred, "I don't know."

With that Bill jammed his arm even further until he heard a loud cracking noise.

"Oh my God, you're breaking my arm," he screamed. "Stop, I'll tell you everything."

"You better talk fast, or you won't be alive when the police arrive."

"All right — all right," he blurted out. Then after sucking in a quick breath he whispered, "Some guy paid me five thousand dollars to rough her up. He told me he didn't want her to be able to work for a long time." Then after another quick mouthful of air, he wheezed. "He said she'd make a good piece of ass — if I felt like it."

"What did he look like?" Bill asked, while Mary awkwardly taped his wrists behind his back.

"He was a tall thin man," he slurred, again gulping for air between each groan. "He had dark eyes and a black beard — that's all I remember."

"That sound's like Dante all right," Mary said. I've got a picture of him in my briefcase," she shouted, quickly running out of the room.

Bill could now hear the police siren in the distance as Mary breathlessly crouched on the floor, shoving the hospital newspaper right in front of his face.

"Is this the man?" She shouted.

"You better tell the truth," Bill yelled, pushing the gun barrel deeper into his neck.

"Yes — yes that's the man. He paid me five thousand dollars."

"That dirty son-of-a-bitch," Mary screamed, just as the police siren went quiet. Quickly she ran out of the room to meet them, tears running freely down her face.

In only moments the police took over, while Bill nervously explained what happened.

"He just told me that Doctor Dante paid him five thousand dollars to rough me up and rape me — am I right," Mary screamed at him.

"Yes — that's right," he groaned as the officer pulled him to his feet, blood dripping everywhere.

Mary pointed defiantly at Dante's picture, "This man's an attorney at the hospital where I work as the Nursing Director, she explained."

"Well, you certainly got more out of him than we could have," the officer said.

"It took a little persuasion," Bill growled. "But I don't have the same restrictions you have. I probably should've shot the son-of-a-bitch."

"You're right on that, but I'm glad you didn't. If you had I'd be taking you in instead of him," the officer explained, "and that would have only complicated things. At least we now know who's behind all this, but we'll need to get you downtown and record your statements."

They talked a bit longer before the police officer explained that they'd need to secure the crime scene and get their lab to check things out.

"We'll put you up in a hotel for the night, and we'll need your house key," the taller officer said, looking at Mary.

"We won't need a hotel," Bill said. "We have a place to stay."

"Alright then, if you could follow us to the station, we'll document your story."

"We'd be happy to," Bill said, impressed by their efficient response to everything that had just happened.

* * * * *

It was almost two in the morning before they finally returned to Bill's townhouse, and they both rolled and tossed much of the night before getting up and walking to the Hatch Cover for breakfast. It was a cold dreary morning, and as they sat down at their favorite table, their friendly Scrub Jay cocked its head at them, as if questioning where they'd been lately.

"Bill, it's time we leave this place, and I'm going to type up my resignation and place it on Bakencamp's desk first thing Monday, with a few choice words — I also need to make some personal phone calls."

"Okay," Bill nodded. "And I agree, it's time we get the hell out of here, since we've more than served our purpose. I only have two more cases to go, and they'll probably settle out of court, so I may not even have to come back here."

"When can we leave?" Mary asked.

191

"Why don't I have a moving van pick up our things as soon as possible? I bet they could have us packed and out of here in just a few days."

"Good. — I'm all for that," she said, thinking back to how close she came to being killed.

"I'll turn my car in on Monday, and stay with you. And I don't want to go back to my house again."

"I wouldn't have it any other way," Bill agreed.

* * * * *

On Monday morning Mary arrived at work with her resignation in hand, and immediately asked to meet with Bakencamp. His secretary told her he was meeting with Dante, and she'd call her as soon as he was available.

"No. Just tell them I'm going to meet with them right now, and what I have to say concerns both of them — it will only take a moment."

As she opened the door and walked into the office they both looked like two kids that had just been caught smoking in the garage.

"Gentlemen, what I have to say will only require a moment of your precious time," she scowled, walking right up to them and placing both hands on the conference table.

Glaring at Dante, she snarled defiantly, "I got your God damned message Saturday night, and perhaps you're wondering what happened to your messenger. Well, let me tell you what happened," she smirked. "After we took his knife and gun away, he confirmed that you — you bastard — paid him five thousand dollars to rape me and rough me up so that I wouldn't be able to return to work."

Then after turning her head away, just long enough to regain her composure, she continued. "My husband was a well known surgeon, who followed the Hippocratic Oath very closely, and he would often tell me about people like you, but I'd never really understood what he'd meant until now."

Again she started to choke-up, but she quickly firmed up her jaw, holding back any further emotion as she resisted any breakdown on her part.

"I can tell you with full assurance," she said staring directly at Bakencamp. "You, Dante, and McGrath are three sick puppies."

With that she threw her resignation on the table.

"Here's my resignation, which I'm sure you're anxious to receive. I have thirty days vacation due, and that piece of paper serves as my notice, since I'm leaving today. I've already turned in a copy to the personnel department, and I've typed a letter to your Board Chairman, just in case you fail to tell him what's really going on in this *Nut House.*"

Then looking at Dante she whispered, "The police will soon be contacting you, and I'll be available if they should ever need me. But knowing you, you'll probably squirm out of your rat hole — so I want you to know something right up front."

Then lowering her voice even more, so it couldn't be taped, she continued.

"I have a friend in Las Vegas who'd make your torpedo look like an amateur. In fact, he's one of the best in the business. I met him when I was a nineteen-year-old showgirl, and I found him to be a complete gentleman. He'd put your guy to shame."

As their faces turned ashen, she hesitated a moment so they could fully digest what she was about to say. "I called him yesterday, and we had a long discussion about my situation — and I asked for his advice. He persuaded me to buy some security, and we both agreed to an unwritten contract. What that contract says is that if any member of your corrupt *Dinosaur Club* even breathes in my direction, my friend will turn off your headlights. It also says that if anything happens to me or any of my close friends, with or without cause — like perhaps an accident — he'll be sure that all three of you are taken care of permanently."

Dante looked at Bakencamp and was about to interrupt, but Mary held one finger to her lips. "Shhh — no conversation please," she whispered.

Then once again, leaning forward over the table, she continued. "My friend wants to be sure you get the message because he doesn't want to make any mistakes. So, in the next few days or weeks he's going to leave a special calling card with each of you." Mary raised both eyebrows and kind of tossed her head back so her hair was off her forehead. "He may leave it in your bed, or on your desk, or even under your windshield wiper one day, and it will confirm my contract with him."

With that, Mary turned and walked toward the door. Then suddenly she stopped and slowly walked back. "Oh yes — I forgot one thing. There is an addendum to our agreement." Continuing to whisper she explained. "If Doctor McGrath's surgical clique ever gets back in business, or anyone ever experiences another epidemic, my friend will take it just as personally as if you performed your stupid surgery on me. Do you read me gentlemen?"

It was obvious they both understood what she meant immediately without saying another word.

With that she turned. "Well, TA-TA. It's been a real pleasure," she smiled — softly closing the door behind her.

* * * * *

That Friday, as Bill and Mary left for Florida, and as they watched the mountains fade into the distance, Bill finally spoke.

"Mary, I really am very anxious to start writing again, and since Adams isn't free to write about the McGrath epidemic — someone has to inform the public. Don't they?"

"Oh, that reminds me," Mary said. "I bought a lap-top for the boat. We can't have you fishing all the time — the public needs to know what these powerful international bankers have been up to."

"You mean the Wealthy Oligarchy, don't you?

"Whatever it is, I now know this problem is a lot bigger than just our dysfunctional doctors and politicians."

"You know, this whole thing reminds me of the world's first democracy, when the Athenians were invaded by the wealthy Palestinians," Bill said. "Many writers have tried to explain that a democracy can only serve as a temporary form of government, until the wealthy discover that they can vote themselves money from the public treasury, and thereafter a democracy always collapses from loose fiscal policy before it once again becomes a dictatorship. Some have described how this democratic cycle moves from bondage to faith, to courage, to liberty, to abundance, to complacency, to apathy, and then all the way back to depending on some wealthy Oligarchy, just as the Athenian culture returned to bondage back in 45 BC. In fact some authors have said this whole cycle takes only about two hundred years for a democracy to fail, and we started our democracy back in 1776, just a little over two hundred and thirty years ago. And I think we're in the apathy stage, totally dependent on this Oligarchy that will inevitably force the working class back into bondage — taking away our freedoms, while we foolishly languish in some sort of sustained state of apathy."

"Bill, you really do need to write about all this, and I now fully understand that there is an honest to God Oligarchy behind all this."

"Well let me assure you these things just didn't happen by accident," Bill explained. "Mary, I don't think I ever told you how I met President Ford, or what he said to me. While were driving, let me tell you how I met him and what he told me," Bill said, going on to describe when he'd previously accepted a job as the administrator of a hospital in Lansing, Michigan, to help them back on their feet financially.

"As I recall, it was in the mid to late 60's when a huge snow storm buried Lansing in several feet of snow, with some drifts reaching the roof tops, virtually shutting down the entire city. Since Lansing was the Capital of Michigan, we had in place a State Disaster Plan that involved the National Guard and the local Police Force — and since the phone service was out of order, I was notified by a police officer on a snowmobile that he was to take me into the hospital, since all the city streets were impassable. I remember how the snowmobile kept sinking in these ten foot drifts with two of us on it, and we struggled for a good half hour to get to Saginaw Avenue, which was a main thoroughfare some ten blocks from my house. When we finally got to that street, there was a National Guard track like vehicle waiting to take me to my hospital, which was located on the far west end of the city. As I climbed inside this strange vehicle I was even more surprised to see both Governor George Romney and Senator Gerald Ford enjoying a hot cup of coffee — and as we made our way to our respective offices to implement the Disaster Plan, we got to know each other quite well."

"Now that's really interesting," Mary said.

"Since I had to affect the Emergency Plan for the sick and injured they dropped me off first, and as a result of this unusual meeting, the three of us became good friends. Then later, after Ford had served as President — I was appointed by Doctor Jerome Heustes, who you now know very well, to serve on an NIH committee that was to define the Diagnostic Related Groupings of Diseases, for Medicare. He appointed me because I was the Principle Investigator for this computer based medical record research study that involved some five Universities, including Michigan, Michigan State, Minnesota, Iowa, and the University of British Columbia. After one of our DRG meetings, Doctor Heustes and I discussed the dangerous trends toward the deregulation of our once nonprofit healthcare system and the potential cost threat it posed to other important infrastructures, which the working class depended on. In our conversation, Heustes became aware of my friendship with Gerald Ford and he asked if I'd contact him, to see if he would help us try and stop any further deregulation of our health insurance and pharmaceutical systems."

"Your not going to tell me you could just pick up the phone and call him, are you?" Mary grinned

"No, since Jerry lived in Palm Springs at that time, I called my close friend who ran the Eisenhower Medical Center, to ask if we could meet there — and since Betty Ford, and Delores Hope were on his Board, it was a simple matter to persuade Jerry to meet with us. Eventually that meeting took place at the Gene Autry Hotel in Palm Springs, where we all stayed, and Jerry invited the Honorable Richard Gephardt, the Democratic U.S. Congressman from Missouri to also attend so he could review their plan to "Promote Competition in the Healthcare field." This discouraged us because it was this very same competition for profit that was destroying the professional image we'd all held so sacred for so many years. He also agreed to invite Orin Hatch, the U.S. Republican Senator from Utah, and Robert Dole, the Republican Senator from Kansas to join us and discuss Medicare, Medicaid and its effect on our Voluntary Healthcare Sector. By the time we had the meeting, our group had grown to twenty or more Administrators and Board Chairman that were all interested, and then on Saturday morning eight of us met privately with Jerry Ford for a full day. Doctor Heustes described some of the serious problems he'd been having, and since I was working in the front lines, trying to protect private hospitals from being taken over, I described some of these earlier Dinosaur conflicts that were challenging us on a day to day basis. I also reminded him of how the Flexner Report of 1910 — once warned this country of the danger of the uncontrolled proliferation of advertising, competition and money incentives in this professional service to humankind. I explained how Flexner had warned us how this would lower the whole plane of professional conduct, which would eventually lead to the overall demoralization of the healthcare profession. We also discussed how *community* rating under the Blues once privately owned nonprofit prepayment system was deregulated by the McCarran Ferguson Act of 1945 — permitting profit insurance to spiral healthcare costs unfairly under their new *group* rating system. Heustes described how Medicare had once again split the system into a two level system, one for the poor and one for the wealthy — and how regional planning no longer existed."

"Then after almost eight hours, I finally looked directly at Jerry, and asked, 'Isn't there anything we can do to turn this thing around?' And Heustes quickly added, I agree totally with Bill, and we're getting between a rock and a hard place, he'd snarled."

"That's just terrible," Mary said. "That just goes to show you how dysfunctional we've become," as they both sat in thought for a moment contemplating this horrible dilemma.

President Ford just sat in thought for a moment, and then he stood up and walked to the chalkboard and drew a large cross on the board. As he pointed at the board he said, "This was my *Iron Cross.*" At the top of the cross he wrote, *The Congress, Senate, and Bureaucrats.* Then on the left arm of the cross he wrote — *The Military* — and on the right, *The Industrial Complex, Lobbyists, and the privately owned Federal Reserve.* What we now know as the Oligarchy. Then at the foot of the cross he wrote in smaller letters, *The People.*

"The Administration's primary job is to balance things between these various power groups," he explained before picking up a piece of red chalk and writing in the center of the cross, t*he Administration and its Cabinet,* which he circled. "You'll note that I put the administration in red because it represents the hot seat, which I've actually survived being in." Then as he walked back to the table, he loudly cleared his throat. "When I was in office, I spent eighty percent of my time trying to balance these groups so they were not fighting, and as a result I very seldom got to do what I or the people wanted from a President." He then went on to explain — "In my position, I could never let too many gifts flow to any one power, for things would then quickly get out of balance, kind of like a loose string on a Stradivarius destroys the tone of a beautiful ballad. And that's exactly what's happening with today's military and industrial complexes, as our dysfunctional congressmen, our military, and a few favored executives who are granted so many gifts and benefits that our economy grows weak and the world becomes an unfriendly and fearful place. Worse yet, *We the People* eventually become fatigued, apathetic, and vulnerable from all this. I guess what I'm saying is, that in real life, the President actually has little to say about what goes on in this struggle for wealth and control. So where do you think the power rests?" Without waiting for an answer he continued. "Well, it usually flows from the high born to the politicians, since they hold the best hand at any given time. My job was to not to let things swing too far toward this Shadow Government, and I can assure you that's quite a balancing act." Looking at me he said, "Bill, I don't recall the pressures that the wealthy private owners of the Federal Reserve put on our politicians to pass the McCarran Ferguson Act because that was before my appointment, but I do know the public would never voluntarily ask this Shadow Government to open this can of worms in any service to humankind. I also know that this wealthy Oligarchy and today's politicians will never close it. Teddy Roosevelt, FDR, Eisenhower, Kennedy and myself — as well as many other honorable politicians have often threatened to expose this shadow government — but they were all quickly stopped, and in some cases even killed. These guys are intent on someday controlling the *World Market* through what they refer to as their *New World Order* — an order that hides behind Globalization and today's dysfunctional UN."

"Are you saying we're going to have to live with this mess?" I asked.

"Bill, I'm saying that it will be virtually impossible for any President to unilaterally stop this without exposing who's behind it all. And that just ain't going to happen."

"Yes, but you must have some recommendations, so we can at least hope for a future," Bill replied not yet discouraged by what he'd just heard.

"In my humble judgment, the healthcare system will have to eventually collapse, which will perhaps offer a new beginning — or if that doesn't occur, you'll probably need to promote a revolution that exposes all this corruption before you can change the track this Shadow Government is currently on. I know this much, the current power structure will not willingly budge from their current path, because there is just too much money at stake and far too many crooked deals have already been made."

"Well at least we know where we stand," Heustes finally growled, starring hopelessly at me. "We thank you for your candor Mr. President — and perhaps we will someday promote a revolution."

"That evening, after a full day of discussion, a bus picked us up for dinner at Bob Hope's home, which was a huge dome shaped building located at the top of the foothills overlooking Palm Springs, where Delores Hope was waiting to greet us. As we entered the huge circular center room we noticed a man in a tuxedo playing soft dinner music on the Grand piano, while waiters scurried in and out with trays of hors d'oeuvres and drinks. Then suddenly Bob Hope magically appeared, walking right up to my wife Susan and giving her a big kiss on the cheek as he whispered 'hello doll.'"

"You have to be kidding," Mary said. "What a compliment!"

"I can remember Susan was both shocked and flattered, and after we visited with them, we were all directed toward the buffet. Then as everyone was finishing their dinner, a power failure sent the room into darkness — and the waiters hurried to light all kinds of candles, which cast a variety of interesting shapes and shadows across the huge domed ceiling. Bob Hope was quick to capitalize on the moment, as he climbed half way up a flight of stairs that circled the wall to the second floor. Holding a huge candle under his chin he said, 'I told Delores to pay the light bill last week, but she never listens.' While the lights remained off, he kept everyone entertained, and it soon became obvious why he was so successful at comedy — keeping us in stitches for a good half hour until the lights finally came back on. He then explained he was leaving on a trip at five in the morning to entertain the troops overseas and graciously excused himself. Mary, although that meeting was a terrible disappointment to all of us — the Hope's dinner made for a memorable occasion for both Susan and myself."

After driving several more miles in silence, Bill finally added, "Mary, the way I see it, I'd be free to write a novel based on actual events if I'd change the names and locations to protect the innocent? What if I titled it, *The New World Oligarchy?*" Bill said, dramatically sweeping one hand through the air."

"Those crooks will probably take you to court for exposing their secrets — and win — but I like it," she laughed — "I like it a lot. And since nobody seems to want to hear the truth, I agree, I think you should write a hair-raising novel based on actual events. I can't think of a better way to educate the public about what's really going on with this upper crust that's screwing the working class of this country. And I now understand why this *New World Oligarchy* wants to level this country to that of others — we're just too strong for them since the Cold War ended."

* * * * *

Bill and Mary married in New Orleans and stayed two days at the Hotel St. Marie on Toulouse Street, where they enjoyed some outstanding sea food and French cuisine. Then after a full day of driving, they finally reached Mary's home in Florida.

"Bill, we need some recovery time," Mary said, "and I really think we need to distance ourselves from our past, like Dr. Heustes did — in other words, let's disappear for a while."

"Do you have any suggestions?"

"We're right on the door step of the Caribbean, and I own a boat — what more do we need? There are thousands of islands within our reach, and you could write in some peaceful bay until your blue in the face." And after she thought about that for moment she added, "And I could stuff myself with fresh seafood, which I never get enough of."

"Need I remind you your boat isn't designed for ocean travel — its fuel dependent, and it would cost a mint. Worse yet, we could get stuck out there, and I'm no mechanic."

"Well then we'll trade my old scow in for a sailboat? Doc was looking at that possibility back when he was alive, and I could check with that same boat dealer he was talking to."

"Do you think Matt could give us a quick course in sailing and navigating the Caribbean? If he could, I'd be willing to give it a try, as long as we could find a safe harbor during the hurricane season."

"Let's do it," — Mary grinned. "At least we wouldn't have to be looking over our shoulder for some sick *Dinosaur* to take us out. Maybe they'll just forget about us if we disappear for a while."

"Perhaps you're right — and we sure don't want to be looking over our shoulder the rest of our lives. Mary, to be honest, we really did damage their image, and they're not the type that can forgive and forget — are they?"

"Bill, if I've learned one thing, I know that this cancer is well beyond the treatment phase, in fact it's everywhere as Dave said. Perhaps President Ford was right, maybe healthcare does have to collapse before it'll get better. So let's just get away from things for awhile."

"Mary, we've certainly done everything we possibly can, and it now seems like we've been fighting this thing forever. I agree with you — and the Caribbean really would be a great place to write."

"That settles it," Mary shouted. "I'll call Matt in the morning and ask him to give us a quick course in navigating the Caribbean. And I'll also have him check with that boat dealer and see what's available. If we can find something we like, we'll just trade that big scow off and disappear for a while."

* * * * *

Several months later, they talked well into the night before getting up early and heading to Matt's Marina. As the sun broke over the horizon Bill laughed hysterically at the words, *The Iron Cross,* scrawled wildly in script style over the stern of their new forty-nine foot Sun Odyssey sailboat.

"So you've already named her," Bill chuckled, throwing a bag of last minute supplies on the boat's highly polished teak wood deck. "I like your choice," he yelled, stepping cautiously on deck.

After they finished loading and securing all the storage cabinets they both flopped down to rest a moment.

"Well, let's say goodbye to the good old USA and get on our way," Mary finally whispered.

As Matt yelled out a few last minute instructions, he cast the mooring line to Mary and yelled — "Goodbye and have a great trip, we'll be looking forward to your return."

"Ship ahoy Captain," Mary yelled, ringing seven bells loudly for all the loved ones who were no longer with them. As they pulled away from the dock, Mary's tear filled eyes watched Matt grow smaller and smaller, as she waved at him over the wake of their silently running diesel. Finally she turned from the stern, wrapping her arm tightly around Bill's waist as he switched off the diesel and set their sails toward the open sea.

"It's time to look ahead," she whispered, as they both stared out at the distant horizon.

"I have no idea where our lives will take us," Bill whispered softly, "but I agree with your prescription. We can never even start to recover, until we say good-bye to the past."

Epilogue

Mary and Bill sailed from island to island during their travels through the Gulf and the Caribbean, first making port at Nassau on the island of New Providence in the Bahamas. There they studied the history of the Caribbean and discussed with the residents the many conflicts that occurred during the Spanish, French and English attempts to colonize the Caribbean. After leaving Nassau, they sailed directly south through the Windward-Passage between Cuba and Haiti, on down through the Jamaica Channel before docking at Kingston, in the Greater Antilles Islands. Here they heard how the wealthy English drove the Spanish landowners off the island in the 1650s, eventually resulting in the slave rebellions that started in 1733, details of which were narrated to them nightly by an old sea captain who could be regularly found sipping dark rum at an old wharf pub they frequented. As he narrated his sobering tales, he told how some two thousand white sugar plantation owners of the Master-Mistress Aristocracy tried to dictate to some seventy-nine thousand black slaves — so they could flaunt their wealth and political and social power when they traveled back to their estates in England. He told how these powerful dynasties eventually failed when the black slaves that had originally occupied that island decided to revolt with overwhelming force. The Maroons as they were called, fought back violently once they escaped into the mountains where thousands of them hid, some in holes in the ground, so that they could eventually reclaim control of their own lives.

England's *Eight New Rules of Torture* clearly described the public flogging, burning and dismemberment tactics used to stop this great slave rebellion, and although many of the revolutionary male slaves died violent deaths, the women were only burned with red hot irons as they poured scalding hot water down their throats, allowing them to suffer a bit before returning to their maker.

"Perhaps it's time for the public to sharpen their understanding of our own hypocrisies, and begin to ask some serious questions about these powerful Oligarchies that want to rule the world," Bill explained to the old sea Captain. "It shouldn't take a great deal of thought to realize that the aristocracies that pillaged our human service to our sick and disabled are no different than these Sugar Czars that tortured these poor slaves."

"This is the same tyranny our relatives fled from almost two hundred and thirty years ago," Mary added, "when they were suppressed and taxed so relentlessly."

"Mary, I now see the real difference between an empire and a democracy. Empires are controlled by wealthy aristocracies that totally rule the working class — while democracies are ruled by the working class, from the bottom up. The real danger is when the working class allows some ruthless aristocracy to take over our democracy, just like we're doing now. That's why we voted for a two term limit on our presidency. I remember when we elected Franklin Roosevelt to four terms, and we were worried we'd created a dynasty."

* * * * *

After the hurricane season, Bill and Mary sailed to the Lesser Antilles, where they stopped at San Juan in Puerto Rico, finally making port in Charlotte Amalie in the Virgin Islands. There they took several short trips in that unique cluster of islands. Each night they anchored on the leeward side of some strange new island, snorkeling and spearing fish and Lobster. At Saint Kits, they decided to rent a slip where they spent several months getting rid of their sea legs, staying at the Frigate Bay Resort in Basseterre, and then repeating the same thing at St. John's on Antigua Island in the Virgin Islands, where they docked at Nelson's dockyard, and stayed at a famous five star hotel, the Curtain Bluff Resort. By now, Bill had completed and published two nonfiction books entitled, *A Prescription for Healthcare*, and *Should Corporations Practice Medicine?* But he hadn't yet reached that larger audience. At St. John's, he met a well known author who recommended he reach out to that larger market by writing his first novel based on actual events, so he tried writing, *The Code*

Generator, which sold a few more copies, but was really more of a learning experience.

Finally Bill felt he was ready to write about the tragic consequences of this corrupt aristocracy that has taken over the United States. Sailing back to Florida, he recalled how President Eisenhower once warned this country of the importance in keeping today's dangerous military and industrial complex in balance; and he remembered how President Ford had lectured him on the role he played under his *Iron Cross*, when he said he could not let too many gifts flow to any one power, for things would then quickly get out of balance.

That's exactly what's happening with our submissive congressmen when these powerful aristocracies grant them so many generous gifts and benefits that our economy grows weak and the world more unfriendly and fearful, while the working class only becomes more fatigued, apathetic, and vulnerable. If we'd only take a moment to think about these things, it would soon become obvious that this secretive and powerful inner circle completely controls both our administration as well as our politicians. We're seeing exit poles that have never before varied by more than one percent vary as much as thirteen percent, which statisticians say is impossible. And under this new Patriot Act, we the people no longer control anything. So what's next — martial law or a dictatorship? Bill thought.

"Mary, we really don't understand globalization. When Empires try to globalize other countries, it has always failed. Powerful dynasties led by all the apt or inapt leaders of Rome, France, England, Russia, China, Germany, Japan, and now the United States have all failed in that quest. Yet, globalization of human services such as our environment, our energy, our health, our education, our transportation — do offer a reasonable possibility for world-wide cooperation. Why? — Because they benefit the people as a whole. But, this type of globalization requires leadership by some nonprofit organization similar to the United Nations to coordinate these human services. The flip side is that not all empires and democracies are willing to promote such cooperation, such as China who is now successfully launching the future financial center for the world in Chung King, all because they kept their focus on their own communistic country instead of falling prey to this international banker's credit game. And on top of all that, we're constantly confusing the open market with globalization. It's no accident that our open markets have always been under the control of some wealthy aristocracy that lives or dies by competition and selling a product. We all know marketing's not globalization, its marketing — and marketing functions best without regulation, under a system that allows for open competition and profit. In other words it's the survival of the fittest, a dog eat dog culture, which must win over empires and democracies to be successful. But globalization of human services always fails when they compete, even though these powerful aristocracies thrive in such an environment. When we confuse services to humanity with open and competitive marketing, that's where the trouble starts. In healthcare, Americans have now been marketed to death with all those damned drug ads, when they really have no choice in what they receive for their money."

"Bill, you're so right, and it's time you start writing your damned novel," she growled defiantly as she took over the helm.

With that Bill gathered up his notes and sat down at his computer and kept writing steadily every day, even continuing at Mary's home after they arrived safely back in Florida. Against Mary's advice, the next book was a nonfiction book entitled, *Our Puppet Government,* which Bill had been trying to write for some time.

* * * * *

Yes, Doctor Heustes continued to be their close friend after their return, and for the time being the *Dinosaurs* had perhaps forgotten about all of them, but that was only until Bill finally decided to write the novel Mary had been demanding he complete — *The New World Oligarchy,* and the story of how we must shut down their Federal Reserve, which is currently owned by these powerful international bankers that seek to control the world.